The Poison of Goa

BY THE SAME AUTHOR

The Marvelous Story of Claire d'Amour
The Call of the Beast
Priscilla of Alexandria
The Angel of Lust
The Mystery of the Tiger
Lucifer
The Blood of Toulouse
The Albigensian Treasure
Jean de Fodoas
Melusine
The Brothers of the Virgin Gold

The Poison of Goa

by
Maurice Magre

Translated, annotated and introduced by
Brian Stableford

A Black Coat Press Book

Visit our website at www.blackcoatpress.com

ISBN 978-1-61227-674-8. First Printing. October 2017. Published by Black Coat Press, an imprint of Hollywood Comics.com, LLC, P.O. Box 17270, Encino, CA 91416.
Printed in the United States of America.

TABLE OF CONTENTS

Introduction

This is the sixth volume of a twelve-volume set of translations of Maurice Magre's prose fiction. It contains translations of the novel *Le Poison de Goa* (1928), as "The Poison of Goa," and the prose poems contained in *Le Livre des lotus entr'ouverts* (1926), as "Lotus Blossoms."

Volume One, *The Marvelous Story of Claire d'Amour and Other Stories*, contains translations of early short stories, including the collection *Histoire merveilleuse de Claire d'Amour suivie d'autres contes merveilleux* (1903) and six other stories from various sources, published between 1901 and 1913.

Volume Two, *The Call of the Beast and Other Stories*, contains translations of his first three works of prose fiction in volume form, *Les Colombes poignardées* (1917), as "Stabbed Doves," *La Tendre camarade* (1918), as "The Tender Comrade" and *L'Appel de la bête* (1920), as "The Call of the Beast."

Volume Three, *Priscilla of Alexandria and Other Stories* contains translations of the original version of the story collection *Vies des courtisanes*, first published in *Oeuvres Libres* 23 (1923), as "Courtesans' Lives" plus the additional story added to the version published in volume form in 1925, and the novel *Priscilla d'Alexandrie* (1925), as "Priscilla of Alexandria."

Volume Four, *The Angel of Lust*, contains translations of the novella, *La Vie amoureuse de Messaline* (1925), as "The Love Life of Messalina," the novel published as *La Luxure de Grenade* (1926), as "The Angel of Lust," and the chapter from *Magiciens et illuminés* (1930) entitled "Christian Rosenkreutz et les Rose-croix," as "Christian Rosenkreutz and the Rosicrucians."

Volume Five, *The Mystery of the Tiger*, contains translations of the novella *Le Roman de Confucius* (1927), as "The

7

Story of Confucius," and the novel *Le Mystère du tigre* (1927), as "The Mystery of the Tiger."

Volume Seven, *Lucifer*, contains a translation of the novel originally published under the same title in 1929 and the novella *La Nuit de haschich et de l'opium* (1929), as "The Night of Hashish and Opium."

Volume Eight, *The Blood of Toulouse*, contains translations of the novel *Le Sang de Toulouse* (1931), as "The Blood of Toulouse," and the chapter from *Magiciens et illuminés* entitled "Le Maître inconnu des Albigeois," as "The Secret Master of the Albigensians."

Volume Nine, *The Albigensian Treasure*, contains translations of the novel *Le Trésor des Albigeois* (1938) as "The Albigensian Treasure," and the collection of vignettes "Communication avec la nature" from *La Beauté invisible* (1937), as "Communication with Nature."

Volume Ten, *Jean de Fodoas*, contains translations of the novel *Jean de Fodoas: aventures d'un Français à la cour de l'empereur Akbar* (1939) as "Jean de Fodoas" and the chapter from *Magiciens et illuminés* entitled "Le Mystère des Templiers," as "The Mystery of the Templars."

Volume Eleven, *Melusine*, contains translations of the novel *Mélusine, ou le secret de solitude* (1941) and the collections of vignettes "Le Côté d'ombre des âmes" and "Révélation des mondes invisibles" from *La Beauté invisible*, as "The Dark Side of Souls" and "The Revelation of Invisible Worlds."

Volume Twelve, *The Brothers of the Virgin Gold*, contains a translation of the novel *Les Frères de l'or vierge*, first published posthumously in 1949.

Le Poison de Goa has obvious affinities with its immediate predecessor. *Le Mystère du tigre*, in its temporal and geographical setting, the action similarly unfolding in the mid-nineteenth century, in the exceedingly decadent colony of Goa, which is a frequently-mentioned but unvisited location in the earlier, Malaysia-set novel. However, it features a far more sympathetic protagonist, in its unfortunate Jewish heroine, whom the opening of the story finds in Bombay in desperate straits, and who has to undergo a terrifying ordeal before she realizes that she has found an unexpected opportunity to avenge the death of her mother and brutal torture of her father during a pogrom.

As the strangely tortuous plot of the novel develops, it is eventually proposed that Rachel Jehoudah, like Rafaël Graaf in the earlier novel, might be in need of a philosophical regeneration. Precisely because the reader's sympathy has been so forcefully engaged on her behalf, however, the question of whether she ought to stick to her plan of revenge against the appalling Pedre de Castro or stay her hand, thus breaking the potentially-endless chain of evil sustained by the law of talion, becomes intensely dramatic. In that regard, the novel recapitulates an aspect of the story-line of *Priscilla d'Alexandrie*, and, as in the earlier novel, it is the heroine's father who eventually has to set off on an arduous international journey, with the intention of saving her from herself. Unlike Aurelius, who fails to reach Priscilla in the end, in spite of all his heroic efforts, Manoël Jehoudah arrives in time to intervene in Rachel's project, but his unwelcome admonition only serves to complicate the situation and sharpen her dilemma, while destiny continues to follow its own stubborn course.

The strength and artistry of *Le Poison de Goa* do not reside entirely in its tense and dramatic plot, although that provides considerable narrative traction; the graphic images of decadent Goa, as it is gradually consumed by the march of time, are very striking. They are also entirely imaginary; Magre had not yet visited India, although he had been fascinated by it for some time. In his *Confessions sur les femmes, l'opium, l'amour, l'idéal, etc.* [Confessions regarding Women, Opium, Amour and the Ideal, etc.] (1930) he offers as the origin of that fascination a Hindu glimpsed in Paris at the time of the 1900 Exposition, but there is probably a certain poetic license in that distant connection, and he did not become enthralled with the subcontinent until the early 1920s, when he became interested in Buddhist philosophy and Theosophy, at which point he began to regard it as a key source and continuing refuge of sacred wisdom. Magre had, however, been a lover of exotic traveler's tales long before that.

Prior to *Le Poison de Goa*, the exoticism of India and its religions had been featured with lurid extravagance in "Bagawali," one of his far-ranging accounts of the *Vies des courtisanes*, (whose eponymous heroine is not the person of the same name mentioned in *Priscilla d'Alexandrie* nor the one featured in of the prose-poems in *Le Livre de lotus entr'ouverts*). The exoticism of that vision of India, imaginatively clad in a vague supernaturalism, had also been casually transferred to the forest location featured in *Le Mystère du tigre*, where the ruined temple that is a nucleus of hallucinations and subtle visitations is equipped with Hindu deities somewhat unsuited to its supposed geographical location.

In *Le Poison de Goa*, however, the ruins that fill the setting, still in the process of an uncannily rapid and supernaturally-assisted decay—the poison of the title—are not those of ancient Hindu temples but the Catholic relics of the glory days of the Portuguese colony. Those relics are not merely crumbling stone but also human, in the form of Archbishop de Silva, who believes himself to be in direct communication with God, and in ostensible support of whose dispute with the Pope, Pedre de Castro organizes an ill-fated plan for revolution, which Rachel encourages for her own Machiavellian purpose. Ruined and abandoned Christian churches figure as frequently in Magre's later works as ruined quasi-Hindu temples, and similarly provide imagery that communicates a sense of inexorable historical process on a larger scale than mere human action.

That sense of the mercilessly corrosive effect of time, and the relative helplessness of individuals within the surge of great historical tides, becomes increasingly obvious in the later chapters of *Le Poison de Goa*, and it was to become even more prevalent in the author's subsequent novels, especially when he turned the principal focus of his attention to the troubled history of his own native city of Toulouse. In symbolic terms, that process of inexorable ruination is linked in the present novel with the notion of the corrosive chain of evil that also transcends individual human lives, represented by Manoël Jehoudah as a corrosive toxin opposed to spiritual progress and moral evolution, and in dire need of palliation and cure.

Le Livre des lotus entr'ouverts is one of the items in the present set of twelve volumes published out of chronological sequence, and a case could have been made on that basis for including it in the previous volume, but the reasons for juxtaposing *Le Roman de Confucius* and *Le Mystère du tigre* seemed stronger, and exchanging the former with *Le Livre des lotus entr'ouverts* would have disrupted the chronological sequence anyway. In any case, the prose poems making up the volume were probably accumulated over a number of years, it might be best considered as a work somewhat detached from the chronology of Magre's career, although clearly reflecting the Oriental fascinations that produced the two items in the previous volume, *Le Poison de Goa*, and the first of the author's confessional volumes, *Pourquoi je suis Bouddhiste* [Why I Am a Buddhist] (1929).

Magre always listed *Le Livre des lotus entr'ouverts* among his works of poetry rather than his fiction, and that decision is undoubtedly justifiable, but it is worth observing that many other prose-poems are inserted into his works of fiction as chapters and others are included in his "philosophical" books, notably *La Beauté invisible* (translated in volumes 9 and 11), so that there is a considerable overlap between the particular aspect of his endeavor exemplified in this work and others. The tone of these prose poems is not markedly different from that of *Le Roman de Confucius*, many of whose chapters have a similar poetic character, and the habit of such insertions extended all the way from *Les Colombes poignardées* (1917) to *Mélusine* (1941), spanning the greater part of his career as a writer of fiction. The volume is thus fully entitled to a place in the spectrum of his prose, both in terms of continuing trends already set and laying groundwork for further work in a similar vein.

As a great admirer of Charles Baudelaire and sharing several fascinations with Joris-Karl Huysmans, Magre was doubtless aware of the fact that Jean Des Esseintes, the protagonist of Huysmans *À rebours* (1884), reflecting on Baudelaire's prose poetry, had said that the prose poem was, in his view, the "osmazome" (i.e.,. the savory principle of flesh) of literature and the "essential oil" of art. Magre would probably not have made the same extravagant claim himself, but he certainly employed the genre very extensively, and used it, as in *Le Livre des lotus entr'ouverts* to encapsulate the products of a particular meditative state of mind that is difficult to accommodate in more robustly formulated short stories, or in poetry structured by rhyme and scansion. The items in the volume therefore offer a perspective on both Magre's notion of the exoticism of the East and his commitment to Buddhist philosophy that connects to certain intrusions in his novels and his non-fiction, but is also distinct from and complementary to them. The inclusion of the *Le Livre des lotus entr'ouverts* is therefore a useful and revealing supplement to the narratives making up the bulk of the present collection.

The translation of *Le Poison de Goa* was made from the version of the 1928 Albin Michel edition reproduced on the Bibliothèque Nationale's *gallica* website. The translation of *Le Livre des lotus entr'ouverts* was made from a copy of the 1926 Fasquelle edition.

Brian Stableford

THE POISON OF GOA

PART ONE

The House of the Procuress

Rachel turned round and saw the sun in the distance, about to sink behind the Malabar hill and the new docks under construction, in the square that a patch of water made at the extremity of the street. The globe of that unusual sun was swollen and disproportionate. It spread a light like wine-dregs over the yellow-tinted and abnormally uplifted waves, as if by an unhealthy fusion. The air was damp and oppressive, and the dust, falling back slowly, made a sad golden mist.

Perhaps there's a tornado in preparation, Rachel thought.

Then she took one of the lateral streets that brought her back toward the Mazagon district. But the idea of her mediocre hotel in that suburb of Bombay, haunted by cosmopolitan adventurers, filled her with disgust and she sensed the secret hope of catastrophe that people who have arrived at a difficult juncture in life experience.

For more than an hour she had been walking at hazard, aimlessly, under the colored awnings and prominent balconies, between the bazaars, the shops selling cashmere veils, the basket-weavers and the wood-lacquerers. Sometimes a cunning face brightened as she passed, a bronzed hand held an object out to her with an offer formulated in English or Hindustani. She crossed paths with men of all races. How alone she was among so many strangers! Where would she go tomorrow?

It seemed to her that she was no longer exciting the astonishment in the busy evening crowd that a European woman alone and on foot ordinarily causes in a street in the black city of Bombay. The passers-by were more rapid. The shutters of shops were banging. The horses of the carriages carrying excursionists toward the Esplanade and the gardens of Kolaba were rearing up and then galloping with a singular speed. A seller of balls of dough and colored sweets, who was running, bumped into Rachel, and she glimpsed an expression of fearful hatred on his ash-gray face. The head and shoulders of an Englishwoman appeared at the window of a palanquin, precipitately giving her porters the order to retrace their steps. A Persian in an astrakhan bonnet who had just stood up in his shop and rolled up the tube of his water-pipe shouted something she did not understand to Rachel, pointing at the sky.

In front of the Chinese bazaar the crowd was so dense, and the atmosphere so unbreathable, that the young woman turned left along the walls of the prison.

She found herself face to face with two men who were passing by. They were Europeans, doubtless English. One of them had an enormous pearl in his cravat, like a poisonous insect that had just alighted. Of the other, who had the black garment of a clergyman hiding his collar, she could see nothing except the gold of spectacle rims and the ivory of teeth. The expression on their faces changed abruptly, taking on the joyous idiocy and hypocritical licentiousness that animates a certain category of men in the presence of feminine beauty.

They had stopped, ready to engage in conversation, but Rachel hastened her steps. She had a desire to run. She knew full well that she transported, in the undulation of her body and the magnetic warmth of her blood, an element of pleasure that made her possession desirable.

A Jewess, she thought. *One scorns her with all the more force because one desires her and one would like to enjoy her.*

And she murmured to herself the words she had often read in a Hebrew book that her father possessed, which related the misfortunes of her race: "O Lord Sabaoth, just God, enable me to see the chastisement of these persecutors and tyrants that make us perish, for I have confided my cause to you."

She raised her head and saw that she had returned without suspecting it to the narrow street not far from the temple of Monbadevi where the blind alley opened that she had sworn not to go along, the cul-de-sac whose threshold she did not want to cross at any price. She had thought, however, that she had taken an opposite direction. She recognized the beggar sitting cross-legged at the corner of the uncrossable cul-de-sac. He was gazing with blind eyes, slightly above human height. Drops of sweat were pearling on his naked torso and only the bizarre agitation of his toes interrupted the perfect immobility of his body.

She retraced her steps precipitately.

Look where the just God had brought her! No, no, not that. She had been told, and she believed it, that the greatest sin for a woman was to give herself to a man for money. Money was the pollution that one cannot wash away.

And yet, what would become of her? Was she not about to be thrown on to the street the next day by the proprietor of her hotel?

"Just God, show me the way."

She smiled bitterly. She had just passed a public drinking-fountain and the sole of her foot, where she knew that she had a hole, had just made contact with a little water, with the sad sound of poverty that she knew so well. Her foot seemed heavy, as if it had a sole of lead. She thought about the young women who were once marked with a cross by means of a red-hot iron. She too had beneath her heel the sign of condemned creatures. No one could see it when she walked, but the sign groaned, and Rachel knew that she was linked by the foot to the ugliness of life.

The semaphore of the Malabar hill launched its sad and regular flame over Bombay. The dock workers were flowing, as they did every evening, toward Ahmadadah railway station, making an anguished rumor as they walked. Rachel wanted to escape that flood; but at the corner of a street along which she had already passed she saw, a few paces away, the two Eng-lishmen she had passed a few minutes before. They were look-ing around, and when they saw her they cried, almost at the same time: "There she is!"

Rachel recognized in a second the expression of stupid concupiscence in their features and the idea of having to ex-change words with them caused her to feel ill.

She started to run, followed by the sigh of her shoe. She went to the right, and then to the left. As rapid as her, the night, surging from who knows where, a gray and singular night, descended upon the city galvanized by the storm.

Rachel suddenly perceived the Victoria Docks, toward which she descended between rotting houses.

No one was following her any longer. In the low shops, semi-naked men, chisels in hand, were encrusting little pieces of nacre in small planks of precious wood. At the sound of Rachel's footsteps they raised their impassive faces, but seemed not to see her. Their presence had something so hallu-cinatory that Rachel hastened her pace. A sickening odor of musk was emitted from the houses and mingled with the odor of mud and tar that came from the fermented water of the ba-sins. She was about to reach the quays and had only to follow them in order to come back toward Mazagon and her hotel.

But she stopped. It seemed to her that a voice had just called to her. It was not a voice expressing itself in syllables but a sort of internal appeal that commanded her to go back. Then she went back up the street she had just descended, among the spectral wood-engravers, under the decomposed vaults of balconies.

She started to march without knowing where she was go-ing, through the streets of the black city, until she ceased to take her bearings. And in the shadows of her memory the im-age emerged clearly of an engraving whose terrible subject had impressed her in her childhood.

At the summit of a whirlpool, a fantastic maelstrom, a ship was posed whose masts were broken. One understood that the ship, launched with great speed, was about to plunge, via a white line of foam, into the depths of the gulf. At the prow of the ship, a tiny human figure was expressing his despair with his open arms, and his futile appeal to an indifferent divinity. The sky was a uniform gray, like the laden sky of catastrophe that Rachel had above her at that moment. The sea was streaked with broad stripes and blisters, like the sea at which she had just gazed, and that crudely drawn gulf communicated a sensation of the inevitable and the irremediable.

Rachel had made puerile wishes that the pilot with open arms might benefit from some unexpected current and escape by swimming from those spirals that had to terminate, she believed, in an unimaginable hell.

Why was she thinking about that forgotten engraving? She shrugged her shoulders. But in a second consciousness, something told her that she was launched above the gulf. The crepuscular streets were the sloping lines by which the ship was descending. She had opened her arms in vain, appeal to humans and God. The depths of the gulf were close at hand.

And suddenly, she recognized the place where she was. She had just passed alongside the temple of Monbadevi. A little further on was the beggar with the upraised eyes and the cul-de-sac where the house of the procuress Antonia opened, the house where she was expected at this very moment.

So, that place was like a magnetic pole that was attracting the unfortunate wreck that she had become. The will of destiny intended to take the place of her broken will. Since she had begun to reflect, the manner in which events evolved had always filled her with astonishment. How had she arrived at having no other means of salvation than that house? How had that Antonia known about her solitude and her need for money?

When one falls down in a desert, the birds of prey, it appears, by virtue of a special instinct, come from infinite distances toward the creature on which they want to nourish themselves. Procuresses must have an analogous instinct that guided them directly to young women who have fallen in the solitude of little hotels.

17

"A house on the model of the houses of London and Paris," Antonia with the shiny tresses and the violet silk dress had said to her the day before, raising her index finger as she talked to make the flame of an enormous diamond sparkle.

She only made introductions, and only to render a service. One went into her house, one left again, no one had seen you. The women she received were, in truth, the best there were in Bombay society. Doesn't everyone need money nowadays? As for the men, they were senior English functionaries, important businessmen from Bombay and the surrounding area. The very next day she was expecting a rich Portuguese from Goa, a very curious individual about whom there was a legend. A man who only liked Jewesses—and how he liked them! Was Rachel not both Portuguese and Jewish at the same time? A little good will and her fortune might be made.

Rachel was not indignant, for one does not have the courage to be indignant when one is burned by the hole in one's shoe and the frayed elbow of one's dress. Under the ecclesiastical unction of the words, under the hypocritical pity, under the flash of the diamond, she had contented herself with lowering her head. She lowered it again now in the increasingly compact darkness of the street, and felt herself penetrated by a kind of moral torpor. She was not free. An imperious genius had brought her. It was the just God of her prayers who wanted her to fall.

Above the street, something that the abrupt wind had just snatched up passed like a bird and fell somewhere, noisily. At the same time Rachel felt splashes of warm water over her body, which transpierced her, and the sounds of the city were drowned out by the rattle of large raindrops on the rooftops.

She searched for a shelter between the wooden columns supporting the balconies. She almost tumbled over the beggar with upraised eyes and in the shadows it seemed to her that he was staring attentively at her forehead as if he had seen a particular sign there.

The cul-de-sac where no gas-lamp had yet been lit extended lugubriously before her. A muffled music of a khinnara and a tom-tom, mingled with piercing female cries, gave the place a character of hidden debauchery, of inferior joy.

Rachel recognized the house from which lamplight was filtering and perceived between the poorly-close shutters outbursts of voices, the sound of a violent argument. Something dangerous and crapulous reached her.

Impelled by curiosity, she took a few steps forward and was surprised to raise her hand to touch the metal knocker suspended from the door.

But at that moment the door opened brutally, at a single stroke. By the light of a lantern inside the house, Rachel fund herself face to face with a woman who was running out. She must have been an Englishwoman. She was bare-headed, her blonde hair in disorder. She was twisting a light shawl round her neck, with a mechanical gesture. Her eyes went alternately to the streets steaming with rain and Rachel, who was in front of her. She was murmuring insults between her teeth.

She had already descended the two steps of the threshold and was about to launch herself forward when she changed her mind.

She leaned toward Rachel in a familiar fashion, and, expelling alcoholic breath into her face, she said to her, in a tone of popular pity: "Don't go into Antonia's. It's better to get soaked in the street. The man from Goa's here this evening, the one who only likes Jewesses..."

The whore's familiarity had the effect on Rachel of a physical pollution by which she remained petrified. But at the word *Goa*, the city in which she had been born, she had a singular impression that she had been summoned by a voice that it was necessary to obey.

For a second she had the vision of the blonde turning the corner of the cul-de-sac, her garments so stuck to her body by cataracts of water that she seemed naked. There was a deafening burst of the tom-tom. And she went into the house, murmuring:

"O Sabaoth, just God..."

The Man from Goa

Scarcely had she gone in than Rachel perceived that dread was in the house. She had that perception by virtue of the oblique glance that the mulatto maidservant darted toward the stop of a staircase that led to the first floor, as if some redoubtable possibly might surge forth therefrom. She saw the dread in the faces of excessively made-up women who were in a drawing room rutilant with fake gold, behind a door-curtain, arguing passionately. Rachel was struck by the plaster face of one of them, where the rouge of lips decomposed by the heat made an atrocious rictus. She noticed that another, careless of her dress raised above the knee, was lying on a sofa, nonchalantly and gracefully blowing the smoke of a cigarette toward the ceiling. A Hindu orchestra of four or five white-clad musicians was in another room. They had just completed the tune they had been playing when Rachel came in, and the natouva, who was standing up, betrayed his anxiety by the back-and-forth movement of his enormous turban, made of a scaffolding of muslin.

Rachel hardly had time to dart a glance around the room to observe the ostentation of the dirty gilt of the house "on the model of those of London and of Paris." The walls of the vestibule where she was were covered in mirrors, as if the reproduction on the human form were the symbol of the luxury of Europe. There were mirrors in the drawing room where the women were, and the one where the musicians were, with the result that everything was multiplied, and dread radiated on all sides. Wine had been recently distributed, and its odor mingled with that of tobacco, and the odor of musk that the old wooden houses of Bombay emit. Several empty champagne-bottles were lined up at the foot of the staircase, beside a heap of soiled mosquito-nets.

The ridge of Antonia's nose was more inclined than the previous day. The ecclesiastical character of her face was

20

more accentuated, but fury triumphed over hypocrisy therein. She affected a smiling calm, and made the rapid movements of someone who wants to dominate a complicated situation by her presence of mind; but sometimes, like the mulatto maid, she darted an anxious glance toward the top of the stairs.

Rachel saw her make a sign to the musicians to shut up, to the women to wait, and to the mulatto to keep watch because of an unknown danger, and she was drawn behind a third door by her, which she had not noticed.

To begin with, Rachel heard the word *providence* pronounced several times. Her arrival had something providential about it. It was even said that it was God who had brought her—but an interior voice had already told her that.

As she was about to let herself fall on to a worn sofa, Antonia seized her abruptly by the wrist, saying, in a falsely jesting tone: "No, not there. It's seen too much, that unfortunate sofa. It's caved in."

But Rachel understood, by the gleam in the brothel-keeper's eyes, that it was necessary to stand up courageously in order to be the instrument of providence and accomplish a difficult action.

Time was doubtless passing, for after a few ambiguous and general phrases, Antonia found the appropriate formula: "Let's put our cards on the table."

And that image of an open card game filled her with such great satisfaction that she repeated it several times.

She could have tried to dupe Rachel, obtain what she expected from her by means of some oral trap, but what was the point? Had she not seen the wretched hotel in Mazagon the day before? Did she not know the sordid proprietor, her compatriot? Could she not read in Rachel's eyes the expression of a hunted beast that she had seen in the eyes of other women coming to her house for the first time? If her expert hand palpated a firm shoulder, it felt at the same time the wear of a poor dress. Not the slightest trace of jewelry. The shawl wrapped over the arm for show was cheap Cashmere cloth that must have come from a little bazaar. She could not see the hole in the shoe desperately applied to the floor but she divined it through the foot, as if the clarity of poverty were incapable of being veiled by any terrestrial material.

Antonia therefore laid on the table the cards of the game in which everyone won.

On the first floor of the house there was a man she had known for a long time, one of her old clients, for whom she could answer as for herself. He was a Portuguese from Goa, the descendant of an ancient family.

At that point Antonia began to laugh.

She knew perfectly well what Rachel could respond. All the Portuguese in Goa descend from ancient families. There was not a porter in the harbor who was not called Albuquerque or Castro. But this one was an authentic descendant of the great Castros of old—a descendant who had come down slightly in the world. All the Portuguese had come down in the world at present. But what importance did that have for what one wanted of them, when they were rich? It was better to deal with fallen Portuguese than English puritans, who were all misers and scorned the women of whom they made use. This Castro was a little drunk at present? Well, so what? It was always better to deal with drunken men. He was also reproached for being very fat. A fine thing! She, Antonia had once loved a man with an immeasurably waistline and could not think about him without emotion. Rachel had little experience, but she ought to know that in fat there is a richness of nature that always goes with qualities of the heart, a kind of native goodness. The word goodness was not too strong.

At that point Antonia raised her arms as if to forestall arguments, which the silent statue that Rachel had become did not, however, seem to be about to formulate.

A woman, Antonia agreed, had just quit the house precipitately. Perhaps Rachel had heard that filthy mouth proffering insults and threats as she went away. The girl had been afraid, or rather, had pretended to be afraid. Oh, how one was punished for receiving out of pity the daughters of sailors and half-breeds from the port. It was via the intermediary of that

Whitechapel whore that fear had afflicted the four or five others in the next room. They were putting on airs, but they'd seen many others!

Antonia was about to let her fury burst forth when she remembered what she had said about the aristocratic character of her female clients. She raised her diamond toward the lamplight, as if to assure herself of its purity, and leaned toward Rachel, lowering her voice.

"There are the peccadilloes of youth, assuredly. The traffic in negroes and Chinese on the coast... An old story of a woman, which no one knows, which everyone tells in a different manner, and is doubtless false. Childishness! I've known Pedre for a long time. As soon as he arrives in Bombay he comes here. He makes a noise sometimes, but it's to deafen himself, because he's timid."

Antonia was so charmed to have found the qualification *timid* for her guest that she repeated it several times.

It was at that moment that the sound of a cracked bell began to ring out. The bell-cord must have been tugged forcefully and irregularly, for it had desperate busts followed by shrill notes and brief silences. It translated the anger and impatience of the person who was pulling it.

The idea of a timid man becoming impatient in her house was insupportable to Antonia. She struck the wall several times with her fist, and in response to that signal, the Hindu orchestra caused a monotonous refrain to resound in the next room on three-string khinnaras, accompanied by tambourines.

The last cards of the open game were uncovered.

It was necessary to hurry, for the man from Goa, in spite of his timidity, had one single character defect: he did not like to wait. Now, he was waiting for a woman up there in a drawing room, where dinner had been served. For good or bad reasons, none of Antonia's five-to-seven habitués had consented to be the evening companions requested. Antonia was counting on Rachel, sent moreover by providence with that sole aim.

The envoy of providence felt the vibrations of the bell and the orchestra in her brain. She heard the wind outside that was raging as it was engulfed in the narrow streets, and the pain that was pattering like an innumerable army of dwarf soldiers. And she saw once again the old engraving, with the helpless mariner descending into the gulf of the maelstrom, with no possibility of salvation.

"He's asked for a beautiful girl—well, he shall have one," said Antonia, darting an admiring glance at Rachel, in which there was nevertheless a reservation because of the modesty of her dress.

"Well, you wouldn't be sorry, I'll wager, to have a diamond like this one?" And she strove to laugh as she made the stone sparkle. "Yes, you really are a beautiful girl."

And, as if seized by a scruple regarding the quality of the merchandise that she was about to offer, she took Rachel by the shoulders and palpated the flesh of her arms, in order to assure herself of their firmness.

The beautiful girl gazed into the distance without responding. Her soul was in such disarray, her ignorance of the customs of the place where she found herself was so great, that she would not have been astonished if she had been asked to show the curve of her legs, or if her lips had been lifted to examine her teeth, as she had seen horse-dealers do with colts.

In spite of the noise of the orchestra and the tempest, the bell resounded at intervals.

With a rapid gesture, Antonia removed the hat that kept Rachel's hair prisoner. The aureole of that hair, of such a profound black that it appeared blue, collapsed over the veined marble of the forehead, rendering brighter by its darkness the unreal green light that shone in the young woman's eyes.

Antonia was impressed by that beauty, augmented by the palpitation of the lips, the milky pallor of the skin and the secret despair. Her capacity for pity was translated by a general remark: "Women suffer so much damage for men!" But she hastened to add, in order to correct that regret: "I know him.

When he's drunk, one can get whatever one wants out of him."

Rachel saw again, as in a dream, the Hindu musicians in one room, and in the other, the group of women who looked at her. She noticed a creature with a thin neck who was swaying with a sort of vexation and pretention that made her resemble a pelican, and observed that behind her, on the sofa, the nonchalant young woman with uncovered legs was continuing to launch slow swirls of smoke toward the ceiling.

Almost pushed by Antonia, she went past the empty champagne bottles and up the spiral staircase; she took two or three steps along a corridor in which the sickening odor of musk was mingled with the reek of cooking, and a door opened wide in front of her.

"Here's the beautiful little friend," said Antonia to a man whose back was turned, who was supporting himself with one hand against the mantelpiece and pulling a bell-cord with the other, at the same time as he was looking at his teeth in the mirror at close range, as if he had discovered a chip, with the fixity that drunkards bring to their own contemplation.

On a card table, covered with a pale pink cloth, two places had been set, almost invisible under the shiny mass of two enormous resplendent champagne-buckets. A low bed was to the right, wide, obscene and hallucinatory, with a large rip in its mosquito-net, covered in an indefinable silk that was spotted in places by large stains. The light was coming from a lamp suspended from the ceiling, and as sad and brutal as that of a waiting room. The hand that was tugging the bell-cord suddenly fell, as if the mechanism animating it had broken. The man did not turn round, but his gaze, instead of being fixed on the chip in his tooth, focused on the image of the two women he could see in the mirror.

Undoubtedly, Antonia feared reproaches, a violent manifestation of her guest's impatience. She stammered two or three phrases in which there was mention of the dinner that would be served at the first request, and lovers who needed to coo tranquilly.

Rachel sensed that she disappeared behind her and the frisson of the door-curtain falling back and the little click of the door took on a singularly terrible significance for her.

In that second, she thought that there was still time to flee. The atrocious breath of fear filled the room, giving all the things the immobility they have in nightmares. That fear effaced from the air the sound of the rain streaming over the rooftops, the music of the Hindu tambourines, and a chorus of frogs singing in a nearby garden. It established a perfect silence, like those one imagines reigning in the illimitable spaces of the beyond.

With a clairvoyance multiplied tenfold, Rachel thought that it was sufficient for her to turn round, to open the door, to go downstairs and traverse the vestibule in order to be in the street blessed by the descent of the cleansing water. She thought that her hat was still in the room into which she had initially penetrated. She would gladly abandon it in order to avoid explanations, to be free more rapidly, to forget that wretched scene. With a single surge, in a few bounds she could reach the street. But there are certain qualities of terror that develop curiosity. Now, what might happen attracted her by its unknowability. She could only see the man's formidable back. She looked into the mirror in order to distinguish the features of his face, and what she perceived nailed her to the spot, open-mouthed with astonishment.

The man was staring at her, immobilized and magnetized. He had a cranium like a sugar-loaf, with bushy moist hair. His face was broad, yellow and bathed at the base by a floating double chin. His lips were thick and very red. But what struck Rachel was an expression of keen intelligence abruptly upset by terror. The eyes, small and black, with a fulgurant glare, were immeasurably wide open and projected the eyebrows almost to the hairline. They reflected the most abject fear.

Rachel saw that the man's left hand, which was resting on the mantelpiece, began to tremble, and she made out the little sound that the metal of a ring made against the marble.

And suddenly, the man made a half-turn in order to face Rachel and see her more clearly; but he did it with the rapidity that one has when one loses sight of a redoubtable adversary and fears being struck by him during the second when one is no longer immobilizing him with one's gaze.

Face to face with Rachel, only separated from her by the card table, he considered her avidly. And she, lucidly, observed that he was in his shirt sleeves, devoid of a collar, that the fabric of the shirt was a very fine silk, and overflowed the trousers stretched by his raised pot belly. She noted that his hands were laden with rings, and that his chest was frightfully hairy.

But the man's terror was only augmented by the contemplation of the young woman. His face expressed the fact that he had the confirmation of something redoubtable that he had seen in the mirror, something perhaps feared for a long time and glimpsed in the mirror of meditation. He took his eyes off Rachel again to look to his right at a little door near the fireplace, and it was visible that he was thinking of quitting the room precipitately. But he remembered that the door was that of a toilet that had no other exit, and with a rapid gesture, letting a hoarse gasp escape from his throat, he seized one of the bottles of champagne that were on the table by the neck and snatched it out of its bucket.

He had a weapon now; but the danger he was in, and against which he wanted to defend himself, was so inconceivable, of such an ineluctable nature, that he judged it very feeble, very paltry. Stuck to the mantelpiece, with his left hand forward, beating the air to protect himself, he was more pitiful than terrible; he seemed so scantly redoubtable that Rachel did not think of protecting herself against the champagne bottle, and she even felt any desire to leave vanishing within her.

The breath that emerged from the frightened man's breast became less precipitate, and his eyes less wide; he put the bottle down on the table, slowly. Interior reflection pacified his features, consolidated his limbs, rendered him the usage, temporarily annihilated, of his thought. He considered, by turns, the furniture and the two places set on the table, and his eyes paused on the stained silk of the bed as if on a benevolent altar.

He moved his head up and down slowly, and Rachel understood that he was evoking memories, making comparisons, weighing up some coincidence unknown to her in which her resemblance to another woman must play a role.

The man sketched an ill-assured and prudent gesture toward Rachel, as if he wanted to touch her with his finger, in order to make sure of the reality of her form. He did not conclude the gesture, sensing its ridiculousness. He opened his mouth to emit an explanatory remark, but he realized the impossibility of expressing himself.

All the same, he stammered: "I beg your pardon."

The sound of his own voice troubled him, stirred his nerves. He suddenly let himself fall into a chair. His features resumed the puerile expression formed of ugliness and rejuvenation that tears give to aged men.

At that moment, a sudden squall of rain clattered against the window hidden by curtains, and the song of the frogs rose up more distinctly, like a desperate hymn.

The man got up, with a certain difficulty. He passed his hand over his forehead. He took his collar from the mantelpiece, knotted his cravat and put his jacket on. He took from his inside pocket a long chaplet of large wooden beads, which he threw around his neck, and then he turned to Rachel a face bathed with sweat, but which had become calm again.

It was unnecessary for her to be afraid. She was going to sit down tranquilly facing him. The table was laid. They were going to have dinner. He would try to explain to her the cause of a folly of which he was ashamed.

And it was only then that Rachel recognized him.

The Pogrom

He was linked to her by an impression of water, a sunlit lagoon, and a marsh between clumps of medlar-trees. She had first seen the inverted image of that face with the thick lips and overly bright eyes in the water. And she could say that from the moment that the reflection of that man appeared to her between the aquatic plants and lotuses, her own misfortune and that of her family had commenced.

She remembered that Sunday, twelve years ago. She respired the odor of rotten wood of the Jewish quarter of Goa in the odor of musk that Antonia's old mildewed house emitted. She made a bizarre connection between the cracked bell that she had just heard and the church bells of that Sunday, which had, by the effect of time, the same false and irregular resonance.

She had been walking with her mother alongside the ponds of Banguinim. She was going back toward Goa on the demolished causeways that dated from the times of Portuguese prosperity and, having reached the corner of an orchard enclosed by walls, they had stopped to rest on a stone bench half-buried in the grass. Rachel had started gazing into the water of the lagoon, which was perfectly limpid at that point. It was then that the reflection of the man had appeared to her, that she had distinguished his face. There was another face alongside it. Two unknown men had advanced silently behind her mother and her.

Scarcely had Rachel seen them in the water than a cheerful and imperious voice resounded, addressed to her.

"Continue looking at the water, little girl. Don't turn round."

The tone had been so curt, the surprise so great, that Rachel had remained motionless for a few seconds. When she had turned round she had seen her mother struggling in the arms of a man who was laughing, and who ended placing his lips on hers in spite of her resistance.

She remembered that the man who had spoken to her was less elegant than the European merchants she was used to seeing in the port of Goa, and that he was smiling with an indifferent authority.

But the one who had kissed her mother, the one who had proffered menacing words while she wiped her lips with disgust and she went away, dragging her by the hand, was the man she had before her eyes, the persecutor of whom there was mention in the book of unfortunate Jews, the profaner with the greasy mouth, the pious Castro with the chaplet.

With a fine handkerchief of pink silk he had wiped the sweat from his brow again, and he had just invited Rachel to sit down.

And she, considering him, had seen everything that had followed in the stunning panorama of memories: the obsession, the letters received, the insulting cries uttered by night in the Jewish quarter by young men who were said to be the sons of the aristocracy of old Goa, the ironic sniggers of their friends and the quotidian apprehension.

She remembered her father's words: "And I thought I was coming to the ends of the earth in order to live here in peace with those I love!"

Her father did not know, then, that there is no end of the earth, and there is no place for Jews. It was the time when the Damascus affair had stirred up an anti-Jewish movement throughout Europe and in a part of Asia, and when pogroms were multiplying.[1]

---

[1] The "Damascus Affair" became an international scandal in 1840, following the arrest of thirteen members of the Jewish community of the Syrian city of Damascus, accused of murdering a Franciscan monk of French nationality for the ritual purpose of employing his blood in the Passover festival—the

Twice a week the European newspapers arrived on the English steamship that maintained a regular service to Bombay. Rachel went down to the dock to wait for them with her father, because her mother went out as little as possible, because of Castro—capable of anything, it was said—who was installed with his companion in a harbor-side café and called to her cynically, by her forename, when she went past.

The faces of the Jews became grave when they read the newspapers. They came to her father's house in the evening and commented on the Damascus affair, about which the whole world was talking. Always that accusation of ritual murder, which had served for centuries as a pretext for persecutions! Jewish communities in Poland and Syria were pillaged. Was that also going to reach India? The hatred of a single man was sufficient, as in Syria, to spread the calumny. It was very unfortunate fatality that the one of the sons of the fanatical Christians of old Goa was smitten with Dolça Jehoudah.

In truth, Rachel remembered those Portuguese Jews of Goa as poor men devoid of courage and intelligence. How ugly they were, with their dirty beards, their poorly-manicured fingernails and their ridiculous black frock-coats in the Euro-

---

age-old "blood libel" employed for centuries in the persecution of Jews. At the instigation of the French consul, a Jewish barber had confessed to the crime under torture, and had named other supposedly guilty parties, including the Chief Rabbi and other notable individuals, who were imprisoned and tortured in their turn; several died under the torture. The resultant publicity played a key role in launching a wave of vicious anti-Semitism that culminated in numerous pogroms. The French prime minister, Adolphe Thiers, backed his consul, and the French press did likewise, with only two significant exceptions, although the English press was almost unanimous in its condemnation and the outraged Jewish community in America attempted to organize an international movement of defense for the communities of the diaspora.

pean style, which they wore with loose white cotton trousers and Hindu sandals. What a difference there was between them and her father the intellectual, her father the physician, who lived to aid others and was wise and interested. What a difference also between those women with frizzy hair under 1830 bonnets, with their ruddy patches and hooked noses, and her mother, whose beauty was so perfect that Rachel could not look at her without weeping

"Do you know, Manoël Jehoudah, that Pedre de Castro is saying that he wants to abduct your wife?" one of those terrified Jews, the cashier at a rice warehouse belonging to Christians, had said to her father one evening.

Her father was content to shrug his shoulders. Did not the Portuguese laws require individuals to be respected, even when they were Jews on Goanese territory, and if one wanted to quit that territory one returned to the India under English legislation, which was the most protective of all of the rights of Jews. And then, only women who wanted to be were ever abducted.

But then they had talked about things that Rachel was only to understand later. That Pedre de Castro, married young, had caused his wife to die of chagrin. He had a son of whom he never took any notice. He was haunted by the desire to possess women and his life was dedicated to searching for them. He boasted that he would have Dolça Jehoudah, whatever it cost. A sort of evil genius was incarnate in him.

"A true Christian of the days of the auto-da-fé," said Rabbi Haim, who was a mulatto, and who claimed direct descent from the Jewish tribes that had come to India in the days of the Babylonian captivity. "Does not his friend, the adventurer who called himself Deodat de Vega, whose nationality no one knows and who sponges on the Castros, openly profess to preferring evil to good? Be careful, Jehoudah; women are weak and Christians possess for their pleasure a secret that is unknown to Jews."

Rachel gazed attentively at the coarse features of Pedre de Castro and sought to find there the trace of that secret, or merely the expression that she had contemplated with so much fear when she saw him through the window going back and forth in front of the house.

He sensed the weight of that gaze, but he interpreted it differently. He got up precipitately and, with an obsequious gesture, placed a chair beside her.

Everything that had happened afterwards had unfolded with rapidity, and the cowardice of men had been the cause of it all.

Rachel remembered the impression of terror that had come into her childish life like a tide, an impression that she could not help assimilating to the one that filled Antonia's house, the cause of which was the same: the man sitting in front of her.

Opinion was unanimous in the evening meetings. It was the night that was redoubtable. The latest pogroms, reported by the newspapers, had taken place by night. There was question of repairing and closing the gates of the ghetto. The Jews had once been obliged by law to enclose themselves in their quarter; it was a security measure in their regard, but the custom had fallen into disuse in 1815 when the Inquisition of Goa had been abolished. The gates were worm-eaten and no longer functional. In any case, would it not stimulate the violence to express fear overtly?

Rachel's infantile soul had then had, for the first time, the notion of cowardice, in its pitiless and calculating rigor.

Almost all the Jews of the port of Goa were of the opinion that, since the wife of their coreligionist Jehoudah might attract calamities to their colony by virtue of her beauty, as certain metals attract lightning, Jehoudah's duty was to quit Goa without delay, to flee no matter where. It was true that the Governor General, although vey Christian, had the law respected and showed the greatest benevolence toward Jews, but it was not the same for the district judges and the five magistrates of the appeal court, who all belonged to the noble families of old Goa. It was always the Jews that they held to be in the wrong in all the differences that arose between them and Christians. If there were pillages, there would be no indemnity. If there were blows received and blood shed, there would be no vengeance. And only a merchant of souvenirs for foreigners, who was almost completed paralyzed, opined that rifles should be prepared and brought down into the street at the first attempt at violence.

Pedre de Castro was looking into himself and perhaps remembering the same things as Rachel. He made another, more urgent gesture to the young woman, showing her the chair, and Rachel sat down facing him.

How changed he is, she thought. *Fat has effaced the demonic expression that I found in his face then. Hypocrisy has replaced audacity and I'm sure that he's suffering from that precocious obesity, the man who once affected to show himself with a seductive lightness on the sloping street of the Jewish quarter.*

Tragic events are always preceded by words and signs that might have permitted those they strike to have avoided them if they had dared to listen to the interior consciousness that has heard the words and seen the signs. Rachel remembered that her father had often said, afterwards, that on the evening before the drama unfolded, he had had, not a presentiment of what would happen—that was so horrible and so unexpected that no thought could have conceived it—but a vague knowledge that the only happy phase of his life was coming to an end.

The evening was an evening before the rains, stormy and damp, like the present evening in Bombay, with the same tenacious reek of rotting houses.

The lighthouse of Aguada was rotating its circular beam in the dusk. People were sitting in front of doors chatting placidly. Then furtive assemblies formed. The Rabbi had gone past at a rapid pace. Someone had shouted from a window: "It's written in the Book. We shall all pass one after another. Have pity on us Lord!"

The danger had just materialized. Calumny was threatening to be the instrument of persecution. The rumor had been going around since the morning that a young child, the son of a Christian Hindu, the caretaker of church in old Goa, had disappeared, and the disappearance was being attributed to the Jews. Always the ritual crime! Someone claimed to have seen Pedre de Castro in the process of handing out money to the rabble of the port. It was from the bottom of the street that the persecutors were going to come. But someone else affirmed that Castro had embarked in old Goa at the place where the three towers of the church of Saint Joseph covered the river with their shadow, and was in the process of crossing the seven miles that separated that landing-stage from the new city, at the head of a group of his friends and their armed servants. The road went along the river and then left it to climb the hill. It was therefore from the top of the street that the first cries of death and the noise of weapons would come first.

There was mention of sending a delegation to the governor, but the rabbi had just learned that he had left Goa the day before for Bombay and would not be back for several days. There was talk of going to find the Archbishop or the colonel commanding the fort. Manoël Jehoudah, the only man to have kept calm, observed that they had no precise complaint to formulate, and that the fears were only based on vague rumors.

Meanwhile, the storm that was threatening in the sky had dissipated and the radiant stars were reflected with an incomparable splendor, to the right over the marshes of Banguinim, and to the left over the waves of the phosphorescent sea. The curve of the deserted river was visible like a flood of blue-tinted metal, only troubled by the nagah petals falling like rain from its banks. No sound was coming from the sleeping port. Doubtless the calm of things was communicated to the fearful souls.

Rachel remembered that she had heard the bell of a distant convent before going to sleep.

On the chair where she was sitting, facing Pedre de Castro, she almost jumped. That bell had just resonated, with the same broken sound, a contribution to the evocation with increased clarity of the evening of yore. Castro, his arm extended, was pulling the bell-cord next to the fireplace. Perhaps he was struck by that similarity too, for his eyes widened slightly and he was staring at Rachel as if he expected her to make some remark on the subject of that caricature of a church bell. But Rachel remained impassive, and he contented himself with saying: "I'm ringing for dinner to be sent up."

The mulatto maid slid in, carrying dishes, as furtively as a Jewess would have done in the Goanese ghetto on the evening when the menace had been suspended over it for the first time. Confused words about the tempest that had been unleashed outside, on the less overwhelming temperature and on Antonia's character were exchanged as if in a dream by the man and woman sitting opposite one another. Neither of them was eating, although they were making the gestures, but Pedre de Castro was filing his glass and emptying it relentlessly, like someone who, finding himself in complete moral darkness, believes that he might find the means in alcohol to make an interior light appear.

And Rachel continued to gaze, not at the stout individual who was sitting behind the glittering champagne buckets from which the necks of bottles emerged, but the creature that he had been in another place, a dozen years before.

He was standing in front of a large boat with a deck and playing the guitar. That event had often been described to Rachel and she had taken pleasure in reconstituting it mentally, but she had never imagined it in such a gripping fashion. He was tottering slightly and sometimes stopped playing, in order to burst into hysterical laughter and look at his companion, who was beating time in mid-air grotesquely.

The moon had just risen and the belated boat was seen in the distance by river-dwellers who were filled with astonishment by the music and the songs that departed from it, the great red beacon that illuminated its prow and the wooden cross that a servant was holding aloft at the rear.

The sound of the oars was covered by the voices of the rowers and men crowded on the deck, who were all singling the canticles of the Month of Mary that had just been sung in the churches of Goa. For it was under the pretext of religion that Pedre de Castro had fanaticized his servants, who were converted Hindus, against the Jews, and there was even a mendicant monk, who was sitting cross-legged with a stout staff on his knees.

Castro affected then to despise men, and to treat them as slaves, and it amused him, having roused them against the Jews in the name of the Christian God, to mingle the sounds of his guitar with their pious canticles.

The white nagah flowers were raining down on the nocturnal player, and the boat, with its cross, seemed to be gliding toward some bizarre accursed feast.

No one ran to warn the Jews. At any rate, at the place where the road ceased to run alongside the river and circled the Archbishop's gardens, the entire band leapt out of the boat and ran behind the bearer of the cross, the musician and the man beating time.

It was late. The Jews were asleep. They woke up screaming. The entire street howled with terror simultaneously. When Rachel looked out of the window she saw silhouettes trying to scale the balconies and the cross tipped over in front of her house, which, handled by a group of men, was being used against the door as a battering ram.

She did not have time to be afraid. The events were as unreal and surprising as those of a nightmare. Forms passed in front of her on the stairway. Someone shouted distinctly, with an affectation of calm in his voice: "Bring light! A torch, or no matter what, to illuminate this pitch-dark."

And another voice said: "Be careful that they don't defend themselves."

To which the response was: "They're far too cowardly. Have you ever heard mention of Jews defending themselves?"

A mulatto with an idiotic face came upstairs with a candle. He was holding it close to his eyes, protecting the flame with his hand, and repeating, triumphantly: "I've got a candle!"

There was a brief sound of a struggle in her father and mother's room. And suddenly, by the light of the candle, Rachel had the vision of Castro on the threshold, clasping her naked mother against him. He had blood on his lips, like someone who has received a blow, and he cried, in a voice full of rage: "I'll make him pay for that. Tie him up."

During the few seconds of that apparition, Rachel, who could not see her mother's head buried under Castro's arm, did not recognize that white form, those limpid legs that were trying to strike the man who held them captive. It was the blue-tinted hair abruptly untied and collapsing to the floor, and then the anguished voice that suddenly screamed her name: "Rachel!" that made her identify with that long, smooth and palpitating flesh the person who was for her a kind of immaterial goddess.

Like a dog whose master is being attacked, Rachel had run forward blindly to scratch or bite. But with his foot, as one does with a dog, Castro had sent her sprawling on the ground a few paces away from him. She remained there, stunned, her face against the wall. What struck her when she came round was the number of footfalls resounding in every room in the house, the sound of breaking furniture and the word "money," which returned incessantly to the mouth of several men, calling to one another from one floor to the next. *Have you found the money? The money must be hidden somewhere! Perhaps the money is behind the books?* Then she saw a huge half-breed with the build of a brute, wearing red boots that came up above the knees, carefully spreading out a bedsheet, and, after having piled into it, pell-mell, cutlery, vases and everything he had been able to find, knotted the four corners meticulously and loaded it on to his back.

She went downstairs in three bounds and found herself on the threshold of her house at the exact moment when a wooden box laminated with silver, launched from a window, smashed into a thousand shards.

The street had the appearance of a vast moonlight flit. The fabrics of a cellar of Cashmere veils made a pile in front of a staved-in shop, and two men were exchanging blows while dividing them between them. A Jewess with scarlet kerchief on her head was supine beneath a negro whose white eyes and the lubricious expression of his mouth Rachel could distinguish. A thin old man in a ridiculous dressing gown was running back and forth repeating: "Curse you! May the malediction of God be upon you."

A man who had loaded a heavy chest of drawers with iron fittings on to his back stopped occasionally to draw breath, and shouted in a monotonous tone, like a learned lesson: "Murderers! You've killed an innocent child!"

The cries of the fearful Jews in the house that had been able to remain closed made a continuous plaint only interrupted by the voices of the paralyzed man exhorting his fellows to fight.

Rachel saw the cross that had served as a battering ram turning the corner at the top of the street, in the middle of a compact group.

A cry of delight rang in her ears at that moment and she was seized by the arm and hugged to someone's breast. It was an old Hindu domestic named Abdullah, who did the cooking and accompanied her father when he went to care for a patient in a distant village. He had centenarian parents with whom he lived in Ribandar, with the consequence that he did not live in the Jehoudahs' house but came every morning and left every evening. An instinct had made him get up in the night when he had heard the canticles of the Month of Mary resonating on the river.

There was a rumor in the direction of the port and a shadow barred the extremity of the street. The soldiers had finally arrived. Doors banged, people fled, moans rose up in a shriller tone. Dolor, sensing itself protected, developed more greatly.

Rachel was carried away at a run by Abdullah. Doubtless he hoped that the little girl lifted in his arms would be more susceptible of influencing the hateful Christian executioners than the soldiers with their rifles. He climbed the pillaged street, went under the arch of the antique gate of the ghetto, went around the Archbishop' gardens and launched himself along the road to old Goa, to the point where, after zigzagging between abandoned houses, it rejoined the river.

He arrived too late. The band of Christian canticle-singers, with its drunken guitarist, its booty of stolen objects, its prisoner and its naked living prey had just cast off on the tranquil water and were heading upriver toward the ancient Portuguese city.

Then the Hindu started running along the road parallel to the river, only departed from it by clumps of mimosas, but odorous pandanus, while camphor-tress inundated by rust, and nagahs with their rain of white flowers. Sometimes he parted the foliage, uttered a desolate cry, raised the child above his head and held her out toward the boat.

It was then, through the parted branches, that Rachel had the unforgettable vision.

Pedre de Castro, struck in the face by a Jew whose wife he had just stolen, had sworn an oath on the cross borne by his servants to avenge himself. And between him and his friends, while they went back to the boat, amid by wagers and bursts of laughter, the possibility of that vengeance had been discussed. The unanimous opinion was that he would not dare to accomplish the vengeance that he projected—and that was what impelled him to act.

He cross rose up slowly in the prow of the boat and Rachel saw that her father had been attached to it, his arms outspread, with a face that he had clad in a scornful calm.

She did not hear the phrase repeated several times to the servants by Deodat de Vega; "Above all, don't do him any harm." For he was thinking of the consequences that the affair might have with the Portuguese authorities and how important it was that he was neither wounded not dead.

She only saw a very young man, who had the large head of a degenerate, place on her father's head by derision, a hastily-woven crown of white flowers plucked from the nagah that made a vault above the water.

All of that appeared to her to be devoid of meaning, incomprehensible.

It was Deodat de Vega who picked up the guitar and began to play.

Pedre de Castro advanced toward her father and said to him, at close range, face to face and pointing to his still-bleeding lip, a phrase that she did not hear, any more than the other: "She's the one who'll drink from my mouth the blood that you've caused to flow."

At the same time he drew away a cloak of yellow cloth that hid something immobile lying on the deck at the front of the boat, near the erect cross. Then he made a sign to a man who was crouching beside him, pointing at the opening that led to the space below the deck

What happened was as rapid as an image in a dream.

The removed cloak had uncovered something long and white, a form of supernatural brightness that seemed to store the ambient light of the moon, with the result that everything around it as darker. Rachel only recognized her mother when she stood up, with a single surge, the movement and decision of which gave her body an extraordinary beauty of proportion.

As if she had become fluid and intangible, the admirable form slipped between the two men, took two or three light steps over the deck, traversed the line of oarsmen with as much ease as if she had passed through them, and threw herself into the water. The droplets that sprang up after the fall of the body made a circle of little bright stars. But there was no splashing, no effort of someone drowning and who wants to live: nothing but a broad indifferent undulating that was seen to disappear in a circle.

The oarsmen, rowing forcefully, did not stop to striking the water. It was necessary to shout an order to them to go back, and that order came a little too late. The boat turned, with difficulty, because of the faster current coming from the other branch of the river.

When they got back to the place where Dolça Jehoudah had disappeared, there was no trace of her, and it was only for form's sake that Castro ordered two Hindus to dive several times. The boat wandered hither and yon without anyone paying any attention to the clamors of an old man and a little girl on the bank.

Consternation and the fear of responsibilities took possession of the souls of the pious Portuguese. The glare of the red beacon on the water suddenly became so sinister that everyone turned their eyes toward old Goa. The half-breed domestics and the Hindu Christians, who did not estimate the death of a Jewess as any great loss and who felt covered by their masters, resumed the canticles of the Month of Mary in chorus. But under the declining moon, with the crucified man crowned with nagah flowers, whom no one any longer dared take down, the canticles took on such a lugubrious resonance that the voices faded away one by one, and when they arrived at the first landing-stage, alongside the ruins of the Church of Saint Joseph, only the brute in big red boots was still singing.

Everyone dispersed with rapidity along the old walls, along mossy flagstones pathways, between the low buildings and demolished towers. It was the persistently drunken half-breed who assumed the responsibility of detaching Manoël Jehoudah from his cross, and who left him with his damaged wrists and his crown over his ears, haggard and solitary, between the sparkling surface of the waters and the three-headed shadow of the Church of Saint Joseph.

"Oh, render him, Lord Sabaoth, in accordance with his wickedness."

Rachel had read that phrase in the book in which the misfortunes of the Jewish race were enumerated. In that book there were many descriptions of the pogroms that had once taken place in Spain, Portugal and elsewhere, which were more terrible than those in Goa. Those ancient pogroms resembled those of which she had read accounts in the newspapers, which had taken place recently in Russia and Poland. They all began with the accusation of ritual murder and continued with the pillaging of riches, whether those riches were the bodies of women or money in coin.

But although the author of the book made the ardent wish, the Lord Sabaoth never rendered according to wickedness. The Jews were often massacred, always despoiled, sometimes forced to changed their homeland. They never received anything in compensation for their woes. Rachel recalled having read that in Spain, all the Jews of one community had been expelled entirely naked, without hats on their heads or sandals on their feet, because the Christian inhabitants had claimed that it would be a pity to abandon even a small piece of cloth to those accused individuals. Once, in Germany, the fire that had consumed the houses had been so ardent that a neighboring church had burned down and its great bell had become a formless lump of bronze. The monks of Malta, having encountered a ship full of Jews fleeing toward the Levant, had attached them to the masts and bulwark and used them as targets for their arquebuses.

The old author of the sixteenth century sometimes added to the end of an account of a massacre that some Provençal bishop who had ordered it had been stricken with leprosy by the wrath of the Eternal. He tried hard to establish a connection between the defeat of some Austrian prince by the Turks with the evil treatments that the prince had inflicted on the people of Israel. Rachel, less prejudiced and believing less in justice than the religious author, had not seen with the same evidence as him any relationship of cause and effect between the crime and its punishment

What had astonished her most in her youth was that the men who had robbed and humiliated her father were able to continue to live without being troubled and that, having been taken before judges, they had been able to emerge from the tribunal with their heads held high and a smile on their lips.

The pogrom of Goa had been followed by a parody of pursuit and judgment, but the day after the night when it had taken place, Castro and his friends, impelled by fear, formally accused the physician Jehoudah of having abducted a Christian child in order to make use of his blood in abominable religious practices, and they had even gone too far as to demand his immediate arrest. The district judge thought he was showing a great spirit of clemency in leaving him at liberty, because of the violence to which he had already been subjected and the misfortune that had struck him.

One the day when the youngest son of the caretaker of the solitary Church of the Magi had disappeared, Manoël Jehoudah had gone to give his cares to the caretaker, afflicted by elephantiasis. Jehoudah had often been called to old Goa because he cared for poor sick people gratuitously. He sometimes went on foot by road, and at other times he went upriver in a little dinghy, of which Abdullah plied the oars. That day, he had gone to the Church of the Magi without being called by the caretaker, out of pure charity, taking advantage, he said, of having come to old Goa to see how his patient was.

The house was a wretched shack backed up against the church, and one reached it by way of a winding path through brushwood, which prolonged a long avenue bordered by mango-trees. Jehoudah had seen the child, well after the avenue, at the place where the path rejoined the road. He was sitting at the foot of a tree, and the physician was astonished, after having passed by, that the child had not run toward him as he usually did.

A little further on, while traversing what had once been an outlying district of old Goa and as now a mass of ruined walls, he had recognized the silhouettes of Pedre de Castro and Deodat de Vega some distance away. The sight of those two men, by whom he and his wife were spied on and followed, had caused him a movement of repulsion and he had, he remembered, swiftly passed the cloak that he had over his left arm to his right. That gesture had been the fragile pretext for the accusation. The two Portuguese affirmed that on perceiving them, Jehoudah had been tempted to turn back, that he had, by an instinctive movement, tried to disguise something that seemed very heavy and was rolled up in a cloak. Then he had drawn away with a rapidity that would have been incomprehensible if the physician had not had something to hide.

They even added that Jehoudah's attitude had been dishonoring. They willingly admitted that they had a few inoffensive pleasantries for which to reproach themselves in his regard, and they expected that, finding themselves face to face with him in a solitary place, he would have demanded an explanation from them. At the time, they had put his singular flight down to the well-known cowardice of Jews.

Rachel had always shivered with humiliation on thinking about that encounter. Why had his father not had the courage to march toward the two men and slap the one who had kissed her mother by surprise? Alas, in the physician Jehoudah, thought alone was audacious. As he was obliged to explain subsequently, in order to justify his attitude, it was the possibility of an altercation, the dread of having to materialize his anger in action and the incapacity to do that, that had hastened him along the road, ridiculously, in a cowardly fashion.

The two Portuguese claimed that after having laughed enormously at the flight of the cowardly husband, a suspicion had occurred to them. They wondered what might be in the package enveloped in a cloak that Jehoudah was carrying. The physician affirmed that he had nothing over his arm but his cloak, which he had taken in spite of the April warmth, because of certain fits of fever that caused him to shiver in the evening, but the Portuguese were ready to swear to the truth of their accusation on the Christ. They could not, they said, think of a theft, in view of the poverty of the caretaker of the Church of the Magi, but they thought about some profanation of a sacred object. They went to the church. The caretaker was already astonished not to have seen his child return. They waited with him and spent all night and the following morning searching the surroundings, fruitlessly.

Under the influence of indignation, and knowing that, if they accused the Jewish physician before the law, the latter would have time to make the evidence of his crime disappear, they had resolved, with a few friends and servants, to make an immediate incursion into the Jewish quarter and to search the physician's house.

It was in the course of that incursion that Castro had been struck in the face by Jehoudah and had resolved to take him away, with his wife, who was perhaps an accomplice, to the Church of the Magi. He thought, by intimidating him, that he might obtain a confession. He regretted having involuntarily driven a woman to suicide, but a host of witnesses affirmed that he had not done any harm to any of the Jehoudahs. They had merely been taken on to the boat by force. If Dolça Jehoudah had preferred death to the vision of the Church of the Magi and that of a father weeping over his lost child, it was because she must have had a conscience that was not tranquil.

Castro also regretted that a few blows had been struck here and there in the Jewish quarter, a few doors broken down and a few objects broken by the Christians, whose virtue it had not been possible to moderate. That was very minor damage compared with the shedding of the blood of an innocent. Even the death of Dolça Jehoudah was insufficient to avenge that bloodshed, and Castro maintained his complaint and his accusation against the physician.

He had not been able to bring any evidence of that other than his moral certainty, affirmed by reiterated oaths on the Christ. Those oaths, supported by the oaths of all the young noblemen of Goa, were so numerous and so solemn that, for all those who attended the trial, the idea of Christ was bound to the pogrom of Goa.

It was Christ that had visited it. A cross had been erected on the boat that transported the administrators of justice. All those what had participated in it were soldiers of Christ. Castro and his companions were innocent of the death of Dolça Jehoudah, because the events made it obvious that the death in question was the will of Christ. Manoël Jehoudah was found innocent of the death of the child, because there was no proof against him, but he quit the tribunal indirectly scarred, suspected by everyone of having shed blood for mysterious practices. His defense had been imprinted with sadness and not punctuated by the sincere cries by which hearts are conquered.

The king's prosecutor, a just man in the measure that one can be when one sees things through the shadows of one's mediocrity, had not requested any penalty against him, but he had pronounced the word "magic" with sufficient real terror to make the audience shiver. For him, although Manoël Jehoudah could not be convicted of the ritual crime, the ritual crime was not in doubt. He believed that it had happened in other places, and that learned Jews, inheritors of old traditions, fabricated unleavened bread at Passover with a mixture of flour and infantile blood. The more learned Jews were, the more it was necessary to beware of them.

The king's prosecutor knew personally, he had it from a very reliable source, that the blood was not only used to make unleavened bread, that it had other maleficent uses and that those uses were related in books written in Hebrew. He regretted, for his part, that a Jewish physician accused—without proof—of the murder of a child, had in his possession a vast library of books incomprehensible to Christians. He had seen those books while searching Jehoudah's house, for—the king's prosecutor observed, regretfully—they had been spared

47

in the pillage, and in leafing through them he had been struck by their antiquity, their mystery and certain typographical dispositions of the text in which he thought he recognized invocatory formulae.

The king's prosecutor was an obedient servant of the law. He showed that in a striking fashion, in proclaiming that one could not condemn a man when there was no conclusive proof against him, but he could not help deploring that fact that the law did not arm those who defended it better and that the king's prosecutor no longer had, as in the times of the Inquisition, the right to have what he did not understand burned.

Manoël Jehoudah had been obliged to lave Goa. Christians who saw him at the end of a street retraced their steps ostentatiously in order not to pass close to him. His coreligionists did not pardon him for having been the origin of an anti-Jewish movement in the Portuguese possessions of India. Many of them, including the rabbi, insisted that, by way of a concession to public opinion, he destroy the books that had become legendary since the prosecutor's speech at his trial.

He had departed without regret. His window overlooked the sea and one could see the river widen into a broad estuary there. He was unable to look at the white line that formed a stripe at low tide or the disquieting eddies in the water at high tide. It was out there on the strand of Aguada that he had bent down, full of horror, over a form so eaten away by fish that he had been obliged, in order to recognize it, to wash the long blue-tinted hair soiled with mud, with his own hands.

And now, Rachel was looking the author of so many woes in the face. He was there, sitting placidly, with slack cheeks and a fat belly, indicating that he must eat well and doubtless enjoyed a tranquil conscience. He had insisted several times that she eat and drink, and had said banal things that he tried to render amiable, reminding Rachel by the inclination of his head of the movement of certain malevolent dogs when they lick your hand.

Now he had taken a cigar out of his pocket and was launching large puffs of smoke toward the ceiling. He must have the habit of coming from Goa to enjoy himself with women in that brothel in Bombay, the only one where Europeans could be found. He was a client. They knew him. They knew his tastes, his habits. He liked champagne. He was violent. He detested waiting. This evening, after having trailed through the bars of the port, he had decided to dine with a woman. And that woman was her, Rachel.

So, there was no justice. The injustice was even about to be aggravated. Rachel had often imagined the unexpected circumstances that might put her in the presence of Pedre de Castro, and would permit her to take revenge upon him. In the fantasy of dreams, she had seen herself, by a series of bizarre events, thanks to an immense fortune, enjoying a discretionary power and humiliating the detestable being. She had imagined him on his knees, imploring her. Not only had none of that occurred, but it was her who was now at the mercy of the man, and in the most miserable and shameful conditions possible. He had certainly recognized her, by virtue of her astonishing resemblance to her mother. Impressed at first by the evocation of the ancient drama, he had calmed down, he had dined, and now he was reflecting.

Miserable race, he must be thinking, *whose children one finds in the dubious places of big cities*. He hadn't had the mother; well, he was about to have the daughter.

Doubtless, in accordance with his habit, he had dined first. Rachel had seen him look at the bed complaisantly. He would soon get up, seize her, and shove her on to it.

At that thought she sensed a warmth run through her body and make her ears buzz.

No justice! Never justice! There were the weak and the strong, and the strong were almost always the wicked. She thought about her father, out there, in the little town of Cochin, from which she had fled. He had wanted to live with the people known as the black Jews, the most wretched of all, twigs of an entirely bastardized branch of the race. And he had

49

never thought of avenging himself! She saw again a deserted road, at dusk, and her father almost running in order not to have to quarrel with two Christian insulters.

At that moment, she had difficulty not standing up and crying out. She felt suddenly light, strong, and invincible. What no Jew, to her knowledge, had ever dared do, she was about to accomplish. She was astonished herself that the task was so easy.

A large carving knife was on a plate, amid slices of roast beef. Rachel, whose elbows were on the table only had to let her arm fall in order to seize it. She calculated that by standing up at the same time, she would be able, almost in the same second, to traverse with that weapon, which seemed very sharp, the broad belly that was in front of her, making a cushion over the table.

She glimpsed what might happen then. The man's cries, what she would say as she struck him again, the police in kha-ki uniforms and turbans, the prison before which she had passed during the evening, a trial in which all the past abomination would be evoked, but a trial in Bombay, before English judges.

The rain outside was no longer beating the window-panes with such force, but it could be heard running in streams over terraces. There was a lassitude about the wind. The song of the frogs rose up with a regularity that rendered it sadder.

The resolution taken gave Rachel's face a sort of illumi-nated serenity that transformed its expression. And then, fac-ing her, Castro's gaze became more fixed. He considered her as if he had ceased to recognize her. He bit his lips like some-one who perceives an error and, pushing the table in front of him, he got up. He took one or two steps and Rachel thought, with an interior laughter, that he was about to lift the mosqui-to-net to make access to the bed easier.

The knife was still within reach of her hand.

With an immense effort, in a low voice, Castro said: "I'm not mistaken. You really are the daughter of a physician named Jehoudah?"

Rachel's hand had brushed the plate where the roast beef and the knife were. To gain time, she said: "Me!"

"Yes," said Castro. "Manoël Jehoudah, who once lived in Goa."

So he wasn't sure! It was to her that it belonged to tell him. But why? Why give him that further victory, the fall of Jehoudah's daughter? That might perhaps suffice for him to find death less frightful.

Rachel's eyes expressed tranquil surprise. She shook her head. "My name is Rachel Soarez," she said.

That was the name under which she was registered at her hotel, under which Antonia must know her.

Castro uttered a deep sigh, as if he had been delivered from a terrible threat. He stammered: "I told myself that.... It was such an improbable coincidence!"

With a visible satisfaction, he repeated: "Rachel Soarez!" Then he said: "Oh, if you knew, if you knew!"

What? Was he talking about the drama in Goa? In that case, Rachel knew. But she thought she understood that it was a matter of another drama, interior to him.

What? What could he be thinking, exactly? Did deeply evil beings enjoy their wickedness in the same manner as those who do good?

Rachel expected some abrupt attack on Castro's part at any moment. She was ready to bound to her feet and she never lost sight of the knife. But she searched in vain in the thick face, in the tremor and the moistness of the lips, the gleam in the little eyes, for the animation that sexual fervor puts into them.

He spoke to her without moving forward, and his voice seemed to come from much further away than the distance that separated them.

When he first pronounced the words: "Perhaps you're the instrument of providence," Rachel, recalling Antonia's very similar words, thought that she would have burst out laughing in other circumstances. She contained herself, but the gravity of what Castro said then was diminished, retaining a sort of comical stain, and everything that followed had the appearance for Rachel of being a parody of another, true scene, more moving, and lived elsewhere.

"I'll explain to you later what just happened within me, but it's necessary that you don't say here a moment longer. Since you've come here, it's because..."

At that point he stammered, and Rachel understood that he could not find the delicate formulae, doubtless never pronounced before, by which he would have promised her the money she was counting on from her visit to Antonia's.

She shrugged her shoulders. The tension of her upper body indicated the passionate curiosity that animated her. She tried to understand. The gleam of the knife n the table seemed to fade.

"We're going to leave together. I thought of all that during dinner. You're God's witness."

That formula must have satisfied him, because he repeated it again.

Suddenly, the bell announcing the pogrom of Goa resonated in the distance, amid the chorus of frogs. Castro had pulled the bell-cord. He asked for his coat and hat, which he had left somewhere, and he made a sign also to bring Rachel's hat and coat, if she had one.

The mulatto maid deposited those objects on a chair with a disconcerting rapidity, not without darting a pitying glace at Rachel. The latter even had the sensation that she was holding herself back in order not to give her some advice, to make her a recommendation of prudence. But the sentiment of her own security prevailed, and she disappeared.

Rachel remembered the advice of the blonde woman on the threshold of the house. What more was there to fear on the part of the man from Goa, the one who liked Jewesses? Had he taken other women away as he was taking her, or was what was happening new, special to her?

Castro had looked at his watch and had murmured: "With a vehicle, we have plenty of time."

Then, indifferently, he added: "Doubtless you live in Mazagon. It's scarcely a quarter of an hour from Mazagon to the port. The ship doesn't leave until five o'clock in the morning."

What ship? He wanted her to take a ship with him? He was disposing of her, without consulting her, as if she belonged to him! He didn't suspect that, on the contrary, it was him who had become her possession and that, during the time that remained to him to live, she would be attached to his execrated form, to his blood, with the same tenacity as the crustaceans that had been found on her mother's body and that it had been so difficult to detach. He was right. They had time. She would not strike until the moment chosen by her...

As he had just parted the curtain over the window to make sure by the panes that it was still raining, she seized the knife from the plate with an abrupt gesture and rolled it up in her shawl.

To leave the room, Castro bowed ceremoniously before her, but he summoned the invisible mulatto maid sharply because the corridor and stairway were not sufficiently illuminated and Rachel might not be able to see.

On the contrary, she could see very well. She walked with her head high and breasts jutting, and a vague smile even wandered over her lips. Down below she saw the closed doors behind which a vague terror still stirred, and then the sinister and streaming street where one gas lamp was lit, like an astonished eye; further away, her gaze plunged into the darkness of what was about to happen.

She was not astonished that the blind beggar continued to stare at a point on her forehead. She felt that she was marked by a sign. Castro had just told her so: she was God's witness.

The Agonizing City

The stars of a serene night were reflected on the waters of the river Mandavi with the broader and brighter reverberation that comes from the proximity of the dawn. Eight Malabarans were plying the oars of the boat and, and the sound that the oars made as they struck the water was the only one to trouble the nocturnal silence.

Castro was sitting beside Rachel, in the front of the boat, and sometimes leaned over to remind the oarsmen that he had promised them a tip if they crossed the distance separating the new city from old Goa with the greatest possible rapidity.

Rachel wondered what could be impelling Castro to arrive a little more rapidly, and what was making him look anxiously to the sky to see whether the first pallors of sunlight might be appearing. The twenty-three hours of the voyage of the steamer that maintained the service between Bombay and Goa had told her nothing about her companion's intentions. Castro had shown himself particularly respectful in her regard and everything he had said to her betrayed the fear that she might change her opinion, that she might cease to want to accompany him on arriving in the port of Goa. He had been reassured when she had affirmed that she did not know anyone there and that, in consequence, nothing could retain her there. He had returned several times to the resemblance between Rachel and a woman he had known, he said, and who was dead. But the young woman had been able to recount such a plausible history of Rachel Soarez that he no longer suspected that she might be the daughter of the Goanese physician, and her resemblance to Dolça Jehoudah did not appear to trouble him as much.

In the distance, beyond the tops of the trees accumulated along the banks, Rachel saw outlined on the bareness of the ruddy hills the silhouette of a ruined church, the elongated skeleton of a ruined convent.

When the boat passed the village of Ribandar, Rachel saw that her companion was profoundly absorbed by the contemplation of the water. Was he searching for the face of Dulça Jehoudah, who had disappeared there? A nagah petal traced an uncertain furrow through the air and came to settle like a moth on the young woman's nee. She caress the pale tissue, as soft as a wing, and raised her hand to her forehead as if to place a crown thereon—but Castro did not see the gesture.

He only emerged from his reverie when the boat bumped into the worn stones of the jetty. Then he made a sign to Rachel to follow him without losing any time.

For the traveler who arrives via the river Mandavi, nothing allows him to believe that between its waters and the distant mountains, beneath the shady masses of vegetation, there are the vestiges of what was once the ancient city of Albuquerque, the great Portuguese metropolis, the ecclesiastical queen of India. Only the church of Saint Joseph, with its three towers crowned with tattered crenellations, like three heads of tenacious old men beneath ragged hats, attests to the struggle of stone against the forest.

When she was a child, Rachel hardly ever went into old Goa. She only had a very vague memory of it, but what she saw in the moonlight appeared to her to be different, transformed, singularly more savage and abandoned.

Behind Castro, she first went along a path so narrow that the reeds bordering it struck her face. Then she crossed a bridge and Castro shouted: "Be careful!"

The bridge had no guard-rail and one sensed that certain planks were rotten, yielding underfoot.

Rachel wondered whether she would not do better to finish it right away, and whether the stagnant waters that she perceived between the slats of the bridge would be an appropriate tomb for the man whose death she had resolved. She imagined the fat body swaying abruptly between the aquatic plants, and he frightened frogs. But the solitude of the place would have given her action a sinister quality that she found repugnant.

She traversed the ramparts, and a place where there ought to have been gates, marched across waste ground where sections of wall still stood, passed under Albuquerque's triumphal arch and then went into two little churches, low and similar, like two old sisters crouching down together to die, and abruptly found herself in a broad paved avenue, solemn and straight, between the facades of palaces covered in sculptures, with Gothic portals and Renaissance turrets. Long grass grew between the flagstones; sometimes a coconut palm loomed up in the middle of the avenue; there were arborescent ferns that spread out before the doors, and Rachel remarked that the majority of the palaces were devoid of roofs and that their windows were like great open wounds from which long pandanus branches dangled in sheaves, and bignonias with vine-like stems. The magnificent dwellings were only appearances; they had only kept the skeletons of stone to give a figuration of grandeur to that phantom avenue.

Castro was walking with difficulty because of his pot belly. He passed to draw breath, and as if he had divined Rachel's thoughts and wanted to excuse the decadence of the city, he said: "This part of Goa is now the most uninhabited of all. A few years ago there were still a number of Portuguese families living here, but once there was a fire, another time a storm." There had been an earthquake, and then an epidemic. He did not pronounce the name of the disease, out of superstition, because of the force of appeal there is in the syllables of the name. But neither the earthquake or nor the epidemic were the true causes of the evil.

He resumed walking, looking to the right and the left, as if he feared seeing something redoubtable suddenly surge forth.

"I can't know whence it came," he said, in a low voice. "No one knows that. It began a long time ago, before I was born, I think. It was a sort of curse. Life ceased, almost abruptly, to bring its sap. Commerce declined. People had fewer children. Then faith diminished. The convents emptied. The monks went elsewhere. Some returned to Portugal, others settled in China. One might have thought that an order of abandonment had been given."

They had walked as far as the Rua Derecha. It was there that what remained of the activity of old Goa had taken refuge. Castro, whose head was bowed, raised it, as if the sight of a few inhabited houses had rendered him his pride.

"And to think that elephants of war were stabled over there, then the workshops for the founding of cannons, then the shipyards where galleons were constructed, and the city extended even further, with a girdle of convents and churches. Now, the sons of the first conquerors of India live in a veritable tomb.

Between the sections of wall Rachel saw a vast cloister, whose quadrilateral was bounded by four ruined chapels, and which was all that remained of the power of the Jesuits. She went past edifices that were evidently empty and deserted, which were the former palace of the governor and that of the Inquisition. An equestrian statue lay in a square, fallen and broken.

"Vasco da Gama!" said Castro. "Isn't it a pity?"

They went around the statue, and, after going alongside a wall pierced by crenellations, in the shadow of dead dwellings, a light finally shone. It was a small light that illuminated the panes of an arched window. In the mortuary darkness of the defunct city, that gleam had something supernatural about it.

With surprise, Rachel saw her companion fall to his knees. It seemed that behind the lighted window she had seen the passage of the head of an old man with a pointed bald cranium and a circle of hair around the neck.

"The patriarch," said Castro, getting to his feet. "When he starts to walk in his palace, daylight isn't far away."

And he hastened his pace.

Rachel recalled everything she had heard about the Archbishop of Goa, the Primate of India. He was partly responsible for the religious decadence of the old Portuguese capital. For many years, he had been at odds with the Pope. He had scorned his authority, caused a schism.[2] The Christians of the Orient were divided into two parties, and had even come to blows several times. Driven by an intractable pride and claiming to receive revelations directly from God, the Archbishop of Goa, in order to create partisans, had ordained anyone who asked for it, including adventurers come from almost anywhere, and even African negroes. His great power had diminished, but he was ninety years old and, possessed of a tenacious vitality, refused to die.

"I've always thought that the life of Goa was linked to that of the Archbishop," said Castro, as if talking to himself. "He knows that, and he gets up at night to struggle against the destruction."

At a place where the collapse of several facades allowed the sight of inclinations of various stories and fragments of staircases whose spirals led nowhere, Castro stopped again and gripped Rachel's arm.

"Listen!" he murmured, breathing heavily.

Rachel listened, but only perceived an anguishing silence.

"It has often happened to me to get up at night in order to take account of that nocturnal activity of the dead, the active presence that is hastening the end of the old city. It's a real, palpable entity, albeit without precise form, which circulates over he runs and draws nourishment from them.

---

[2] The Archbishop to whom the story refers is presumably supposed to be José Maria da Silva Torres (1800-1854), who was appointed in 1843, did indeed fall out with the Pope with regard to questions of his authority, and contributed to the so-called Goan schism of the 1850s. He was dismissed from the post in 1848 and returned to Portugal, although some sources give that date incorrectly as 1851, which is more likely to be the year in which the story is set. The account rendered in the novel is, however, considerably melodramatized and largely fictitious.

"Then, it seems to me that the disintegration of things is more rapid. I can hear the wood rotting, the molecules of stones dissolving. Sometimes it's an old beam that cracks, sometimes the sound of a rat gnawing the marrow of a door. The bones that sustain the limbs of monuments are decaying internally. A putrid decomposition flows in the water under the aqueducts. It's as if an immense army of silent termites were animate in the shadows, devouring the mosaics of the parvis, the steps of colonnades and the iron clasps sustaining the vaults."

Rachel felt the relief of a ring imprinting itself on the arm that Castro was squeezing.

"On some mornings, I've found pillars of the cloister lying on the ground, which I had seen the precious day in their place in the gray file of pillars. I've heard rubble falling and I can swear that the bell of the Church of Mercy rang, one night, without anyone being able to discover who pulled the rope. There's an active force that hastens dissolutions, precipitates putrefactions, making use of autumnal damp and the pestilential exhalations of marshes. It's an extrahuman force that is employing itself in the annihilation of the Catholic Goa: Goa, the city of God.

A nocturnal bird cut through the air with a heavy wingbeat. The reality of the sound reassured Castro.

"We've arrived; this is my house," he said, indicating a dwelling that had a large closed portal, reached by means of several steps.

Arrived! Rachel thought. *The voyage has to be longer.*

The Church of the Magi

As she approached the portal, Rachel saw that it was only a wall, doubtless recently built, following collapses and
repairs, but on which a door with two battens had been crudely
painted, the color of wood. Castro took a key from his pocket
and opened a very small but real door a little further on. He
made a sign to Rachel to pass before him.

A half-breed, who was doubtless the doorkeeper, was lying on fragments of carpet, asleep. Castro pushed him with the
tip of his foot and gave him orders in a low voice. At the same
time he put a finger over his lips, and Rachel understood that it
was important not to wake the residents of the house—or perhaps only the other servants.

After a few minutes, a lantern blinked and swung at the
back of the room and Rachel saw the servant returning, laden
with formless objects. Then she distinguished a large vestibule
with crucifixes on the walls and portraits that seemed to her to
be corroded by damp. She had the impression of faded gold,
pious images, dust and obsolescence.

Castro took a few steps in the shadows and unhooked
one of the long Portuguese capes, dark brown in color, that fall
all the way to the feet, giving their wearers the impression of
monks, by virtue of their broad sleeves and hood. He threw it
over Rachel's shoulders, saying: "This is in order that no one
will guess who you are when we come back in daylight."

Rachel thought that that scruple was quite unnecessary.
The curiosity that had brought her was about to be satisfied.
With her hand, she felt the blade of the knife rolled up in her
shawl. The hours, even the minutes, of Castro's life were now
counted.

Bur suddenly, the eyes of the Portuguese had a haggard
gleam. A thought had just occurred to him. He stared alternately at the obscure wall, then Rachel, and asked the young
woman point-blank: "Do you have a knife"

She took a step back, and had the sentiment that she had been divined, that he had seen the weapon that she was carrying, and that he was about to throw himself upon her to forestall her.

Emotion prevented her from saying a single word, and paralyzed the movement she attempted to make beneath the cloak in order to disengage the knife from the folds of the shawl.

But with a slight shrug of the shoulders that meant: *That's true—the question is absurd!* Castro turned to the half-breed and said to him: "Give me a knife."

He turned away and with all his might he spat in the direction of a painting that represented an individual with delicate features, a large drooping moustache and a lace collar over silver armor.

The half-breed, however, having searched his belt, replied in the low tone of someone making an apology: "I only have a pen-knife, and it's chipped."

Castro almost snatched it from the hand that was holding it out to him. He stood on tiptoe and inflicted two long thrusts, vertically and horizontally, on the portrait of the man in silver armor.

Rachel heard the sound of the canvas tearing, and saw that Castro, unable to reach the face, had made a cross on the portrait, at the place of the heart.

He turned round, sniggering.

"There's a force in images, which it's necessary to kill if one doesn't want to submit to it. I shall burn this portrait, the portrait of Pedre de Castro, the genius of evil."

He threw away the pen-knife, made a sign to the half-breed to load the package he had gone to fetch on to his back, and he drew Rachel outside.

Stray dogs were going along the deserted street. A cock crowed. An elephant trumpeted in a distant enclosure. A freshness, of marshes and wet grass, spread through the air.

They walked as rapidly as Castro's obesity permitted. They traversed empty squares, went along walls, and crossed further ramparts. A door opened and closed as they passed by in a low house constructed in bamboo, and in another, Rachel saw an old woman crouching down and blowing on a meager fire between two stones

They had traversed the ancient outlying districts of Goa, and Castro said with a certain solemnity, pointing to the line of trees ahead of him:

"The Church of the Magi is there."

Things were beginning to stand out with more clarity. The road they had followed had brought them to a hilltop. Rachel had the Ghat mountains in front of her, whose shadowy mass was slowly tinted pink. To the right, the Mandavi river took on a more delectably blue-tinted hue, and all the meanders of its channels made azure circles around dense clumps of palms. To the left, and avenue of mango-trees descended a slope toward a sort of flattened colossus dormant beneath a tower. It was the Church of the Magi.

Perhaps it's at this very place, Rachel thought, *that in a similar twilight, my father didn't dare to confront two men, and fled.*

She understood, as they arrived at the church, that her curiosity was about to be satisfied.

"Father Vincent won't have left for his hermitage yet," said Castro, lightly. "We've arrived in time."

A few naked Hindus emerged from the church and passed them. They seemed surprised to see Europeans, and fled at a run. Castro uttered a sigh of satisfaction.

"Mass has scarcely finished," he said. "Father Vincent, who is a saint, celebrates a mass here every morning for the inhabitants of the village of Boma. They're so poor that they don't even have a piece of cloth to cover them. Father Vincent says mass in the dark expressly for them, in order the God will not be offended by their nudity." And he added, with a sort of pride: "Father Vincent is my confessor."

On the threshold of the church, Castro's servant unfastened the cord of the package he was carrying. A number of pieces of wood slipped out, crudely painted white in imitation of candles, one extremity of which was colored red, doubtless with the aim of representing the flame.

Castro made a sign to the Hindu to go and deposit the fake candles inside the church.

Father Vincent appeared on the threshold. He was a very old Hindu with white hair, who had been a late convert to Christianity and who, instructed by the Franciscans, had acquired a reputation of sanctity by virtue of the purity of his heart. He only knew the Tamil language, but Castro, who spoke that language, must have found it more convenient to confess to him in Portuguese, because it was in Portuguese that he explained what he expected of him.

The old priest must have been habituated to the ceremony of the fake candles, for he smiled benevolently and helped the half-breed dispose them. His visage filled with the naïve admiration of someone contemplating an excessive luxury when he saw that two genuine wax candles had also been brought, which Castro lit himself, and placed to either side of the altar.

The Church of the Magi was constructed on the plan of a Latin cross, but its vault was singularly low. It was as if the nave and the choir were crushed by the weight of the ancient tower that weighed upon them, making the arches bend, breaking the surge of the curvature and the circular arcs of the stone barrel-vaults. The low side-chapels gave the impression of sinking into the ground, and the squat pillars constructed in the Hindu style, with inverted lotuses around the capitals instead of volutes, resembled exhausted giants, ready to disappear among the moving mosaics over which swarms of mosquitoes swirled. Damp had turned the columns green, enabling moss and parasitic vegetation to grow on the Virgin Mary and the Christ.

Castro was on his knees now, his hands crossed, his head leaning forward theatrically toward the old priest, who was giving him absolution. He accused himself of sins in a low voice, and purely as a formality, since the individual who was about to grant him pardon in the name of God did not understand Portuguese.

The light of dawn, filtered by the nacreous shells that replaced stained-glass in the windows, caused pools of stagnant water to shine and gave a strange value to an enormous angel in teak-wood, which resembled a Christian seraph in the wings and a Brahmanic god in its seven arms and the enigmatic expression of the face.

Immobile by the entrance door, Rachel saw Castro stand up, and was struck by the transfiguration of his face. He no longer had any expression of sensuality in the thickness of his lips. His little eyes, widened, were gazing beyond the things that surrounded him, as if they were transparent and he had glimpsed a more beautiful world through them. He marched toward the altar, with a deliberate nobility that might have appeared ridiculous. because of his belly wobbling to the right and left, but his sincerity gave his entire person a grandeur of sorts.

"I have an oath to make to God," he said, turning to the old priest. "A vow of which no one can relieve me."

On the threshold of the church, Rachel sensed great warm sheets of sunlight behind her, illuminating the trees the waters and the mountains. And it seemed to her that she saw before her the accumulating darkness of a greater injustice than she had ever been able to imagine; and that injustice was without recourse, for its origin was in God.

Those who committed evil deeds were always the masters of those they had made to suffer. Things were always arranged in that manner. In the domain of the material, they were always the first, they had money and the advantages of life. Those who were subject to an unjust oppression those who were despoiled and scorned, might at least have been able to say that the spiritual domain belonged to them and that they would be consoled by the possession of a realm that the evil could never attain. But no—not even that! There was no more beautiful realm than the one she had just glimpsed in the shining eyes of the man who had killed her mother. By the artifice of religion, the prestige of ancient rites, the magic contained in the hand of the benevolent old man, a grace had penetrated into the evil soul and had cleansed it of its sins.

The man she had seen the previous evening in shirt-sleeves, drunk on champagne, full of terror at the sight of her in a room in a brothel, was advancing, rejuvenated and purified, toward an altar where God was considering him with complaisance. Oh, how beautiful the sunlight must seem to him now! Undoubtedly, he had thought of that emotion, as a dilettante of the voluptuousness of forgiveness and innocence.

Rachel took two or three steps along the wall and arrived at the foot of an angel with the face of a Buddha. Under her brown cape she unwrapped the folds of the shawl and gripped the hilt of the knife with her hand.

A very short man whose legs were immeasurably swollen by elephantiasis dragged himself against a pillar and adopted a posture of prayer. The light augmented rapidly. A water-snake leapt up in a puddle and made a luminous circle of splashes. The face of the old priest filled with a divine mildness.

Then a voice resonated, with a moving timbre, charged with human sadness, so different from Castro's that Rachel thought at first that a man other than him was speaking in the church.

"Lord, you have extracted me from perdition and you have shown me the way. You have manifested your will be sending me a messenger to whom you have given the form of my nightmares. Be praised, Lord! Before this creature that you have molded in the image of the other, in order that she should be at my side as the witness to the evil that I have done, I beg you no longer to allow me to succumb to temptation, to deliver me from the evil that has always been around me, to permit me to be just and pious, to love you and to love men, my brothers. I make the oath to consecrate myself to your service and I ask you humbly to enable to dwell with me the one who is similar to the other, in order that my soul, which was doomed, might be saved by her, in order that the cause of the sin might be light and salvation. Oh Lord, grant me that it might be so!"

The old priest had raised both hands and he was waving them gently. He did not understand the words pronounced, but he knew that vows always surpass the powers of realization, that oaths to God are rarely kept, and he would have liked to attenuate its force. The caretaker of the church seemed to be asleep. Castro, having touched his forehead to the stone, got to his feet. He had mud stains on both knees and between the eyes. The half-breed slid rapidly toward the altar and started removing the simulacra of candles. Something very pure, emanating from the prayer and the benevolence of the priest, was suspended in the air.

But Rachel did not sense it. Vengeance filled her soul and spoke to her. She pictured what she was about to do, and suddenly saw how contrary to her intention her action was.

Was not what the Christians called absolution the remission by the priest, the intermediary between God and a man, of all the evil he had done in his life? Innocent as on the first day! Like a new-born child! That was what the benediction was intended to make of the sinner. But who could tell? Were there not individuals who, by the purity of their life, ended up acquiring great powers? Perhaps that old Hindu filled with ingenuousness had conferred, by means of his wrinkled hand, a grace of which he possessed the secret, a spiritual shield for the afterlife. And she was about to strike a man who possessed such a perfect certainty of being sinless that she saw him advancing toward her with a childlike expression in the eyes.

He was no longer the same as before. She was about to kill a man other than the drunken and debauched Castro that she hated. This one would go straight to the Christian paradise, as he imagined it, and he would sit at the right hand of the God who only loves the strong and the powerful. And his last thought would doubtless be to thank her, for having chosen that unique moment of temporary perfection, in which he could, by the subterfuge of grace, benefit from an endless happiness.

There was a slight sound of iron on the stone, which no one heard. It was the knife that Rachel dropped, beneath her cloak.

The vengeance could not be so simple. Was the crime simple? The vengeance must follow it step by step, take the same detours, to arrive at a scene as strange and complete as the one on the boat in the moonlight, in which a naked woman was violated in front of her crucified husband. What a folly she had nearly committed in killing this blessed Castro, this pardoned Castro, this angelic caricature of the fat lustful man!

She had the time now. She had him. For him, she was the envoy of God. She had understood that she was simultaneously the symbol of his remorse and his desire, and that he could no longer do without the sight of her. Well, she would cause him to redescend the terrible ladder, the obscure steps of baseness and wickedness. Of that by which a man is valued, the little part wrenched from the darkness, she would deprive him. The divine light that he had glimpsed in his mind would never shine again for him. She would precipitate him among his peers, his true brethren, those down below, even if she had to be dragged down with him, and once, at least, the justice that God did not deign to give on earth, or granted so late that it was not worth the trouble of receiving it, would be realized.

As Castro arrived beside her, Rachel smiled. She could not take her eyes off the water-snake that was advancing toward the altar in regular hops, through the puddles between the sunken flagstones. The half-breed saw it, and tried to drive it away from the altar with the end of a wooden candle, but the old priest made a sign to him that there was no need.

A snake could hop around an altar without offending God.

PART TWO

The Archbishop who Conversed with God

The rumor had run around old Goa and the new city, and had spread among the villages in the surrounding area. A miracle was going to occur that day. That was not particularly extraordinary. Miracles were frequent in that narrow fragment of the land of India submissive to Portuguese authority. They had begun when the first of Albuquerque's galleons had cleft the waters of the river Mandavi and had multiplied, with the tombs of the saints, the consecrated chapels and the places of pilgrimage. Since Monsenhor Joseph de Silva had conversations with God, the miraculous was quotidian and permanent. It descended over the demolished dwellings and ruined convents of old Goa like an inexhaustible river of light, although it lost its force by virtue of its continuity.

But the miracle that was due to take place that day would be the sign of a solemn divine approval. After years of negotiation and hesitation, the governor of the colony had received formal orders from Lisbon. The King of Portugal, threatened personally with excommunication, was renouncing the struggle in which his clergy had engaged with the Pope. The aged schismatic archbishop was to retire to a convent. Senhor de Lima, the governor,[3] had full powers to have the force of the royal will respected by force.

This news had thrown Goa into great effervescence. Many portraits of the King had been displayed on doors, head

---

[3] An interim governor named Lima did serve in Goa in 1840-42 but he cannot be the one featured in the story, who is fictitious.

down, as a sign of scorn. It was known that the governor, a weak and taciturn man, was incapable of any action. That action could only be manifest through the intermediary of the colonel who was at the head of the eight hundred men of the garrison. The colonel was a great drinker, who never had an hour's lucidity to devote to military matters, but a ship from Europe might one day disembark an extraordinary envoy with a supplement of troops. It had been agreed that a manifestation would take place in old Goa, the pretext for which would be the blessing of the banner of the True Christians, presided over by Pedre de Castro. The Archbishop, who had not been seen for a long time, would emerge from his Episcopal palace, and a miracle would have occurred.

There had been some thought of celebrating that ceremony outside the Church of the Magi, but the ground there was singularly marshy, and the sands bordering the river Mandavi at that place were unstable. It was feared that some believers might disappear, which would have been the inverse of the desired effect. Then again, the Church of the Magi was too close to Boma and its wretched inhabitants. Those recent converts were all devoted to the Archbishop, but they were obstinate in living in a complete nudity that was irreconcilable with the sacred character of the manifestation. The main square of Goa, on to which the shaky door of the cathedral opened, was the most appropriate place, but the fallen statue of Vasco da Gama was too telling an image of the splendor of the colony and its decadence. A hilltop north of the city had been chosen, alongside the debris of the Church of Saint Anne.

Great discussions had taken place regarding questions of precedence. Who would march behind the Archbishop? Would it be the Albuquerques, the Gamas, the Cabrals or the Pereiras? There were only families of fabulous antiquity in old Goa. Unfortunately, successive cross-breeding over four centuries had deteriorated the purity of the conquerors' blood. The Albuquerques were entirely black and the last descendant of the Gama family had the wooly hair, the flattened nose and the ebony tint of the negroes of Zanzibar, who, toward the end of the eighteenth century, had been transported to the coast in large numbers by French and Dutch slave-traders. The half-breeds that were known as topas—which is to say, men who wear hats—were a majority. Those who held the highest status were the few families that, like the Castros or the Mascarenhas, had retained white skin. That high status was guarded so jealously, and with such insolent arrogance, that it had excited grim hatreds.

It was agreed, in the end, that the members of the Association of True Christians, a group whose goals were the grandeur of Goa and the glorification of Christ, would march at the head, whatever their color. They would, of course, as a sign of their aristocracy, be clad in the European fashion, with a top hat and a black frock-coat.

All the bells that retained a little musical quality had been ringing since sunrise. That May afternoon was particularly hot. Rugs, colored fabrics and bed-sheets decorated the inhabited houses, and wreaths of foliage or pieces of muslin had been hung over the gaping thresholds of those that were not.

Pedre de Castro had been awaited for a long time in the house of the Mascarenhas, from which the True Christians were to set forth in procession for the Archbishop's palace. Someone had gone to knock on his door, but he had left home some time before. Very late, just as the True Christians were about to set out without him, the mother of the entire family of Mascarenhas, a fat matron who gave birth to scandals as easily as children, had uttered sniggers of delight from the height of the mirador, where she was perched, in order to keep watch and take note. Then she had run downstairs in her low-cut crimson scarlet dress to announce with loud joy that the President of the True Christians had just come out of the house of his Jewess, where he had doubtless gone to obtain some advice before the ceremony.

She was not mistaken. Pedre de Castro had emerged from the house in which he had installed Rachel. The more degenerate societies become, the more their rigor increases, and, at the same time, the further advanced a slackness becomes that renders them indulgent to everything that goes against that rigor. The True Christians were content to smile, wrinkling their eyes. The majority were preoccupied with the appearance of their frock-coat and the movement of their trousers, hired from a clothes-dealer in the port of the new city. And then, if Castro had that Jewess, newly arrived in Goa, for a mistress, did not Cabral have the wife of his best friend, and did not Mascarenhas have a hunchbacked Hindu from Panjim?

On the rumor of the miracle, people had some from far away to old Goa and the Christians were mingled with Muslims and Parsees. Cashmere silks sparkled, unfurled headscarves were waved, unusual gleams shone in the eyes. The trumpeting was heard of elephants that had transported travelers and were tethered on the old quays to iron rings that had once served to retain caravels.

The Portuguese aristocracy was deployed behind the wrought iron of balconies and beneath the broken ogives of windows. Obsolete costumes overflowed with magnificence, and lines of hands were held out to make a display of enormous fake rings. The beautiful Conception Colaço, beneath transparent black lace, allowed the sight of her breasts, whose beauty was famous, and, lowering her amber long-lashed eyelids, launched a provocative gaze at the young men, by whom she was never sated, as they passed by. A little further on, her rival Juana de Faria, as rigid as a statue, extended toward her the face of an angel in dull wax, congealed with envy. The collar of her dress rose up to her chin and its sleeves hid her hands. She was accused of being afflicted by an incurable skin disease, and her lovers did not did not deny the rumor.

Before the aged Marcora, who had contracted in Mascate habits of buying and selling human flesh, stood his four scarcely-nubile daughters, whom he trafficked openly. He directed them like a flock, with a bamboo rod, and laughed incessantly behind his venerable beard, for he was a cheerful man. Although old Marcora was pale of complexion, his daughters were as black as it is possible to be. A curious and inexorable physiological law dictates that the descendants of Portuguese and Hindus are blacker than the blackest Hindus.

In accordance with an ancient custom, the archbishop, before the ceremony, had taken a meal in the great hall on the ground floor of his palace, the doors of which were opened in order that the people could go in and see the Archbishop eating. In the times of Goa's splendor he had had the governor to his right and the commander of the war-fleet to his left. Behind him, standing, stood the most powerful man in India, the Great Judge of the Inquisition. All the Portuguese nobility, an entirely white-skinned nobility, was grouped around them. The Archbishops were great eaters and drinkers and the meals were very long. Now, there was no more Inquisition, the Portuguese fleet only consisted on a single three-master whose captain was a nonentity, and as for the governor, he had gone to earth in the new city for fear of being compromised. The meal had only lasted a few minutes, just time for fake roast meats and heaps of fish or game to file past. Everyone knew that the Archbishop never took any nourishment, scarcely a glass of water per day, and that he was nourished by the light of Heaven, which an invisible angel distilled for him, by virtue of a special grace.

It truly was a great miracle that Monsenhor Joseph de Silva was able to emerge from the darkness of his place to appear between the thick walls of the threshold and then walk beneath the awning without being consumed by the sunlight or carried away by the wind. He was translucent, immaterial. The fabric of his robe did not seem to shelter anything beneath its folds. He held himself upright, like a young tree, in spite of the crushing weight of his miter. The stem of his finger did not seem to feel the burden of the amethyst. He leaned on his crosier, but lightly, for he scarcely brushed the ground. His face was covered with wrinkles, but those wrinkles were unreal, as if designed by a dream chisel. His extinct eyes were a green washed by time, which gazed much further than the people or the distant hills. As he advanced, he moved through an atmosphere of delight and purity.

A Swiss Guard with an unkempt tattered uniform marched at the head, adjusting his long moustache and causing an enormous halberd to resonate. Children, dressed for the occasion in muslin robes, threw flower petals, and a topa beadle who directed them with the end of a large metal cross sometimes criticized them violently in a mixture of Kanara and Portuguese. Behind the Archbishop's awning was Castro, alone, carrying the blue banner of the True Christians. He was sweating and panting, sometimes sponging his brow with a multicolored handkerchief. A few paces away from him, as he had demanded, came the black frock-coats and the hunchbacked hats.

Then the monks were huddled together. Their host was less numerous than anyone had thought, for the convents were being depopulated with an incredible rapidity. Of the immense community of the Franciscans only five members remained. There were no more than two Carmelites: the prior, who was an adolescent, and the cook, who was so fat that he was obliged to lean on the prior. The Trinitarians had donned the cowls that their order had once worn during the Inquisition's auto-da-fés.

A black Albuquerque held at arm's length the helmet of his reputed ancestor, the great white Albuquerque. A Gama of Zanzibar had put over his frock-coat the breastplate that had once covered the torso of the Great Gama of Portugal. Statues of the Virgin were also transported, removed from the shade of their sanctuaries, and saints who healed the sick. And their faithful followers, on recognizing then, cried "Mercy!" and prostrated themselves in the dust. Beggars paid by Castro took advantage of the noise to utter a few cries of "Down with the King!" and those cries also found a faithful echo in the crowd.

Voluntary penitents, to show that they merited the fire, had had robes painted with devils and menacing faces. They marched in those robes with pride, as if they were promised to the pyre, holing a piece of wood for a candle, bemoaning their sins. Sometimes, they were recognized by one of their less pious friends, who were watching the cortege pass by, who made vulgar remarks, laughing; then they stopped moaning to reply in the same tone, with similar laughter.

There were also free priests, missionaries who never went anywhere, and church caretakers in bizarre ecclesiastical uniforms, who wore long, rusty sixteenth-century swords in their belts. An old beggar who made money by showing his deformities to foreigners, affirming that he was the last victim of the Inquisition, dragged himself along at the rear with a knowing expression, as if the ceremony were being held for him.

Incense swung by the beadles or burning in windows perfumed the streets. The bells vibrated with more profundity in the evening air. Benedictions fell from the transparent Episcopal hand. And thus, slowly, the Archbishop traversed the city, like the living image of spiritual ecstasy in the midst of a cortege of caricatures.

On the hill, in front of the debris of The Church of Saint Anne, there was a temporary altar. It was there that the Archbishop extended his hand to consecrate the blue banner of the defenders of the faith, the men who wanted to render to Goa its ancient power.

Castro was on his knees. He no longer felt the sweat on his brow. On the contrary, he was invaded by a delightful freshness. He now had the certainty that God had sent him a messenger. Were not all Rachel's words in accord with his interior conviction, with what all the sensate men of Goa thought, which what the man who conversed with God doubtless thought, even though he had not expressed it, and who was transmitting his force via the channel of his benediction. He would do what she had advised him to do and what he considered to be his duty.

He had had doubts for a long time. Could the messenger of God be a Jewess? Why not? For one thing, he would be able, a little later, to convert her. Then again, everyone received in accordance with his merit. There were angels, apparently, floating in the old halls of the Archbishop's palace, but the Archbishop was a saint; he was a sinner. It would have

74

been too much pride to hope for an angel. A Jewess had come, however, bearing in her face the testimony of his past sins. It was necessary to listen to her and believe her. A little while ago, when he had perceived her ivory profile behind a shutter, he had lifted up the blue banner and he had felt as young as he had at twenty.

The monks, the penitents and the distant crowd on the spiral of the road, were all on their knees. The Archbishop was speaking now. No one could hear what he said, his voice was so weak, not even Castro, who was prostrate at his feet, but the Archbishop was not making any effort to make his words audible. He was addressing himself to Heaven rather than to human beings. He was replying to questions that had been asked of him in other conversations by invisible mouths. Doubtless the satisfaction of those responses must be great for his visage reflected an incomparable suavity and he was trembling slightly.

When he finished, it was as if a ripple of love spread out in a circle, to die away at the extremities of the earth, and there was no one who did not feel better.

No visible miracle was produced, but no one was disappointed. Everyone took away in his soul a little shard of splendor, which he held within him.

As he stood up first and raised the banner, Castro saw, from the height of the altar, the entire city on its knees. His breast swelled with contentment. Was he not the foremost of all those people, the richest and the most intelligent? It was to him, personally, that the holy benediction had come. He saw his life under the color of domination. But in going back down toward Goa he remembered, confusedly, that he had learned from the catechism as a child that the sin of pride is the first by which Satan is manifest. He did not want to pause on that memory.

The vapors of burned incense were mingled with the odor of the putrescence of Goa and the vegetal breath of the neighboring forests. The sun had just disappeared over the waters of the river Mandavi, only leaving a flamboyant illumination on the red stone bell-tower of the convent of Chovas.

Father Vincent was still at prayer in the place where he had fallen at the moment on the Archbishop's blessing. He had spent a part of the day sending away the poor Christians of Boma, whose complete nudity would have shocked Portuguese society. He had only done it because he had been told to do it, for he had never been able to understand why nudity, a sign of innocence, was susceptible of causing scandal. Then he had run to the Saint Anne hill, and had arrived just in time.

It seemed to him that the night touched his shoulder. The time had come to go back to the bamboo shack in which he lived on the hill overlooking Boma. For that, it was necessary to go past the Church of the Magi.

When he began to go down the avenue of mango-trees he was the victim of a singular illusion. The enormous Church of the Magi was lower and more compact than before. It seemed to him that it was crouching down more broadly, that its formidable contexture had spread out among the sands on which it was built. How marshy the ground was in the vicinity! Stagnant waters gleamed between aquatic plants. In the distance, there was nothing but the glitter of pools, undulations of mud and the melancholy hymn of frogs.

That the mass of stone in question, with the cyclopean blocks of its pillars and its fortress tower, had not yet sunk into the mobile ground of the sands was the greatest of miracles, thought Father Vincent. God maintained the stones, the paving-stones and the cupolas by means of a permanent will, an effort devoid of inattention. And perhaps that was because he, the most humble and most ignorant of priests, got up well before dawn and went down to the rocks of Boma, careless of wild beasts, to say mass to very simple people, so poor that they were obliged to walk stark naked. He had surely been deceived; he ought to have been able to say the mass in broad daylight; God did not disdain the nudity that he could, in any case, see in the darkness and the purity of which he could measure, and he wanted there to be a church there, for the most wretched.

That thought gave Father Vincent an extraordinary joy. How solid the ground seemed to him, that sandy ground sustained by divine force! How important his life became!

The moon had just appeared, illuminating the tops of the mango-trees. He was running now, amid the shiny puddles, for great happiness makes solitary pedestrians run. The frogs did not flee as he passed by, and did not interrupt their song.

Pride, Cupidity and Lust

Rachel passed her hand over her forehead and got up from the wicker sofa where she was lying. She thought she was the victim of a hallucination. She had just heard the sound of a khinnara, a Hindu three-stringed guitar. She dropped the fan of woven straw that she was using to drive away mosquitoes and took a few steps under the veranda.

The heat of the evening was overwhelming. The air, charged with the miasmas of pools, was displaced in dense gusts. A Hindu maidservant was going back and forth in the room adjacent to the veranda, laying the table for dinner.

"Can you hear a khinnara?" Rachel asked the Hindu woman. "It's coming from the waste ground beyond the garden. Who can be playing there at this hour?"

The maidservant made a vague gesture signifying: *Who knows?*

Rachel went down the steps the steps of the veranda and went through the garden. Wild cacti were growing in the middle of the paths and she was obliged to part foliage with her hands. Her hair, gathered in several tresses, came loose. In the movements that she made, her indoor dress, made of Chinese silk, stuck to her body, and, as the fabric was transparent, she had the sensation of being naked.

She looked through a breach in the ruined wall. There was no one there. Who had she expected to see, anyway? She shrugged her shoulders and went back, slowly. The sound of the guitar had an effect on her nerves that she could not explain. It was a tune played on a khinnara, on a similar evening, that had decided her life. Would she have loved that Italian fantasist and braggart, that shiny-haired liar, if the guitar had not ornamented him with the poetry of music. No, and as her existence in Cochin was in the quarter of the black Jews, she would never have decided to quit her father if she had not been intoxicated by the sensuality of the three vibrant strings under the ivory fingers of a young man. Fundamentally, if she had gone with him to Bombay, it was not because of his eternal cheerfulness, his superb conceit, or his insensate promises; it was not because of the attraction of a new life and a mirage of pleasure. It was because of something else, and something very small.

She remembered the successive stages that she had passed through on the road of disillusionment. That had begun on the steamship that was bound for Madras and on which they had booked second-class passage for Bombay. Michael could not really have only been able to think about music and had neglected the formalities that would have permitted him to collect money from the correspondent of his banker in Cochin.

On the deck of the boat she had been gripped by a frisson of anguish, a bizarre desire to go back. She had gazed, in the morning sunlight, at the hand of the man she loved placed on the brass rail of the side of the ship. That hand had just dropped, negligently, a miserable yellow valise, a valise that was evidently astonishingly light, because all Michael's luggage had been sent ahead in error and was waiting for him in Bombay. And that hand, by a curious mystery, was no longer the same one that she had seen the previous evening: the long artist's hand, the plucker of strings. This one was coarser, redder, connected to the arm by a powerful and hairy wrist. It clutched the brass rail like an implement, and the extremity of the fingernails was geometrically square.

That had only lasted a few seconds, for afterwards, Michael had laughed —he was always laughing—he had thrown back his hair romantically, and had then put the light valise on his shoulder, as if it were a crushing burden.

It was only on the quay at Bombay that Michel had confessed that he did not possess the beautiful dwelling so complaisantly described, with a gilded gate and an English garden. There was not even one of the modest bungalows that petty functionaries inhabited, and with which Rachel would have been content. He had no habitation in the Mazagon quarter, of which he spoke incessantly as the most agreeable place on earth. He admitted that, but as one admits a fact of no importance. In the place where the ideal house should have stood, opposite several ill-famed bars backed up against an abandoned mosque, stood a small hotel run by his compatriot Ricardo. There was nowhere better than that hotel. True, Ricardo did not have a very engaging manner. That was because he had been very unfortunate as a result of his great generosity. A society of Italians met in his house. Many were unemployed. Life was so hard under the English! But the majority were singers or musicians, and isn't the essential thing to be able forget reality, with music and amour?

Michael had admitted, gradually, and without great difficulty, that nothing he had said was true. The old man that Rachel had glimpsed with him in Cochin was not his father, but a stranger to whom he had hired himself out as a guide to visit the Malabar coast. He had abandoned him without even collecting his wages because he could not do the same thing for long, nor see the same faces. He did not have a position at the Italian Consulate in Bombay. He had no position anywhere, except sometimes that of musician in a hotel orchestra or functionary in a small coastal casino.

Rachel remembered that all those things had not appeared so terrible because of the secret hidden in the music of the guitar. It was sufficient, in the evening, that the dome of the old mosque and the silhouette of a palm tree appeared, that the guitar resonated and the hands playing it became aristocratically ivory again, for all the lies to become real, for her to be in love and be beloved.

Feminine folly! she thought. It was that little thing that had been the beauty of her life. It was because of that little thing that she had been so desperate the evening that Michael did not come back. She had been foolish enough to wait for him facing the mosque and the palm tree, and to go, late at night, into a few taverns in the port where she knew that Michael was wont to spread his gaiety. Then she had reflected. Michael wept as easily as he laughed. He sometimes had a violent remorse at not being able to give Rachel a life worthy of her. Then he sank to his knees and begged her pardon, and then he played her very sweet airs on his guitar. But that remorse was always accompanied by a desire to escape the suffering it engendered. Certainly, Michael must have left, in order to have no more remorse, to see other faces elsewhere, to make new promises, to laugh at his ease, to live for a while with the illusions of magnificence.

Rachel no longer knew now whether she had loved that man. She considered him as an instrument of her destiny. She had even ceased to hold anything against him. He was the one who had caused her to know the solitude and despair thanks to which she had gone through the streets of Bombay toward Antonia's house of ill repute, and the guest sitting in his shirt-sleeves, as surely as toward a goal fixed in advance. Thanks to him, she had encountered the human creature about whom she had been thinking since her childhood. The idea of vengeance, she realized now, was the primordial sentiment of her soul. Since the death of her mother, she had only loved her father in part, and with an affection mingled with scorn, because he had not had the courage to avenge himself. She had always had the sentiment that it would be necessary one day to fulfill a task, and her youth had been obscured by that hidden agenda.

She darted one last glance over the garden, where the wind was stirring the trees.

Feminine folly! she said to herself, again. Now the task was before her. She had vowed herself to its accomplishment, and yet it had only taken a guitar heard in the distance for her to run, like a schoolgirl, to a breach in the garden wall.

She had dined rapidly. The evenings were long in the lugubrious house in which only the rooms on the ground floor had been cleaned and fitted out. In those rooms there was a random mixture of modern furniture that had been brought in haste from Bombay and old furniture in the Indo-Portuguese style.

In order to distract herself, Rachel decided to remove a statuette depicting Saint Francis Xavier[4] baptizing a kneeling Hindu from a niche hollowed in the woodwork of her room. The naïve sculptor of that statuette had wanted the saint, entirely occupied with the sacrament he was giving, to be looking at the pious Hindu. In spite of that, he had left a kind of inattention in the facial expression, and Rachel went to bed with the sentiment that Saint Francis Xavier was staring at her with a certain reprobation.

She was about to transport the statuette to a neighboring room when she noticed that the wood panel forming the back of the niche had been eroded by damp. She touched it with her finger, and the rotten wood immediately gave way. A metal object came away and fell into the niche. Several reflections sprang forth from it at the same time, and surprise nearly caused Rachel to drop the oil-lamp that she was holding in her left hand.

The object enclosed in the hiding-place was a solid gold cross with a thin chain of the small metal attached, that must have been very valuable. There were black pearls embedded in the arms of the cross and four large diamonds at the extremities. Time had tarnished the gold and dulled the pearls, but had not altered the living flames of the diamonds, which shone like four lidless eyes. Something sad, magnificent and secret was exhaled by the jewel.

As Rachel was studying it she heard the door knocker resonated, and the trailing footfalls of a servant who started walking slowly. It could only be Pedre de Castro. Two or three times already he had come at a similar hour to tell her about his projects and rejoice in the sight of her. It had been agreed that in the eyes of society, Rachel had come to Goa preceding her husband, a great entrepreneur in Bombay who intended to

---

[4] The Jesuit missionary Francisco de Jasso y Azpilicueta, better known as Francis Xavier (1506-1552), only worked in Goa from 1542-45, but his pioneering work there had a long-lasting influence,

buy and cultivate vast terrains in the environs of the city. With the title of a married woman, appearances were saved. When Rachel went out, she was assumed to be going to examine plantations, former fertile fields transformed into marshland by Portuguese negligence, and Pedre de Castro's visits had the pretext of the affairs of buying and selling that he was in the process of negotiating.

Naturally, everyone said in whispers that the beautiful Jewess was his mistress—but everyone was mistaken.

It was, indeed, Pedre de Castro who had knocked on the door. Rachel recognized his heavy tread. She could easily have hidden the cross that had just emerged for her from the darkness of the past, but she did not think of that. She immediately had the presentiment that she could make use of that treasure in the goal that she was pursuing.

Pedre de Castro lowered his eyes. He stammered, seeking a plausible explanation for his visit. This evening, more than ever, he had need of amicable words. That very morning, his son had returned from the Jesuit College in Bombay where he had concluded his studies. He had found him, as he had always been, hostile and taciturn, with the same muted snigger with which he greeted everything his father said. Castro had sensed immediately that he was going to have a quotidian contradictor who would turn to derision what he was doing, and diminish it with his laughter and his doubts. And yet, he felt capable of doing great things, if he were aided morally, if someone believed in him.

He let himself fall into an armchair. The same servant with the dragging feet lit a large lamp whose shade was crimson and which gave faces a hint of passion. Rachel had a bottle of rum bought and poured a glass for Castro. In the Church of the Magi he had promised God not to drink any more, at the same time as he had made a vow of chastity. He had respected his promise of temperance for a few days, but then he had quibbled over the terms employed. He could drink as long as he did not get drunk. And Rachel had agreed with him.

He talked about his projects. Events were moving swiftly. The blessing of the banner on Saint Anne's Hill had produced an immense effect. He was overwhelmed by letters and propositions. The colony was with him, ready to defend the Archbishop. If the King of Portugal had been weak enough to sacrifice him to the Pope's rancor, it was up to believers to maintain by force the man who conversed with God. The governor was a wretch. He could be set aside. The troops were not numerous and would side with the stronger party. Their colonel was perpetually drunk. Castro's eyes sparkled in affirming that it was just to suppress a man who was perpetually drunk.

He remained silent momentarily and, encouraged by Rachel's approval, he contemplated greater hopes.

Why not? There were other examples. Sainte-Domingue had detached itself from France sixty years before, and that island had not had at its head the men that Goa would have. One only had to read the history of the Spanish colonies of South America. Goa could become an independent State—a republic or a kingdom, what did it matter? They would see when the moment came. Oh, his son did not believe in him. He would learn to know him. The essential thing was that Rachel believed in him.

She believed in him. She exulted in Castro's words, she overbid them, smoothing over the difficulties, affirming the necessity of acting immediately.

Castro was now pacing back and forth, stopping sometimes to drink a mouthful of rum. Yes, act quickly, that was his opinion. He had tried to consult the Archbishop on the matter; the Archbishop's opinion was the opinion of God—but his responses were always enigmatic, for he had lost the habit of speaking to humans. Then again, it would need money, a great deal of money. Castro's fortune was perhaps the largest in Goa, but a fortune based on mortgaged domains and fallow land, a fortune that scarcely permitted him, in bad times, to go to Bombay twice a year—twice, no more, and not again!

Rachel knew how necessary to was to mingle Providence with the actions of practicing Christians. She seized Castro's arm and she said to him, giving her voice a mysterious character: "This evening, Providence has brought the necessary money. Come." And she drew him into the next room.

Saint François Xavier and his Hindu were lying on the floor. On the white sheet there was the stain of the black pearls and the four flames of the diamonds.

Castro considered the hiding-place in the woodwork of the niche, he weighed the gold of the cross, evaluated the quality of the pearls and the diamonds. His face was animated by an extraordinary cupidity, the signs of which Rachel was seeing for the first time.

He knew the jewel without ever having seen it. That cross was celebrated in Goanese history. Two centuries before, the Portuguese aristocracy had clubbed together and had ordered that jewel from a goldsmith in order to send it to the Pope as a gift. It was his ancestor, Pedre de Castro, the one whose portrait he had slashed on the morning of his confession, Pedre de Castro the debauchee, who had received the cross from the goldsmith and, after having it blessed with great pomp, had placed it on the ship that was to set sail for the Occident. Now, Pedre de Castro, who did not believe in anything, had had a fake cross blessed. He had kept the true one, thinking that he would take it with him when he fled Goa. He had been living in this house at the time. Doubtless he had hidden the inestimable jewel and had died without being able to retrieve it.

Rachel was not unaware of the influence that the strange personality of his ancestor had had over Pedre de Castro. At twenty, he had taken for his model the thief of the cross, the abductor of women, the killer of Jews. He had tried to renew on a small scale the exploits that had rendered the former Pedre de Castro famous. He was aware of the legend that his ancestor had sold his soul to the devil, but the devil did not exist, and under the influence of his friend Deodat de Vega, Castro had professed, during the early years of his youth, that evil was superior to good, and that the characteristic of superi-

85

or men was to do evil consciously. He had explained that to Rachel during the long conversations he had had with her.

His objective, for years, had been to enjoy life egotistically, to drive back within himself everything there was of pity disinterest, good sentiments, and he admitted that a new, singularly voluptuous and profound enjoyment had gradually come to him in seeing creatures suffer because of him. Either by virtue of hazard, or by his unconscious will, he had been let to repeat the criminal acts of the man he called his master, the great Castro. Many years later, when he analyzed his past conduct and the state of his soul in those days, he had been obliged to conclude that there had been a sort of substitution within him, as if the evil will of the ancestor had taken possession of his own and had directed it.

His effort of evil—he did not give the details to Rachel—had stopped with the death of the young woman that he had loved and whom Rachel resembled. That had coincided with the departure of Deodat de Vega. Then religion had regained the upper hand in him. He had felt remorse. Had he not even thought of entering a convent? Oh, if he had encountered a true priest, a man of God! But the clergy of Goa were so degenerate. They demanded money for confessions, and even when the sum demanded had been paid, the priest demanded more for the absolution. There were some who said mass while completely drunk, and it had been necessary to transport to the new city almost all the sacred objects in the churches, because those who had custody of them would have had them melted down and gone to sell them in Bombay. Father Vincent had too much simplicity of heart, and the Archbishop was too close to God, to understand human sins.

Left to himself, Pedre de Castro had seen the love of evil that had haunted him in his youth disappear. He had had crises of a sort. At the moment when he least expected it, a surge of lust, an interior storm, devastated him. He dared not tell Rachel what he was then obliged to do. The actions of his youth, which were only the feeble echo of the actions of his ancestor, presented themselves to him for realization again, with a pow-

86

erful force of suggestion. The nights of drunkenness at Antonia's, with Jewesses of the lowest order, paid generously to allow themselves to be humiliated, were only the most anodyne form of his so-called pleasures. Remorse came afterwards, as surely as the sun after the rain. And that had endured, and would still be continuing, if Rachel had not come and he had not gone with her to the Church of the Magi.

"Lord Sabaoth, they are prey to three scourges: pride, cupidity and lust. Oh, pour them into them without measure, in order that they may be accursed for eternity!"

Rachel remembered those words from the old book. They were still present in her mind. How she congratulated herself for having acted with cunning, patience and courage! The three scourges were unleashed, whose power would draw the eternal malediction of the Christian who had attached her father to a cross and killed her mother.

Under the red light of the tall lamp that Castro had brought into the bedroom, she gazed at the fat man colored by the lampshade, and he seemed to be covered in blood, vile and grotesque. He was standing straighter than usual, inflated by an unusual self-importance. Was he not the future President of the Republic of Goa, perhaps the King? He rubbed the old gold of the cross to make it shine again; he palpated the pearls or admired the marvelous clarity of the diamonds, and the amour that enchains men to precious metals made him breathe heavily, as if he had run a long distance.

He darted a glance around at the walls, which appeared to be ablaze, passed his tongue over his lips and said: "The entire cross might not find a buyer for a long time. The rajahs are ruined and only the English in India are rich enough. But each jewel might be sold separately. The pearls are large, and the diamonds too. With that..."

He did not finish. His thoughts had turned abruptly in another direction. He had looked at Rachel to obtain approval from her, and his gaze had wandered from her mobile mouth, where her teeth were shining, over her milky neck and the birth of her shoulders, over the undulation of her body, visible under the silk, and more desirable than if it were naked.

Rachel saw Castro's little eyes fill with an intense flame, and his entire body subside, as if it were storing an immense sum of desire. Alongside him, the bed displayed its white surface, and the sheet raised over a light hollow seemed to be awaiting human forms in order to cover them with warmth. Rachel measured his insensate temerity. The passions were unleashed one after another. Was she not about to be the first victim of the lust that she wanted to reignite?

Castro took a step forward and stumbled over the statuette of Saint Francis Xavier, which was still on the floor. He picked it up respectfully and replaced it in its niche. Rachel took advantage of that to seize the tall lamp and head toward the door, slowly but glancing over her left shoulder, keeping watch to see whether the beast was about to pounce.

The breath that the bedroom had set ablaze died down in the drawing-room. The crisis died when scarcely born, but would doubtless be resuscitated later. The cross made a bump in the interior pocket of Castro's jacket and the chain attached to it rendered a metallic clink. Two large nocturnal moths flew into the wall, with a sound of crumpled wings. The night was splendid. On the threshold, Castro kissed Rachel's hand ceremoniously, and it seemed to her once again that there was the sound of a guitar somewhere—but she did not know where.

The Submarine Quarter

When the rainy season had concluded, the water of the pools that covered the Goanese countryside began to go down. The cool of the night, succeeding the ardor of the sun, produced rather dense fogs that the dawn had difficulty dissipating. It was the moment when, it was said, one could glimpse beneath the waters poured out by the two arms of the river Mandavi the terraces and domes of the quarter of Goa that had collapsed into the sands a century earlier, following a flood.

Desirous of taking account of that, Rachel had herself accompanied that morning by a Malabar boatman. She had gone down the river in a canoe hollowed out from a tree-trunk and, leaving the Church of the Magi to the left, had been rowed to what was known as the pool of the drowned city.

It was early and a dense mist covered everything, enveloping the chain of the Ghats in the distance, giving islets covered in fig-trees the appearance of confused masses, outlining the coconut palms on the banks like bizarre creatures issued from the night, which were about to disappear with the triumph of the light.

The boatman had made her a sign to indicate that they had arrived at the approximate location where the ruins of the Dominican quarter were supposed to lie. On leaning over the side of the boat, Rachel perceived nothing at first but the bleak and indefinite mirror that calm waters are. On gazing more attentively though the blue transparencies, however, she thought she could distinguish a monumental perron ending in a collapsed portico, lines of columns, a stone stairway disappearing under lianas and a recumbent marble form, like a goddess asleep among the mobile scintillations of water-snakes. Further away, there were the tangles of edifices, something akin to an inclined Arabic mirador and the truncated body of a tower. Still further away, through the undulations that the oars made, Rachel saw—or thought she saw—the long perspective of an aquatic cloister, and the majestic frame of an enormous empty portal under which a slender fish with green fins was passing.

The Dominican quarter bore the name of the convent of that order that had been installed there, but it was mostly composed of pleasure houses in which the rich inhabitants of Goa had desire to enjoy the cool air coming from the almost parallel arms of the river. Were those the sumptuous dwellings of old that Rachel had just glimpsed? Were those the gardens where beautiful Portuguese women had wandered, in ruffs and taffeta corsages, and where the feasts given by the Castros or the Altaides had been held? She wondered whether it was not her imagination that was creating the images, and whether she might have been deceived by the play of reverberations through the liquid depths.

Suddenly, very close to her, in the fog, she heard the same guitar resonating the music of which had already intrigued her a few days earlier. It was a melancholy tune, which she did not know, a lament that made her think of some defunct chagrin, of the amorous adieu of two lovers who were signaling to one another from distant balconies in the midst of falling palaces, amid the engulfing waters.

At her gesture, the boatman ceased rowing, and a few moments later, a boat following her own emerged from the fog. There was a young man, almost a child, in the boat. It was him who was playing. He was standing in the prow, and had not expected to find himself so suddenly in Rachel's presence. He stopped playing abruptly. His face reflected a surprise so ingenuous that Rachel started laughing. The canoes were side by side and a conversation began almost involuntarily.

Rachel did not find him sympathetic at first glance. He was narrow-shouldered and his gaze had something pretentious about it that myopia sometimes produces. He was beardless, but with stray hairs on his chin. His forehead was too broad and his hairline too straight. He spoke hesitantly, in a slightly muted voice, but suddenly, he produced certain words with the warmth and quiver that reveal an enthusiastic nature.

He said no matter what, at hazard, about the Dominican quarter and the possibility of glimpsing its domes at certain times, in order to gain time and master the heartbeat that was elevating his bosom.

As the two boats brushed the edge on an islet planted with frangipanes and mangroves, he proposed walking for a while, to await the moment when the fog cleared, leaving the water clearer. Rachel accepted.

The fog persisted for a long time. Rachel perceived that she had the affinities with the young guitar player that permit a first conversation to unfurl without any effort to maintain it, and for the first silences not to bring any embarrassment. She enjoyed it, confusedly. As the heat increased, with a gesture in which there was familiarity and abandonment, she took off the cape that was placed over her shoulders and put it over her arm, saying in a low voice, as if it were an intimate confidence; "The heat comes so rapidly in this season."

He received that statement as if it were a precious secret and lowered his eyes. When he raised them again, he saw that Rachel's arms were naked and that her loosened corsage allowed a glimpse of the milky amber of her cleavage.

He blushed, and hastened to say, in order to hide his confusion, pointing to the long grass through which they were walking: "Aren't you afraid of snakes?"

"Oh, no," she said, "look!"

And, lifting up her skirt slightly and holding out her leg, she showed him that she was wearing supple leather boots that were almost knee-length. She sensed immediately afterwards that that entirely natural gesture had shocked him. At the same time she wondered: *How old is he? He's not much younger than me. Who is he? What is he doing in Goa?*

At the summit of the Ghats, the clouds were suddenly ripped apart, and a red light cut the landscape in two, like a blade.

"I haven't yet told you who I am," said the young man. Timidly, he added: "My name is Joachim de Castro."

And he immediately cast an oblique glance to see what effect that name had on Rachel.

It produced a considerable effect, which she did not let him see. Since the moment when she had seen him in the prow of the boat it had not occurred to her that he might be Pedre de Castro's son. And yet, should she not have been able to recognize in the young man all the characteristics of the execrated family? He did not resemble his father, but she consented to recognize certain analogies. The hand reminded her of the hand that had trembled on Antonia's mantelpiece and had palpated the black pearls. A certain grasping movement of the arm was analogous to the movement that she had seen before her, near her bed, which she had been able to avoid. She strove to find a common appearance between the son and the father, but unwittingly, the charm of the first conversation acted upon her and she remained enveloped by it.

"I know your father," she said.

He knew that. He hastened to say that he was aware of the land deals that his father was making. He added that he, personally, did not believe in the future grandeur of Goa. The city had had its time of splendor and was dying now. One could not struggle against evolution. In any case, cities in their decline had more charm than commercial cities in full prosperity.

Rachel listened to him distractedly. So, she thought, the fable invented by Pedre de Castro had seemed plausible to his son. What credulity! She strove to be scornful of him for that, but could not succeed.

The mists had dissipated, uncovering the immensity of the train. They agreed rather abruptly each to go their own way, but as they went back to the boats they turned round at the same time to say that they would soon see one another again at the same place.

As she went away, Rachel continued to scrutinize the depths of the pool with her eyes. But it was mechanically that she searched for the apparitions of towers and palaces, the contours of old Portuguese dwellings with Moorish architectures consumed by aquatic plants, and the skeletons of drowned cloisters and chapels. There was in her soul an immense engulfed city that she scarcely distinguished, with more hopes than cloisters have pillars, and more desires for beauty than terraces have pure marble.

The Root of Passions

The man who was going up the Rua Derecha in old Goa looked to the right and left as if he had not seen the houses along it for a long time and was astonished to find it so little changed. He affected to straighten his head beneath a large and very worn felt hat. His ridiculously short jacket with shiny elbows as tightened at the waist with an affectation of elegance. His trousers were grimy, his shoes worn out, attesting to long journeys on foot. His person radiated an extreme poverty in spite of the effort he was making to give his appearance and easy and slightly arrogant superiority. His face, freshly shaven and excessively powdered, contrasted with his wretched garments.

He passed in front of the overturned statue of Vasco da Gama and then the archbishop's palace. He was visibly heading for the Castro house. However, when he had arrived a few paces from the large walled-up portal he stopped, seemed to hesitate, and turned back.

It was mid-afternoon. The torrid heat made the streets deserted. A stray dog went along the walls, its tongue hanging out. The man followed it with his eyes for some time and smiled, shaking his head because of the resemblance there was between himself and the animal.

He had been pacing back and forth for some time when Pedre de Castro came out of his house. The man noticed that there was something furtive and urgent in his manner. He took a step forward in order to be noticed, and even sketched a gesture of recognition, but Pedre de Castro only darted a distracted glance at him and passed by. Then the man started walking behind him. He was not holding himself as straight, his head was inclined forward and his stride was less certain.

When Pedre de Castro arrived at Rachel's house and knocked, the man had a surge of energy; he ran forward, shouting: "Pedre!"

Castro considered him with surprise. He searched his memories sincerely; then, suddenly, his eyelids fluttered, he pinched his lips and put an icy expression in his features.

"Come on! You don't recognize me?" the man said.

And as if it were sufficient to plunge his gaze into Castro's to recover an authority momentarily lost, he smiled and extended his hand with a certain condescension. Castro allowed his to be shaken, reluctantly.

He certainly recognized his old friend Deodat de Vega, whom he had not seen since Jehoudah's trial. The other had left the country at that moment. They had written for some time and then their letters had become sparser. Afterwards, Castro had learned that his friend had been arrested in Calcutta with regard to a deal in the slave trade, and then convicted of an attempt to blackmail a woman and transported to Australia. He thought he would never see him again, as he thought that he had finished with many things of his youth.

The door had just opened. Castro indicated with a gesture that he was in a hurry, putting off the conversation until later, but Deodat de Vega did not intend it to be thus.

"It's necessary that I speak to you immediately," he said. "I've come a long way to see you. I know that you're in the midst of great things. You'll need men like me."

Even while flattering his friend he retained a tone of ironic superiority.

Then Castro gestured to him to go in with him.

Rachel was in her bedroom; dressing after the siesta. The two men traversed the veranda and started walking in the garden while waiting for her.

Rachel's garden overlooked the garden via a narrow barred window before which one of the rare paths passed that the wild plants had not invaded completely. At the sound of footfalls Rachel looked through the window and did not recognize the powdered man at first. Gradually, however, that manner of walking while trailing one leg slightly and that smile expressing the negation of everything returned to her memory. Stuck to the wall, her face crushed against the grille of the window, she considered passionately the two men who had caused her misfortune by their mutual love of evil.

She understood their conversation by the grandiloquence of Castro's gestures and the prideful swelling of his features. He was experiencing pleasure in shining before his friend. He was subject once again to the ascendancy by which he had once been dominated. He allowed himself to be drawn to confidences. A savor of youth came to his lips.

As they passed the window, Rachel overhead one phrase in passing. They were talking about her. She understood that by the crease of Castro's eyes, and the fashion in which she saw him lean on his friend's shoulder. He must be flattering himself for having her for a mistress.

Rachel heard Vega say: "Perhaps you're wrong. It's necessary never to be proud of women. You know what I've always thought about that."

Castro was laughing now at evoked memories. A greater baseness was painted in his physiognomy. Oh, yes, they scorned women and they had certainly shown that by treating them as slaves. The two men rejoiced together in the actions they had once accomplished. Rachel trembled with rage at the idea that they might be talking about her mother.

It seemed to her that Deodat de Vega was explaining to his friend that the experience of life had not brought him, as it had others, even a hint of repentance.

The two men stopped not far from the window and Rachel heard this:

"One is sometimes punished. I've been at Port Jackson and felt the whip of the English overseer on my back. But now I'm here. I'm free. I said to you once, and I still believe, that evil is logically stronger than good, for it isn't embarrassed by ridiculous considerations of morality or pity. It's better to be on the side of evil."

It had been agreed that in the interest of their common projects, Deodat de Vega would show himself as little as possible in old Goa. He was installed in an isolated villa not far from Panjim, and it was only by night that he came to visit Castro.

Naturally, his visits took place in Rachel's house. But nothing in his costume any longer recalled the wretched individual who had walked in the garden a few days earlier. As in the times of his youth, Deodat de Vega wore impeccable white gloves, soft silk shirts and a cape retained by a golden chain that he threw negligently over his shoulder.

Castro had thought at first that it was necessary to reassure Rachel. Life and tribulations had changed his friend's character. A man like him was necessary to his projects. He counted on using him without allowing himself to be influenced by him.

Contrary to his expectation, however, Rachel immediately testified amity to the newcomer. That amity was so apparent that Deodat de Vega sensed its excess and was surprised by it. Nevertheless, he attributed it in part to the ennui that Rachel must be experiencing among the ecclesiastical ruins of old Goa, and in part to his own seduction.

Almost every week he took the boat to Bombay, where he devoted himself to the purchase of weapons and negotiations with adventurers of his acquaintance to whom it was necessary to make appeal when the moment came. He had also been charged with the sale of the diamonds and the black pearls. That sale had brought Castro more than he had hoped, and his confidence in his friend had increased. He knew full well that Deodat de Vega was above the desire for money. In addition, the latter had explained his difficulties with the English law. He did so with the sort of cynicism that can also be called sincerity, and which consists of excusing one's sins by recounting them with exactitude and glorying in them.

The abolition of the trade appeared to him to be a monstrous hypocrisy on society's part. Was not slavery the goal of all social organization? A free man like him was obliged to struggle incessantly in order not to be a slave. Why, then hide oneself in enslaving wretched black brutes? He had been wrong to let himself get caught, that was all. As for the so-called blackmail of the English lady, that was a story that would have made one die of laughter if it hadn't ended so badly for him. The widow of an English general who had pursued him for two years with declarations of amour and love-letters! An old crackpot from Calcutta who had offered him her fortune a hundred times over! He had finally decided to accept one of her offers. Unfortunately, it was at a bad moment, after he had abducted one of the lady's nieces, another girl from whom he had had nothing but ennui. In order to avenge herself, the general's widow had made use of a letter he had written her. God knows why! She had organized one of those plots that only women can conceive, out of spite. It had then been perceived that the niece was a minor, and the prudery of the English magistrates had been so effectively unleashed that he had been sent to Port Jackson.

Deodat de Vega had recounted all that before Rachel, over whom he had no doubt that he possessed as great an ascendancy as over Castro. Also before her, he talked about the preparations for the armed coup that would deliver the colony to Castro and the partisans of the archbishop.

It would be necessary to show the greatest energy from the start. One only imposed oneself by fear, one only succeeded by violence. What was most to be dreaded was advice to be prudent from timorous individuals.

Sometimes, Deodat de Vega lowered his voice and his tone became graver. That was when he made allusion to a sect by which, in the course of his travels, he had been initiated into a singular philosophy that was the basis of his convictions.

Rachel once heard him say: "When one wants to realize an important project like ours, it's necessary to consider before anything else that human life has no value. The men who instructed me at Khiva went much further, since they claimed that every time one suppresses an existence, one augments one's personal strength by as much, and that the strong are those who have the most deaths to their credit."

That evening had been an evening of enthusiasm. In Rachel's drawing-room, the last arrangements had been made that would conclude in the autonomy of the colony of Goa. They had discussed that fate of those who remained faithful to the King of Portugal and the religious authority of the Pope. The few priests rebellious to the authority of the Archbishop would be expelled. The governor was a man so dead by nature and so weak in character that no one had thought his death necessary. The only serious danger came from the colonel commanding the troops. He was almost always drunk, but he had moments of lucidity. Enclosed in the fort of Aguada, which was impregnable with the means at their disposal, he could bombard the new city.

Deodat de Vega shrugged his shoulders and cut the conversation short with a negligent gesture of his white-gloved hand. He would take charge of the colonel. That could be left to him.

By the light of the punch that was burning on the table, illuminating faces congested by the sentiment of their importance, positions were given and received. Castro would immediately replace the old Aguilar as President of the colony's Council. He was entirely designated to be thereafter the President of the future Republic. Mascarenhas would be the Minister of the Interior, and Marcora, a former long-haul captain who had spent his life at sea, would command the war fleet. It was on that fleet that the salvation of the new State would depend when Portugal sent its ships. Castro announced that Deodat de Vega had just negotiated the purchase on his behalf of a three-master of the latest model, with thirty guns, of which he would make a gift to the Republic of Goa.

Hands were shaken. Mutual felicitations were exchanged. They drank to the inspiration of the muse of the imminent revolution. It was only late at night that the conspirators slipped out to return to their homes.

Rachel was struck then by the fashion in which Castro opened the communicating door between the drawing room and the veranda, saying: "How hot it is in here. I need to breathe."

And she saw that he leaned out to listen to the sounds of the night.

Apart from a bird perched on a branch in the garden, which uttered a sad whistle at intervals, the night was almost silent. Camphor trees and wild frangipanes exhaled a heavy odor mingled with the damp odor of the nearby marshes.

"You didn't hear anything?" said Castro to Vega, taking him by the arm.

Vega shook his head negatively. "Still the old idea of the specter of destruction wandering the streets of Goa by night, knocking over a column, attacking the arch of a porch..." And he shrugged his shoulders lightly.

"Yes, we've just been talking about future prosperity, making full use of the land, and I'm convinced that there's an element of death prowling around us."

Deodat de Vega returned to the table and poured himself a drink.

"For you, then," Castro went on, with a broad gesture showing the sky, and the intonation of someone continuing a conversation often resumed, "there's nothing there, there's nothing anywhere?"

"Not nothing. There's a possibility of pleasure in us that tempers our belief in good and evil—if we have one, of course."

Castro's eyes illuminated momentarily, and Rachel felt herself enveloped from head to toe in a gaze of desire.

"Once, you remember," Castro said then, "we thought of nothing but our pleasure. We dared to put that before everything. That was a good time."

The two men, motionless beside one another, gazed in the direction of the mountains, and the hunched form of their backs expressed the regret of everything that is lost with age.

When they picked up their hats in order to leave, the thicker lips on Castro's face gave the impression of being painted red. The irony and willful superiority of Vega had given way in his features to an expression of ferocious bitterness.

On the threshold of the house, Rachel watched the silhouette of the two friends dwindle in the sloping street. Something indivisible linked them together.

Their mutual love of evil, Rachel thought.

And when she had closed the door again, on finding herself among the empty punch glasses, the chairs aligned around the table and the cooled smoke of cigars, she had difficulty not laughing, alone, with satisfaction.

She measured the road that she had covered so rapidly. She was tranquil now. The man she had seen one morning in the Church of the Magi, rejuvenated and purified by a sincere impulse toward God, had rediscovered the road that had led him back to evil by a circle from which he would not emerge. How well hazard had served Rachel by bringing back that companion in debauchery! Castro was attached solidly to his youth by the root of passions.

And Rachel wondered whether the moment had not come.

But no, not yet. It was necessary that he be on the cross, like her father, that he suffer, that he knew for what crime he was being punished by Rachel, the daughter of the physician Jehoudah. And she promised herself to find an unexpected and terrible vengeance.

"Lord Sabaoth, you shall be redoubtable to the wicked!"

And she leaned close to the mirror and stared mechanically at her own image. She stepped back and passed her hand across her face as if to remove a mask. She had an ugly expression that she had never seen before.

The Form of Vengeance

In the same way that good actions only have value by virtue of the manner in which they are made, Rachel sometimes thought, vengeance is only just if it is given a form equal to the crime. And it was almost involuntarily, as if engendered by her long imaginations on the subject, that the form of her vengeance, confused at first, appeared in her mind.

That morning, she had met Joachim at the moment when she arrived at the water's edge, and they had descended in the same canoe the broad channel that runs alongside the isle of Divar. They had gone a long way, but neither of them was in any hurry to go back.

They had resumed the interminable conversations in which two young people who are glad to be together strive to tell their story and to show themselves in the light that ought to be the most seductive for the other. Rachel had depicted herself as an unfortunate and oppressed woman and had made a story of her life analogous to the one that she had given Pedre de Castro. An instinctive prudence had impelled her to conceal the manner in which she had left Cochin for Bombay, and she had adopted the version agreed since the first day with Pedre. If she was in Goa it was to wait for her husband, a buyer of land that he proposed to put to use. She allowed a mystery to float over her life with that supposed husband and Joachim was too timid to interrogate her categorically. He asked her indirect questions, however; he was astonished by her solitude, and he sought above all to elucidate the reasons for his father's frequent visits.

Joachim de Castro had not known his mother. He had been brought up by his grandmother, a creature whose mind narrowed by devotions and the terrors inspired in her by her son. Joachim had only been twelve years old when she died. Her father had then put him in a college run by the Jesuits in Bombay. Pedre de Castro only saw his son during the vacations and he even took advantage of those times to go hunting in the Ghats. The father and the son had not exchanged affectionate words. They had remained strangers to one another, separated by the insurmountable wall that sometimes rises up between beings of the same blood. Joachim de Castro had remained apart from the vulgar pleasures of adolescence. He was pious, but avid to love. Since he had arrived in devastated Goa, everything was a subject of astonishment for him. Rachel frightened him because she was a Jewess and her beauty threw him into states of excitement analogous to those he had experienced in hours of mystic ardor. He loved to hear her talk, but he sensed that the best of her was escaping him.

Rachel had all the more difficulty replying to his questions in a plausible fashion because she acquired in the presence of the young man an imperious need for sincerity, the force of which she could not explain. She had ended up living in the lie as in a familiar element, and, as had happened to her in the early days of her sojourn in Goa, she no longer suffered from showing sentiments that she did not feel or disguising those that she did. But Joachim de Castro radiated a current of verity, a rectitude of the soul, that influenced her. And gradually, in the stories of her life that Joachim's questions obliged her to recommence, she drew gradually closer to what had really happened. Although her stories were never sufficiently clear, Joachim knew that Rachel's youth had been poisoned because of a man, and that that man had caused her mother's death in dramatic circumstances, the details of which she did not want to reveal to him.

"There is one virtue that I admire above all others, which is courage," Rachel told him.

Joachim did not know whether he was courageous. He had not yet been undergone the proof of action. He sensed within him something like a surge of ardor, a need to attain Rachel's admiration.

"I'd like to be courageous for you," he said.

And Rachel, still preoccupied with unveiling to the young man the veritable depths of her own soul, said then:

"Don't you think that the man who does evil ought to be punished by a similar evil? Veritable justice consists, in my view, of rendering with a rigorous exactitude the good that has been done to you as a recompense, and the evil that one has suffered as a punishment. And humans acting thus are then the instruments of God."

"Why not speak to me more sincerely?" said Joachim, who was following Rachel's thoughts less by means of the words he heard than his own intuition. "I sense that there's a constant obsession within you. You see again, perpetually, an image that is in the past and from which you have suffered."

They had stopped walking. They looked one another in the face and she was astonished that his myopic eyes could see so far within her.

"You're wrong to take me for a child," he went on. "I would like so much to show you that I'm capable of defending you and even of avenging you! Tell me……"

But Rachel raised her hand to make him a sign to be silent. It was at that moment that the imprecise thought was sketched within her.

To her right she had a clump of fig-trees, mimosas ad wild organs, to her left the shiny expanse of the waters. The oars of the canoe that was following them while they walked along the path made regular splashing sounds. In the midst of the foliage, pelicans disturbed in their solitude started clicking their beaks lugubriously. The sky was an oppressive blue. It seemed to Rachel that it was weighing on her shoulders. Around her, the earth was infinitely sad under the inexorable sun. She suddenly felt fatigued.

"We must go back," she said. "How far we've come today!"

Jealousy

Since Deodat de Vega had returned, Castro had frequently said: "It's curious; it seems to me that I'm rejuvenated."

He had aged more rapidly and he felt it obscurely, so he felt the need to affirm in speech a new youth. Rachel noticed a change in his manner. He looked at her with sharper eyes, and when he was with her he had an animal fashion of breathing her odor and extending his hand, as if he wanted to palpate her flesh. He had not returned to confess at the Church of the Magi. Once, he forgot to put on his chaplet of large wooden beads, and lost the habit of wearing it.

He also said: "When one looks at things from a certain height one perceives that the past doesn't exist, and that only the present counts."

He reproached himself then for having wasted his time in prayers and confessions. "Redemption! But redeem myself from what? It's enough to think of one's salvation at the end of one's life. It's necessary to enjoy as much as one can."

Rachel impressed him. He acquired the habit of going to her house more frequently. But she remained as distant from him as a Virgin in a church, on an altar.

That has never happened to me with any woman, he said to himself. And as he was unaware of the measure in which his faith had diminished and he was deceiving himself with its formulae, he repeated to himself, in order to excuse his lack of audacity: *She's the good angel that God has sent to me.* At other times he added: *A angel of flesh and blood, all the same. An angel that I found at Antonia's.* And he took delight in imagining her in lascivious poses, dominated and complaisant.

As his self-esteem was immense, he gladly allowed those who talked to him about her to believe that she was his mistress. He laughed in a knowing fashion when anyone asked him for information about the husband he had invented, or lowered his eyes modestly. He sometimes experienced the desire to give her value in order that she might be respected. Once, when Mascarenhas interrogated him he said: "All the land on Divar island, and even that beyond the arm of the river to the north, will belong to her. She's richer than you or me."

But if anyone entered too rapidly into that way of seeing, he was discontented. Nor could he bear the idea that anyone might believe that she exercised any influence over him.

"Jews are never anything but Jews," he said then. "It was manifest once what I thought of them."

However, he realized that Rachel would quickly become unpopular in Goa because of her quality as a Jewess. That unpopularity might rebound on him and harm his position later. He thought that there was a means of remedying that.

One evening, sitting beside Rachel under the veranda of his house, he made her party to the hope he was nourishing of seeing her convert to his religion. She would have the chance to be baptized by a great saint for whom God incessantly marked his predilection by signs and words. That conversion would be an example about which people would talk, and which would serve the common cause.

While he spoke, all he could see of Rachel's face was a mass of shadow with two fixed gleams beneath the aureole of her hair, because they were only illuminated by the lamp that was behind them in the drawing room.

The gleam of the eyes scarcely increased. The response was slow in coming. It was eventually emitted in a muted, atonal voice.

Rachel did not say no. Since she had been in Goa she had become sensible to the beauties of the Christian religion. Before being baptized she wanted to know the dogma better and penetrate it. She would obtain instruction first. Then she would see.

Castro considered those words as a kind of promise. He thanked Rachel, and in a surge of gratitude, for he thought that the gain brought to God would be counted to him, he took Rachel's hand and kept it in his own. That hand was warm, feverish and alive, and Castro felt his heart beating forcefully.

It seemed to him, in gazing in front of him at the design that the pandanus branches made against the dark blue background of the sky, dotted with the unalterable light of the stars, that an unsuspected splendor had been revealed within him for the first time.

Rachel's hand was detached from his own slowly enough for him not to sense the disgust she experienced. The two hands each retained a different burn.

For Castro it was as if a veil had torn, as if he were contemplating a horizon on arrival at the summit of a mountain. And the horizon that he saw before him was that of his soul ravaged by a fire that had burned without him knowing it, and had reached the most secret corners of the substance of his being.

What the half-breed boatman said appeared to him at first to be a lie, a monstrous imagination invented to torture him. But no, the man was speaking innocently, reporting a fact that he considered to be unimportant. The half-breed lived in a bamboo house on the bank of the river; he fished, he hired out his boat, he paid no heed to what might interest the inhabitants of Goa. He had simply related that every morning he took Joachim, Pedre de Castro's son, to the little island in the part of the pool that was known as the pool of the drowned city, and there he met a beautiful young woman about whom he knew nothing, except that she was newly arrived in Goa and that she had thick, almost blue hair, displayed beneath a gray felt hat.

At first Castro thought about striking the half-breed and making him retract his words by means of blows. But his ingenuousness was certain. He preferred to turn his back on him in order to reflect at his ease. Then he started to run along the river bank. It was necessary to know, to know immediately what was what. How long the time seemed that separated him from the moment when he would know. He crossed the ramparts. He headed for Rachel's house. He was out of breath. He was walking with difficulty, burdened by the weight of anguish.

It was only then, in the burning shade of the street, along the old ruined convents and Moorish dwellings full of silence, that he became conscious of what was happening within him. He loved Rachel. He had known for a long time that he desired her, but he had only just learned that he loved her. He had loved her since the first day when he had seen her in the room in the Bombay brothel. And he only realized that today on learning that she knew his son.

So she knew his son. They met on an island, under the trees, in the midst of propitious grass. Nature brought people who desire one another together. He thought about the complicity brought by the morning breath of vegetation, the odor of the sap of the damp earth.

He nearly retraced his steps in order to interrogate the half-breed again, to ask him whether he had seen the two young people holding hands as they walked or sitting down on the ground in order to be more completely together.

And as he reached the perron of Rachel's house, he saw clearly what he had to do.

Antonia had brought Rachel to him herself in that room where there was a bed alongside the table. She was a whore like those he had already known in that house. The envoy of God! Ha ha! Had he not lost his head a little with his vows and his confessions? What mania had taken hold of him then? Had he not been afraid of seeing the drowned woman of old, whom the fish had eaten, under the aspect of a beautiful whore that Antonia was offering him? He should have put the money on the table and thrown Rachel on to the bed immediately after they had dined and drunk the champagne. He saw the whole scene again as if it were painted on canvas. He remembered that he was in his shirt-sleeves and that he had put his jacket on, by virtue of a sort of respect. That thought filled him with fury. She was about to see how he would treat her.

Rachel had prolonged her siesta a little longer than usual. When he was introduced into the drawing room, Castro heard her moving back and forth in her bedroom. Then, as if the compact matter of the door and the wall had become translucent, he perceived the woman with her young, a living, warm, amber body. The mosquito-net over the bed had been thrown back and there was a trace of a form on the sheets, and the hollow on the pillow where her head, with its helm of blue-tinted hair, had rested. On the floor, rounded, a peignoir had fallen from which she had emerged, perhaps naked. Now, he saw her in that chemise of taut, unreal, cloudy linen, of which he had glimpsed the edge over the cleavage of her breasts. She was walking nonchalantly around the room, going from the mirror to the old chest of drawers. She was touching powders, loosening a tress, painting a fingernail. The perfume of her body drifted around her like an invisible wave. She was laden with unrealized pleasures, as languorous as the finishing after-noon.

He could not hold still. He advanced to the door and lift-ed the latch. But Rachel never went to bed in her room without drawing an interior bolt, and the door did not open. Then, con-fused by his futile attempt, Castro went into the garden and started marching back and forth.

He did not know, when Rachel joined him, whether she had seen the latch rise. Her face was impassive, her eyes were brighter than usual, and in the second when he perceived her, Castro measured with a frightful clarity the difference in age there was between them and the physical distance that he must certainly inspire in her. If there had been a mirror beside him to reflect his image, he could not have seen any more clearly his ridiculous pot belly, his double chin, the two large wrin-kles that striped his cheeks to cither side of the nose and his thick red lips, the testimony of his disproportionate sensuality. He sensed droplets of sweat trickling over his temples. It seemed to him that the hair on his head was becoming more impoverished. He thought he could hear the work of the mole-cules in a tooth that he knew to be rotten, in the depths of his jaw.

Vanquished in advance, he spoke.

Rachel immediately had an expression of affectionate enchantment on her face.

Yes, the hazard of an excursion had enabled her to make the acquaintance of Joachim de Castro. She had indeed neglected to tell him that. She liked to get up early in the morning, to go down to the river, to follow the meanders of the channels. Once they had found themselves side by side in the mist. She had had a great deal of pleasure in chatting to the young man. In truth, there was no harm in that.

Then Castro abandoned himself to the surge of denigration that jealousy stimulates.

His son did not love him. He had never loved his father. The foundation of his nature was a hypocrisy that he sought in vain to explain. Raised by the Jesuits in Bombay, he remained, in the depths of his heart, faithful to the sovereign authority of the Pope. He did not want to admit the sanctity of the Archbishop, and his principal reason for doubting it was that his father believed in it. It was necessary to mistrust him. Who could tell whether he might go so far as to oppose his father overtly in the struggle they were about to undertake?

Castro believed, childishly, that a woman might love someone less because he was a bad son, a hypocrite, a traitor to a cause. He did not know that denigration is fuel to a flame.

But Rachel hastened to agree with him. She frowned. Her discontentment went as far as Castro's words.

"I will speak to him about it myself," she said, severely.

No, no—that was not what Castro wanted at all. He would send his son away, whose presence was a danger. He would make him quit Goa, of his own free will or by force.

However, he calmed down, for what is pronounced in words acquires thereafter a power of reality. Rachel's serene face could not be deceptive. Nothing had happened between Joachim and the young woman. One did not know life and the other had been too disappointed by amour to allow herself to be taken in by the young man's first words.

They were both walking amid wild plants, and Castro sometimes moved aside the broad leaf of a cactus in order that its prickles would not hook on to Rachel's dress. The interior mirror in which he had contemplated himself, deformed and ridiculous, had disappeared. He even saw another in which he appeared with all the advantages of fortune and power. Was there a woman capable of resisting the master of Goa? What woman would not be glad to be the wife of the great Castro? He would marry Rachel. The Archbishop would bless his marriage. No one would be able to dispute the beauty of the body that he desired.

They were in the depths of the garden. Rachel sensed that Castro was about to tell her that he was in love with her.

"Look," she said, laughing.

She showed him a cross planted in the ground. It was a cross taller than human height, stout and sturdy, devoid of ornaments.

"It's me who had it planted here," said Rachel. "I found it in the shed, where it was rotting. It appears that it's my destiny to find every species of cross in this old dwelling. At one time it's a gold cross with diamonds, at another it's a cross of worm-eaten wood.

She tore up a plant, which she raised toward the cross.

"When I've converted, it's here that I'll come to pray," she said, without Castro being able to tell whether she was speaking seriously or ironically.

He considered the cross in silence. He seemed to recognize it. He saw that the extremity was crushed, because it had been used as a battering ram. It was the caretaker of this house who, when the pogrom in the Jewish quarter had been decided, had carried the cross behind which the Christians marched. He must have brought it back and it had remained here, forgotten, ever since.

Castro returned toward the house at a slow pace. The words had dried up on his lips. He decided not to talk about love until the next day.

But anxiety had entered into him. He woke up several times during the night, bathed with sweat.

Once, it was to say to himself: "I, the descendant of Pedre de Castro, am going to marry a Jewess, a whore picked up in the gutter."

Another time he saw himself begging Rachel on his knees or extending his hand to set aside a mysterious barrier that loomed up between them. And he repeated: "There's a cross that separates us."

The Knife

Events moved even more rapidly than those directing them had hoped. The Council of the colony proclaimed Castro president by acclamation. The governor did not come to ratify that appointment. He remained locked in the governmental palace, whose great portal remained closed. He was an astonishingly taciturn man, and a servant who dwelt in his house recounted afterwards that he had spent two days motionless, gazing at the toes of his shoes.

When the *Andromeda* called in at Goa before setting sail for Lisbon they did not know how to tell him that he would not be running any risk if he went to the ship and left Goa forever. A child succeeded in hoisting himself up to a window, of which he broke a pane and through which he shouted the advice to leave and a guarantee of safe conduct. No one saw a boat depart from the marble staircase of the palace that plunges into the river. It became known the next day, however, when the *Andromeda* left Goa, that the governor was on board. It was generally thought that he had been favored by fate, for the most violent had thought that it was unwise to let a man return to Lisbon who, in spite of his silent habits, would present events to the Court in a light unfavorable to the colony. There had been talk of throwing him in the sea before he reached the *Andromeda*. It was also remembered that his predecessors had died at intervals of a few months, afflicted by rapid and unknown maladies. That tended to make people think that, contrary to popular belief, sorrow can be accompanied by luck, like joy.

The colonel made the mistake of going to a nocturnal tavern not far from Ribandar. He was retained there until a late hour. As he was coming back to the new city he quit the arms of a few drinkers who were accompanying him and who were all zealous partisans of the Archbishop, because he had heard someone call his name at the extremity of a little path. The drinkers declared the following day that the colonel's name had resounded several times in the night, followed by imprecations proffered by the latter in a jesting tone. They were not in agreement as to the moment when they had heard a rifle-shot, and several affirmed that they had not heard anything. The colonel was found dead in the morning, sitting up with his back against a palm tree, against which he had been thrown after received a bullet in the breast.

The troops, deprived of a leader, did not intervene in the disorder that was produced around the churches. Certain priests, still faithful to papal authority, refused to give way to the new incumbents nominated by the Archbishop. Excited groups broke down the doors behind which they were entrenched. A few houses were set on fire, belonging to functionaries who had left precipitately for English territory.

For several days the rumor ran around that the officer in charge of the powder store at Ribandar, who was the colonel's nephew, was going to set fire to it in order to avenge his uncle. The powder store was almost empty, but the Hindus, ignorant of the mystery of powder, claimed that the entire island on which the new city and old Goa were built was about to blow up. Some of them thought of escaping that catastrophe by remaining on boats in the middle of pools, with the consequence that an entire flotilla was seen in which people were eating and sleeping under parasols, drifting over the waters, until it was learned that the officer whose vengeance was feared had fled to Bombay.

Deodat de Vega had summoned adventurers of all nationalities. A ship coming from Macao had even deposited two hundred Chinamen in the port. They had signed a labor contract, with a wage of one piastre per month, which placed them in a dependency more rigorous than the old slavery. They had assumed that they would be working in the cultivation of land, but it was proposed to arm them and make them a militia of sorts, in case there was a serious struggle to sustain. As they had no organization as yet, they wandered at random, and camped on waste ground not far from the Church of the Magi, seeking their nourishment. However, it was not for rice that they pillaged a shop in old Goa but to procure sticks of incense. They could not resist the dazzle of gold. They commenced the demolition of a church whose pillars were newly gilded, thinking that they were solid gold, in order to carry away the blocks.

Three of them were hanged from an old banyan that stood on the location of the former Jesuit convent on Chovas Island. Their bodies swung in the wind for several days, and were eaten by the vultures. The rest of the Chinese remained prey to terror and despair. They had been forbidden to put the remains of the three hanged men in coffins. Henceforth, the agonized souls of those dead men, which had not been able to return to the land of their ancestors, would wander over the place of their torture tormenting the living and spreading curses. By night, a lugubrious chant of prayers emerged from the miserable huts constructed in haste in the sands near the Church of the Magi. The legend of the three Chinese phantoms was accredited by many minds. Many heard them sighing behind the doors. Many saw them gliding sadly through the silent streets of Goa, with their broken necks and the rope of execution raised in the right hand.

There was a scandal around the relic of Saint Francis Xavier. The Archbishop gave the authorization for the public exhibition of the body of the saint on the threshold of the cathedral. It was laid out in the vestments he had been wearing at the moment of his death, holding a rattan cane with a golden pommel in his left hand. His right arm had been removed in the seventeenth century to be sent to the Pope. Driven by religious exaltation and also the desire of possession, a noble lady, as she prostrated herself, had severed one of the toes with her teeth and carried it away. Since then, the saint only appeared in public beneath a globe of glass supported by a silver frame.

That day, the crowd could not contain its enthusiasm. Perhaps they remembered the noble lady of old. The faithful, singing a canticle and crying: "Mercy!" shattered the glass globe, and overly zealous hands attempted to tear away either a fragment of garment, some hair or an ear. Thanks to the courage of the Swiss guard, armed with his halberd, and the presence of a few members of the new militia, the relic of Saint Francis Xavier was saved.

The cathedral was witness to another scandal. That day, the Archbishop had ordained priests, had conferred minor diaconal orders on young men and was about to consecrate a bishop, as demanded by the extension of the schism. Many churches situated in English territory had adhered to the revolt. It was necessary to send priests into all the suburbs of Bombay, to Bandora, to Corlem and to Mahim. Public rumor had demanded that a bishop be consecrated. That bishop was to be Jéronime Caval, whose popularity was immense.

Jéronime Caval was a former Augustine monk who had received from God the gift of speech, along with the gift of a communicative gaiety. He was extremely violent and sometimes lost his head when he had drunk to excess, which often happened to him. In Seringapatam, where he was resided for a while, he always wore a saber under his soutane, to cut off the ears, he said, of a certain evil priest who was attempting to kill him by casting spells. In that city he carried out an overt commerce in the sacraments and had created for confession a subscription of one rupee per year. In exchange for a bottle of hard liquor he had married people who were already married. It was said that, after having abducted a young woman, he had been a snake-charmer in a large menagerie in Calcutta. He was also accused of having indulged in piracy in Malaysia, and magic with the Sultan of Zanzibar. He welcomed these calumnies and repeated them himself with the most perfect joy. The schism of Goa had attracted him as flowers attract bees.

Fatigued by the morning ceremonies, Monsenhor de Silva had arrived at the moment of the consecration when the imposition of hands takes place. His hands were trembling but his voice pronounced distinctly the formula by which the audience was invited to reveal reasons for the hindrance of the consecration, if they knew of any.

That ought to have been a simple formality, but someone in the crowd called out that there was a hindrance. It was a woman, a half-breed with square shoulders, who advanced full of confidence. She had a livid individual beside her who was brandishing a piece of paper, and she affirmed that she had been legitimately married to Jéronime Caval. Cries resounded. Jéronime Caval tranquilized the assembly by the delight spread over his features, but he suddenly launched himself forward, trying to reach the man with the piece of paper and demanding a weapon in order to cut off his ears. He thought that he recognized him as his old enemy the enchanter. A brawl ensued and blood flowed, while the Archbishop quit the profaned cathedral.

A kind of delirium took possession of the society of Goa at the same time as religiosity was redoubled. Adulteries became more numerous, virgins took lovers. The beautiful Conception Colaço gave free rein to her insatiable amour for adolescents and Juana de Faria prostituted her face of a fallen angel to all the adventurers who wanted to follow her. Old Marcora left his four daughters the care of occupying themselves with the administration of the navy of which he was in charge. On the quay of the new city he dozed, sitting in front of his door, one which *Navy* was written in large letters, and said: "They're very intelligent. They understand business better than me. See my daughters." And there was a childlike, smiling face at each of the four first-floor windows.

Castro drank. His old passion for rum had reawakened definitively. He drank because rum pours a divine warmth into the soul and projects it to sunlit summits, because it was perpetually necessary to talk about the future of Goa by drinking with incapable men, and because he forgot, when he had been drinking, the violence of his arguments with his son and the mental paralysis that prevented him from talking to Rachel about love.

It was on the harbor, in the Palm Tree Café, alongside the offices of the newspaper *L'Abelha*, that the great political dreams were born and took flight. The steamer from Bombay was feverishly awaited, in order to read the European newspapers. They were snatched from hands, but they only brought a renewed disappointment. Neither the Goanese schism nor the events it had provoked seemed to interest the great Occidental nations.

"What the devil can be occupying them out there?" demanded Heliodora da Cunha, who was the most avid for glory, and wore, as commander of the troops, the uniform of an artillery officer.

"Eh! They're occupied with Cuba, of course," replied Marcora, with a burst of laughter.[5]

Cuba, with the support of America, was then in full insurrection against Spain, and the newspapers of the entire world were following the efforts of Narcisco Lopez for its liberation.

A strange jealousy took possession of the directors of Goa. They only spoke about Cuba in order to denigrate that island, its geographical location and the characters of its inhabitants. Cuba had usurped on the planet the place that Goa ought to have held. But they were secretly striving to imitate the heroes of Cuban independence.

"You will be our Lopez," they said to Castro, to flatter him.

"You'll see that they'll send us Concha too," said the pessimists.

Concha was an intractable Spanish general who had all the rebels that fell into his hand shot by firing squads.

But the optimists were more numerous and he repeated with confidence: "We'll obtain autonomy."

---

[5] The so-called Cuban War of Independence did not begin until 1868, but an earlier attempt at liberation had been made in August 1851 by the Venezuelan adventurer Narcisco Lopez (1797-1851), which he did not survive, being captured and shot by forces commanded by General José Gutiérrez de la Concha.

The word *autonomy* was repeated by many half-breeds and Hindus, by dock-workers in the port and Malabar boatmen, who did not understand its meaning. They only knew that there was an Archbishop in Goa who was a saint, with whom God communicated directly by night, and they also knew that from beyond the sea a being of extraordinary but distant power, mythical and formless, the Pope of Rome, wished the saintly Archbishop harm.

And that word *autonomy*, and that distant vision of an irritated Pope in a Vatican similar to a pagoda of Vishnu, were synonymous for them with conversations at sunset, idleness and liberty.

In the evening, in old Goa, many amicable feasts terminated in orgies. Dance music resounded in the houses. There were noisy brawls beneath the shaky towers and in the ruins of cloisters. The mortuary shadows of the ecclesiastical city concealed couplings and combats. And it was necessary to leave certain churches open because faith was such that many Christians got up during the night in order to run to prostrate themselves before God. But it was necessary for those Christians to be armed, because the streets, once peaceful, had ceased to be safe.

Until an advanced hour of the night, Conception Colaço, bare-breasted on her balcony, sang sentimental ballads, for amour was inseparable for her from singling and the mandora. Her rival Juana sometimes tried to respond in a falsetto voice. The whistles of thieves signaling to one another were heard, mingled with fragments of canticles emerging from doors that stood ajar, and the distant ritual prayers of the Chinamen.

People were living in Goa in a vague expectation of the end of the world.

Rachel had noticed the bizarre attitude of Father Vincent in her regard and had not been able to explain it.

That simple and pure man, who always walked with his head bowed over his black robe out of modesty, had raised it several times in her direction. She had seen him prowling not far from her house, hesitating to knock on her door. He visibly wanted to speak to her.

One day, she found herself face to face with him on the bank of the river Mandavi. At the sight of her he drew out an object that he must have been carrying in his belt beneath his robe, which was wrapped in mango leaves. He spoke to Rachel was an extreme confusion. He expressed himself in the Tamil language, of which she only understood a little. He wanted her to take the object he was holding out. It belonged to Rachel.

Unfolding the mango leaves, Rachel saw that they contained a knife, which she recognized as the one she had taken from Antonia's house, and which he had dropped after Castro's confession in the Church of the Magi.

Father Vincent spoke with a humble goodness. So many bad things had happened in Goa! Everyone had forgotten God. It had begun on the day that he had found the knife in the church, or thereabouts. He begged Rachel's pardon. He thought that perhaps the force of evil was in that iron, just as certain divine forces are enclosed in the Virgin Mary's wood, He was returning the iron to the person who had brought it, in order that goodness could return to the poor people of the land of Goa.

Father Vincent had his hands joined and he no longer had the strength to raise his eyes. As he went away he was almost walking on tiptoe, and his innocence enveloped him like an aureole.

PART THREE

Castro's Confession

That night, Joachim de Castro had difficulty sleeping. By the glow of the night-light that was next to his sculpted wooden bed, his eyes wandered over the old portraits of prelates and warriors or stared at the door of his bedroom and its large iron lock. He had the apprehension of seeing that door open and his father standing there, lamp in hand. He had already come twice to wake him up in the night, to order him to quit Goa the next day. He had replied respectfully that his duty was to share the dangers that his father might run. Then he had maintained an obstinate silence. Rachel's name had not been pronounced, but her dazzling image had stood between the two men.

Joachim turned over on his pillow. He had gone to bed early. He closed his eyelids, and in the intermediary state that is neither wakefulness nor slumber, he saw images unfurling.

On the road that rose toward the Jesuit convent in the island of Chovas a host of black robes and white crosses was departing from the door of the convent. They were missionaries, disciples of Saint Francis Xavier, who were going to Malacca and China to evangelize the people. Joachim saw their energetic faces distinctly, in which bright eyes were shining, along with their long beards and the scapulars over their breasts. But three shadows swayed to the right and left over that procession and dispersed it. They were the three Chinamen who had been hanged outside the portal of the convent.

His gaze went further and the saw the caravels of old cleaving the waters of the river Mandavi with their curved prows. Portuguese adventurers were taking off their helmets and breastplates and leaping with joy on the quays of Goa, where a variegated crowd was pressing. And that buzzing crowd plunged between the sculpted porches, beneath the projections of balconies, under loggias in which ladies with ruffs were smiling. The Viceroy of India came out of his palace, among cavaliers, lords with plumes and velvet mantles. The great square before the cathedral was filled with an expectant population, turned toward the enormous threshold of the Inquisition.

From that threshold, Joachim saw the monastic orders that had once filled the innumerable convents of Goa emerging indefinitely. He recognized the Dominicans by their white cowls, the Franciscans by the rope that girdled their waist, the members of the Order for the Redemption of Captives by the red woolen cross that they wore around the neck. The noble orphans of Saint Anne and the virgins of the Infant Jesus had their hands folded over their breasts and were singing canticles. Conception Colaço, half-naked, her breasts crushed over the iron of a balcony, was laughing and showing her teeth, and putting an improbable note of indecency into the gravity of things. But he saw penitents under hoods and candle-bearers with desperate faces, and he understood that he was witnessing a solemn religious ceremony.

And suddenly, over the city, he saw a bell-tower fall, and then another. One bell, which was ringing at full tilt, was detached. A tower collapsed; a cloister deprived of its roof appeared as a procession of skeletons. The delightful faces of women wrinkled abruptly between the marble colonnettes of windows. The wind dispersed the crowd like dust. Nothing remained but one silhouette in the middle of the square, and that was his own. He was face to face with an individual who had just appeared on the threshold of the cathedral, and who was extending a menacing finger toward him: a threat that everyone had feared for a long time, but about which people only talked in low and horrified voices, the menace that hung over the schismatics of Goa, the excommunication launched against him. Joachim could not make out the syllables of the redoubtable formulae, but he understood that he was considered as solely responsible for the religious troubles of Goa, that he had been rejected from the Church, accursed forever.

Everything disappeared: the priests, the cavaliers, the monuments. Joachim, sitting beside Rachel, was gazing at the sea on the quay of the new city of Goa, surrounded by Chinamen.

Several days ago their moaning troop, ravaged by malaria, had come to settle in the port, at the place where a junk from Macao might appear, capable of repatriating them. They had transported the coffins in which they had placed their dead and, careless of threats, they refused to quit the quay for fear of missing the liberating junk.

Joachim was waiting for that junk in his dream. He and Rachel were no longer anything but wretched emigrants, avid to depart together for an unknown land. Rachel's shoulder was close to him, and the presence of that flesh against his own communicated a warmth so penetrating that he woke up.

He searched for a prophetic character in those incoherent images. He was threatened with excommunication. All of those who adhered to the Archbishop's schism would be, at the same time as him. Ought he not to attempt to escape what he considered to be the most terrible of eventualities? But that was not sufficient. His duty was also to attempt to save his father. His father! He was separated from him by Rachel.

Sitting up in bed in the dark, Joachim saw his situation clearly. His father hated him, because he loved Rachel Jehoudah, and he sensed that his son loved her too. To which of the two would that woman belong, who seemed haunted by an idea unknown to him, a project that he could not divine? She could not love his father. The physique of Pedre de Castro was not that of a seducer, in spite of the perfumes with which he covered himself and the slightly ridiculous care with which he chose his cravats and his silk shirts. He had not enough confidence in himself to hope to be loved. He was too young for Rachel. And yet…she had talked to him about her solitude with eyes in which he had seen that emerald glimmer whose

123

gleam made him feel faint. She had kept his hand in hers while saying that she wanted to be aided by someone courageous.

And Joachim said to himself that he could accept being no more, as in his dream, than a miserable coolie working in Macao among the Chinese, if Rachel were with him.

Joachim was needlessly afraid of the appearance of his father in his bedroom. At that same moment, Pedre de Castro was in Rachel's house. He had come from the Fort of Aguada and that of Mary Magdalen. Heliodora da Cunha, who had received command of the army, had disappeared several days ago. He was reputed to be the most energetic man in Goa and he had imposed by his authority a certain discipline on the troops disorientated by the revolution. It was said that he was awaiting events in English territory, in the company of a young negress from Mozambique. Pedre de Castro had replaced him and was directing military affairs as well as civil affairs.

Since then he had had very little time to spare. The future of the Republic-to-be depended on the conduct of the forts when the ship sent from the metropolis appeared. The cannons of Mary Magdalen and Aguada could forbid it access to the port, and perhaps even sink it. Certain malevolent minds claimed that the cannons of the forts had been beyond use for a long time and that, in any case, they could not be of service because the officers capable of directing their manipulation had left. In order to tranquilize minds and affirm his power, Castro had been carrying out almost incessant firing exercises for three days. One of the big guns of Mary Magdalen had exploded.

After a long journey on horseback, Castro had stopped at his house for a few minutes. There he had drunk a few glasses of run to give him courage, and he had hastened to see Rachel.

Now, he was speaking. A strange facility of speech possessed him. He felt a veritable surge of sincerity, analogous to those he had experienced when talking to God in the Church of the Magi. Everything became easy for him. He told Rachel that he loved her and that he had resolved to marry her if she consented to it. He stopped her when she tried to interrupt him. He knew what she was about to say. It was necessary that he lay his soul bare before the envoy of Providence.

Thos two words reminded Rachel of her arrival at Antonia's house, and she laughed internally. The odor of moist cloth that Castro emitted evoked the reek of rotten wood and damp of the old house in Bombay. She saw him again, in a gripping manner, in his shirt-sleeves, gazing at a chipped tooth in a mirror; she heard the sound of his ring on the marble of the fireplace, the cracked bell, and the song of the frogs.

She had placed on the table one of the earthenware vases fabricated in Goa, which was the same color as the skin of the Hindus who baked the clay. She poured out rum from a black bottleneck and pushed a full glass toward Castro. She was beginning to be gripped by a violent curiosity as to what he was about to say to her. She was half-lying in a wicker armchair and strove to diminish the gravity of the conversation by occasionally driving away a mosquito with a thrust of her fan. She did not notice the movement of her peignoir, uncovering her amber shoulder and almost her breast.

"Such as I am! It's necessary that you know me such as I am," he said, in a low voice. "There are obscure things in me that I have never succeeded in disentangling. Am I good, am I evil? I don't know. It's true that good and evil..."

He stopped, measuring a problem, whose solution he had sought for a long time without finding it. Then he dismissed the problem with a gesture.

"It is generally understood, however, that such an action is good and some other evil. Around my twentieth year, I was animated by the deliberate will only to accomplish what is commonly called evil. That was greatly under the influence of Deodat de Vega. He returned from a voyage to Persia and Tartary, having stayed in Khiva, Bukhara and the land of Kafiristan. He said that the cruelest men on earth were in that region. They were Shiite Muslims, but he talked to me as I remember, about a certain sect that worshiped the Devil. He claimed to have been initiated by the local intellectuals to a sort of philosophy, rather complicated, that led its believers to the religion of evil.

"Deodat de Vega did not appear to me then to be a great intellectual; I considered him as a skeptic and a gambler. Although a convinced Catholic, I submitted to his ascendancy. I pretend to mock his feigned religion of evil, but in fact I adhered to it with all my strength. He became my companion, my inseparable friend. We acquired the habit of living a crapulous life, first in the new city and then in Bombay. I tortured my mother to extract the necessary money from her. The unfortunate creature that I had married, without really knowing why, died of chagrin, leaving me Joachim, whose birth had caused me nothing but annoyance."

Castro poured himself a drink. He drank, and wiped his lips with the back of his hand. He looked at the ceiling, and then at Rachel, and he resumed:

"I could say that I felt remorse for having neglected my son's education, for being the indirect cause of the death of that woman of a faithful nature but a limited intelligence; I could say that I regret having spent my youth with whores and men without faith, but no—why say that which is not? In truth, I have no remorse. When I have confessed to a priest I have said, naturally, that I hated my sins, but I was lying. One is more sincere, at certain moments, before the woman one loves than before God. I'm not explaining myself, in any case. But one can explain so little when one considers one's own soul."

Castro was speaking now with the abundance and satisfaction that self-discovery gives. He had had remorse in an external part of his conscience, a surface that was not his profound soul. But in the true depths, there was no remorse. What did it matter, anyhow? Were there not men to whom more was permitted than to others? Well, he was one of them. In the balance, if there was a balance, what could the peccadilloes of youth weigh, compared with the work that he was about to accomplish, the services that he was going to render.

He paced back and forth and he was still drinking. Rachel put a favorable and complaisant smile on her face.

"It's a curious evolution that I've undergone, and even now I don't know whether I understand it very well. I've had returns to the faith, to God. I've sometimes thought of entering a convent. In the midst of my most ardent impulses, I sensed that I had one foot in evil and that something was pulling me by that foot. Do you remember the portrait that I slashed with a pen-knife on the morning when we arrived together from Bombay? It was that of my ancestor, Pedre de Castro. I intended to burn it. Well, I had it repaired and it's still enthroned in my house above the entrance door; he it is who welcomes visitors.

"I've told you about the influence that Pedre de Castro has had on me. If the devil existed, one could say that he was possessed by the devil. It was him who stole from the Pope the cross that I've inherited. He sold a young noblewoman who didn't want him to the King of Visapour. It's him who killed Jews whenever he could. In that epoch, no one put you on trial for killing a Jew. Listen to me Rachel: I don't like Jews. I can tell you that, since you're going to convert, since I've also heard you speak with clairvoyance about the people of your race, and that you share my opinion. I don't like Jews because they're cowards."

He was completely drunk. Rachel got up, took a cigarette from a box, which she lit, and sat down again.

"That's true," she said. "Go on."

"Antonia had the mission of finding me Jewesses in Bombay. I took pleasure in having them, in promising them money, in order to humiliate them, to sense that they were under my domination, to treat them as slaves. I redeemed thus the injury that a Jewess had once done me, the one whose death I caused. Yes, there was another than you who made me suffer. Why was it that woman that I desired rather than any other? That's something I shall never know. One is bound by certain facial features, certain movements of a body. It's that face that one would like to gaze at, that body that will give you pleasure, and not another. I'm talking at the moment about the woman who resembled you."

He looked at Rachel attentively, as if to make sure of that resemblance.

"I'm arriving at the story of the crime of sorts that I committed. One can call it a crime, if one believes in good and evil, and only in that case. I didn't believe in it then. Now, I don't know. And yet, it's the only action that has made me experience, at times—I say at times—a veritable remorse, that lacerating burn that no confession soothes. There are people who claim that one is obliged, in a mechanical fashion, to re-peat certain actions accomplished by one's father or one of one's ancestors. Perhaps that was it.

"Perhaps you've heard mention of the pogrom of Goa. There must have been talk of it in that epoch in Cochin. I was the one who instigated it—me. My master Deodat de Vega did not give me any advice, or any inspiration. I wanted to have a woman and I would have had her, moreover. It was only a question of time. What I say can't offend you. It doesn't con-cern you, who will be Christian tomorrow, but one always has a Jewess with money. Only I wanted her right away.

"Hazard served me. By chance, one evening, Deodat de Vega and I, while out walking, found a dead child at the foot of a tree. He was the son of the caretaker of the Church of the Magi. He had been bitten by a snake. You understand, we found him dead. We had nothing to do with that death. A few minutes earlier we had encountered the husband of the woman in question, a physician named Jehoudah. He must have passed the child without seeing him. Then I had a mental flash of light. We took the child, tied a stone around his neck and threw him into the arm of the river at a place where we knew that it was very deep. He was dead, wasn't he? Whether he slept in the water or under the ground...

"Then we went to find his father and we made hypocriti-cal searches to find him. People helped us. What had become of the child, they wondered? Well, what about that Jehoudah, the physician who possessed books, who must be occupied in

128

magic. Assuredly, it was by magic that he had been able to retain such a beautiful wife. He was going to commit the ritual crime, he had taken the child to his house. I simulated the greatest fury, I gathered a band of good Catholics in old Goa sand that led me, by the favor of a nocturnal pogrom, all the way to the bedroom of the woman of whom I was dreaming. I had her under my arm, naked, or nearly so. She was gentle, and weak. She trembled and begged for mercy.

"One only sees after the event how one ought to have taken advantage of it. I should have taken her in her room as soldiers do when they pillage cities, and everything would have been said. But that Jehoudah, that vile little physician, struck me in the face—I, Castro, had been slapped by Jehoudah. My ancestor would have killed him on the spot. I spared his life, and the idea, rather Machiavellian in truth, came to me of having his wife in front of him, in the boat that was taking me away, to the sound of a guitar...

"What happened then in the mind of the beautiful creature that I was taking away? I've always thought that emotion must have made her lose her mind. She threw herself in the water. She drowned herself. But she did that herself, by her own will. I was accused of being the direct cause of that death. If one goes back through the causes, one perceives that each of our actions has distant and absolutely unexpected reactions. Nothing could have given rise to the thought that that woman would prefer death to...let's call it dishonor, that's the expression that was employed during the trial. For there was an interminable trial. I defended myself stubbornly. Oh, not for fear of a condemnation, naturally, but for a natural liking of victory.

"Well, perhaps you won't believe me, but from that time on I began to hear furniture creaking in my bedroom, which hadn't creaked before, and to have around me on certain evenings the sentiment of a presence, a presence that was not hostile. No one has come to tell us what happens to the dead. One attaches oneself to individuals by the desire that one has for them. Perhaps you'll claim that there's a little madness in that or an extraordinary conceit on my part. I've often imagined that the dead woman was in my atmosphere, that it was me that she accompanied, that she followed, and out of love, and I've even thought that she had the same regret as me, the regret of not having been taken by Pedre de Castro.

"That idea hasn't quit me, and when I saw you appear to me in a mirror at Antonia's—it's said that the dead always appear in mirrors—I was afraid because I thought you were Dolça Jehoudah and the dead always create fear. But I'll tell you something else. That idea is so anchored in my mind that in spite of the material injury I caused him, I've never ceased to hate the physician Jehoudah. I hate him because he had a wife that I ought to have had, because he was more learned than me, because he possessed books that I didn't have the idea of destroying when I sacked his house, because perhaps, in an invisible domain, he disputes with me the presence I mentioned...the creaking furniture...something tender and soft that floats in the air...

"And then, all the same, he slapped me in the face, and the vengeance I took was, in sum, very benign. For, fundamentally, if he had had the choice, that Jehoudah, who had already shown that he was a coward, would certainly have preferred that vengeance to a duel, for instance, a duel that I considered, in any case, to be impossible..."

Castro was interrupted by a kind of exclamation, a bizarre gasp, that Rachel uttered. He stopped and perceived that she was laughing: a hysterical laughter that lasted a long time, and caused her to double up.

"It's the idea of a duel that's making you laugh," he said. "I understand."

Rachel had dropped her cigarette. She lit another. She took two or three steps under the veranda, breathing deeply, and saying: "How hot it is! The heat of these rainy days is heavier than the others." She came back toward Castro and said, slowly: "In what measure, in your opinion, is the terrible phrase in the Bible realized that says that sons will be punished for the sins of fathers?"

"I don't know," Castro stammered, disconcerted. "I've never thought about it. What relationship does that have with what I've just said?"

"Only a distant relationship. I was thinking of good and evil and Joachim."

Castro's brows furrowed.

"If sons receive punishments for their fathers, they ought also to receive recompenses. There can, in a certain measure, be an identification between a father and a son..."

Motionless, Castro waited for what she going to say. Rachel tapped the ash from her cigarette with her fingertip. She was trembling. She raised her head abruptly, and with a jovial expression on her face that creased her eyes, where there was no longer anything but a double green spark, she said: "Would you really be unhappy if I told you that I love your son Joachim?"

Castro's features became distraught. He leapt to his feet and came very close to Rachel.

"Why are you saying that to me? Can it be...? No, there's no possibility that you love that child. Explain yourself!"

He was abruptly breathless. Rachel saw his fat belly rising and falling, and she had difficulty detaching her eyes from Castro's while she saw so much despair and harshness there at the same time.

She laughed, with difficulty. She hastened to reassure Castro. She was joking. She wanted to submit him to a little proof. How susceptible and violent he was!

Castro's eyes moistened slightly. He drank again. He sat down again. He was gripped by the tenderness given by a mixture of alcohol and the sentiment of a great danger that one has just avoided.

"Rachel, I love no one but you in all the world. I've told you that you were the envoy of God. Perhaps you are. If God occupies himself with humans he must guide beings like me as well as the others. Rather than you being with my son Joachim, I'd prefer to know that you were at Antonia's, at the

131

disposal of English merchants morning and night. But it's me that you're going to marry. Why have we waited so long? It's necessary that it be an accomplished fact when the Council of the colony proclaim me President of the Republic. If they protest because you're a converted Jewess, I'll take charge of shutting their mouths."

He stood up. He had been gripped by a sudden idea. Everything could be concluded during the night. He knew a tavern on the quay where Jéronime Caval stayed drinking until dawn. He would pay him generously. He would baptize Rachel, and he would unite them before God.

He had taken Rachel's hand and he tried to lift her up in order for her to go with him. She sensed the odor of rum and rain that was coming from him. She was sickened, but continued smiling.

"No," cried Castro, "Jéronime Caval is a bandit. We'll go wake the Archbishop, have the cathedral opened. The Archbishop can surely marry by night the man who is going to make war on Portugal for him. Come."

He pulled her with all his might. She was obliged to get up.

"Why not, eh? The night isn't far advanced. We have time. By midnight, we'll be married. You'll come home with me. I'll call the servants so that they'll know that you're my wife, and Joachim too. He'll kiss your hand on his knees, before me."

Rachel tried to demonstrate to him that it was impossible. But while she struggled in order not to be dragged toward the door, rage invaded her. Perhaps, if she had had a weapon within arm's reach she would have struck Castro. For a second, she searched for one. But she thought that, in the same way that she had not wanted to kill a man pardoned by God, she would not kill a drunkard who was only semi-conscious.

"Rachel, you are Rachel and you are the other at the same time. You no longer make me afraid, as before. Why did you make me afraid? I want to respire your skin, to lie beside you."

He softened. His head fell on to Rachel's amber shoulder and he felt the feverish warmth of her blood against his temple.

"Be mine immediately," he said. "Come into your bedroom."

He begged her. Rachel understood that she had arrived at the end of the course, that she had now unleashed the male fury that can only be satisfied by possession.

"Well, tomorrow," she said.

"You swear to me?"

"Yes."

"You'll be mine tomorrow."

"Yes."

"It's Sunday. I'll come after vespers."

"So be it."

He left. She closed the door and went to fall, almost unconscious, into an armchair on the veranda.

She remained there for a time she could not evaluate. It seemed to her that someone was in the garden advancing toward the veranda. Her first thought was that it was Pedre de Castro and her nerves were so overexcited that she almost cried out in fright.

She went as far as the three stone steps leading down to the garden and she heard a hesitant voice call out her name.

It was Joachim.

He apologized immediately for his audacity. Unable to sleep, he had got up and he had come to roam around the waste ground behind the house. By the light of the lamp he had perceived the helm of hair and the silhouette of pale shoulders on the armchair. The dejection that he thought he perceived in the pose had made him anxious and had impelled him to climb over the wall.

He was about to apologize again when he sensed a long warm form against him, and the exhalation of a breath whose purity intoxicated him against his face.

133

"It's necessary for you to save me," said Rachel, supporting herself with her arms on his shoulders.

He sustained her, and sat her down. It seemed to him that he had just drunk, in a single draught, an extraordinary wine and that he had been transported into a sublime universe. Rachel was still holding him with her warm hands, shivering, unable to speak. She was at the moment when a woman who has sustained too great an effort is ready to give herself to a man who will profit from her weakness, because she hopes confusedly to recover her strength in the mystery of abandonment. But Joachim had insufficient experience to sense that.

"Oh yes, I want to save you," he said. "I came for that. Tell me what I must do."

And he exposed to her the projects that he had been turning over in his head since the commencement of the night. He doubted the sanctity of the Archbishop. He did not believe in the future of the revolution directed by his father. He expected troops sent from Portugal to arrive at any moment, to reestablish order and institute severe reprisals. Rachel was about to be drawn into the catastrophe for which his father's folly would be responsible. But there was time to flee, if she wished. The port of the new city was watched, but nothing was easier than to come to an arrangement with a Malabar boatman and go to embark on the desert coast between Cabo and Siridao. Many inhabitants of Goa had already done it. If she wished, he would take charge of everything.

But Rachel shook her head. Her weakness vanished and she recovered consciousness of the situation. She found herself in the necessity of acting and she was invaded by the horror of the action she planned. Oh, to depart, no longer to hear mention of anything, no longer to see the man she hated! But then, she would be a coward like her father, who, instead of avenging his wife, had plunged into the reading of his books, like those of his race who curbed their spine under the blows and awaited, instead of fighting for justice, the chimerical advent of the Messiah.

She spoke in a low voice, in a desperate one: "Haven't I told you, Joachim, that I'm here to avenge my mother, killed before my eyes. It's not a matter for me of going away but, on the contrary, of being here until tomorrow, when the man will come who has ruined my life and whom I reproach as much for the death of my mother as the death of my own soul, avowed, because of him, to hatred."

She stopped suddenly. What she had just seen filled her with such surprise that she detached herself from Joachim's timid arms and got up.

In the moonlight, which mingled with that of the lamp, the contour of the young man's head had just appeared to her to be strangely similar to that of his father's head. The sugar-loaf form of the cranium was more attenuated, and the neck did not have that characteristic compaction between the shoulders, but the thrown-black hair had a similar undulation. Rachel knew very well that the visage she could not make out in the dim light of the veranda had neither the thick lips that she found repulsive nor the little eyes sparkling with malice, but the shadow that was beside her was nevertheless a reduction of Pedre de Castro.

Like his father, the young man was possessed by the desire to clasp her in his arms, to render her a slave, to have her for himself. He too aspired to see her converted to the Christian religion, he too spoke about God. The only difference there was between them was that for one of them, God was represented by the Pope, while for the other, God had sent Monsenhor de Silva especially to Goa. They were two enemies of her race, and if she, by exception, had escaped for them the malediction that struck all Jews, it was only because she had a face that pleased them, a skin delicate to the touch, a body that they considered as the receptacle of their future pleasure and which they wanted to enjoy.

Was she going to be the dupe of the amorous words of a young man, as she had been duped by the music of a guitar?

How wretched it was to be a woman, to have nerves, to tremble, to lose sight of the goal!

She turned her head in order not to see the myopic gaze in which she knew there was sincerity, perhaps goodness. Rapidly, she said: "Haven't you told me that you'd be happy to defend me, and even to avenge me?"

"I'm entirely yours. You can dispose of me. I swear to avenge your mother as if she were my own."

"Well, the moment has come. Be here tomorrow before the end of vespers. Only remember that courage is not always as easy as one believes."

Joachim was about to protest. Rachel stopped him.

"Go now. No, not one word more. I don't want to explain anything to you for the moment. Until tomorrow."

She continued to turn her head. She drew away into the garden.

She murmured: "Oh well! Isn't it written in the sacred book of the Jews, which is also that of Christians, that the sons will be punished for the sins of the fathers?"

The Chain of Evil

Manoël Jehoudah tore up the letter that he had just read. It was from the rabbi of Goa, and had been written in Hebrew in order to have a more confidential character. Jehoudah leaned over his balcony, which was suspended above the port of Cochin, and threw the little pieces of paper into the water.

He looked around the low room whose walls were covered with old books, and for the first time he had the sentiment of his perfect solitude. Even when his wife had died, even when his daughter had left him, he had not been surrounded by such a great void. It seemed to him that the circular limits of the earth, with their life and their humanity, recoiled, leaving him irremediably alone in a desert.

He sat down and reflected. But what he had to do imposed itself rapidly on his mind. He stood up again. He had to leave right away. Nothing could retain him.

He wrote a letter to a young English physician recently installed in the new quarter of Cochin to give him a list of his sick patients and recommend them to him. He put a little underwear in a small valise. He cast a glance, in which there was no regret, over the things surrounding him. His library, which had been his blessed refuge, the living garden of his thoughts, the road of knowledge with a thousand characters, had the effect on him of a spiritual tomb in which he had slept a sterile slumber.

For one last time he touched the *Source of Life* of Solomon ibn Gabirol,[6] in which the philosophies of the ancient Kabbalistic books were summarized, the *Vale of Tears* of Ha

---

[6] The eleventh-century neo-Platonic dialogue known in Latin as *Fons Vitae* [Source of Life]—the Arabic original has been lost—seems to be the principal source of Jehoudah's morality.

Cohen,[7] which he had often made his daughter read in order that she would learn the long sequence of misfortunes and persecutions that had struck the Jewish communities of all lands, and he murmured:

"Perhaps my daughter would not have left me if I had talked to her about everyday things, little pleasures, petty duties, about everything that is life. But no, I wanted her to attain the truth, to achieve interior wisdom. And the one who believes he is ascending with descend again."

Manoël Jehoudah had no servant to inform. Since his daughter's departure he had served himself, for the love of simplicity and solitude. Having turned the key in his door he headed for the port. There he learned that the steamer from Madras that served the coastal ports had departed the previous day. There would not be another for a fortnight.

But to wait a fortnight was impossible. His mind was in Goa, near his daughter, in the midst of events whose redoubtable character he glimpsed and for which he judged himself partly responsible. He made an arrangement with the owner of a sailing ship that was about to transport a cargo of cinnamon to Mangalore, and obtained, by paying generously, that he would be dropped off in Goa. He might be there within a week.

Jehoudah knew that by fixing in thought a being who is familiar to you, and examining from all angles the known motive of one of their former actions, one can arrive at deducing the unknown motives and reconstituting the sequence of events that one wants to know. He applied himself to that for a week and his anxiety only increased.

It had been dark for a long time and the lighthouse of Saint George's Isle had not been sighted when the sea suddenly became stormy and heavy rain began to fall. The sailing ship had a great deal of difficulty reaching the harbor entrance.

---

[7] The Jewish historian Joseph ha-Kohen (1496-1575), whose *Emeq ha-Bahka* [The Vale of Tears] is the book from which Rachel continually recalls quotations.

There it was necessary to be recognized, to spend several hours in formalities. Marcora demanded customs duties so crushing that there was no longer any commerce. He had also organized taxes of individuals. No one had the right to disembark without depositing a surety in his hands.

It was very late when Jehoudah was able to reserve a room in a hotel in the port. He noticed with surprise that in spite of the advanced hour, the cafés installed in the European style were brilliantly lit and that songs and dance music were emerging from them. He saw the silhouettes of gamblers in improvised gaming dens; women were prowling along the houses, and the Chinamen lying at the extremity of the quay formed a somber mass. No one noticed him when he walked with a long stride up the street ending at the road to old Goa.

He marched without paying any heed to the rain. Memories flooded from all directions: Dolça Jehoudah holding the hand of the infant Rachel and smiling at him tenderly. There they had sat down on a stone bench to gaze at the countryside. At that place where the river and the road are side by side he had perceived Abdullah from the boat where he was tied up, running at lifting up his daughter in his arms. It must be somewhere in that darker part of the waters that Dolça, his beloved wife, had thrown herself in order to die. She had died in the most redoubtable conditions of the soul, prey to despair and terror. Jehoudah thought that the emotions of the last hour of life are the portion of the dead in the beyond.

O my God, you are the witness that I have struggled with all my might against the thoughts of vengeance and that I have not wished a similar death upon the man who caused the death of my beloved. O my God, be not redoubtable to the wicked!

Manoël Jehoudah thought he could hear the canticles of the Month of Mary decreasing lugubriously; he breathed the phantom perfume of nagahs, of which a crown had once been driven down over his eyes. A gray daylight was beginning to filter through the clouds when he arrived at the landing-stage of Saint Joseph's Church. One of the three heads was a little more damaged than before. He stopped in their triple shadow.

Suddenly, he felt cold, and the terror of action paralyzed him. Before, also, in the same place, he had found himself prey to an unspeakable horror. Manoël Jehoudah only had audacity in the intellectual domain. He knew once again the power of fear, and it required an immense effort for him to triumph ever it.

He got his bearings. He passed under the triumphal arch of Albuquerque and he headed toward the sloping street at the bottom of Saint Anne's hill, which the rabbi had mentioned in his letter.

Day dawned in the rain. Shutters clacked. On the ground floor of an old stone dwelling the panes of two large windows were illuminated by a lamp. Manoël Jehoudah saw, confusedly, a slender silhouette, and a heavy helm of blue-tinted hair. He recognized the creature issued from him, whose beauty had always filled him with an almost sacred wonderment.

Was she alone? He was almost sure of it. He refused to believe otherwise. He could not be mistaken in his hypotheses. His heart was beating very forcefully; his teeth were chattering. He was afraid, a fear that would have made him flee if his will had not retained him.

He placed his hand on the door-knocker and let it fall. The knocker rendered a feeble sound; there was a silence, and footsteps in the house.

Rachel had never thought that her father was so small. She considered him with astonishment. It was impossible that he had shrunk in a few months. It was not chagrin that had arched his back. He stood up straight and spoke gently, without anger. As she listened to him, Rachel could not help being tormented by that ridiculous preoccupation with stature. She had sensed as soon as he began speaking that he had only come to thwart her projects and, with her eyes fixed on the ceiling, she now remained enclosed in the taciturn silence of those who are resolved not to allow themselves to be convinced.

"You're astonished that I've divined your thinking," he said, "And that I've even followed its phases step by step. It wasn't so difficult. There was only one other hypothesis that could explain your presence in this house. That appeared to me, however, less frightful."

"I don't understand," Rachel said. "You would have preferred..."

"Yes," he said, without hesitation, "I would have preferred to know that you were degraded to the point of abandoning your body for money, even to that man. Those who do not want to go any further than appearances, like Rabbi Haim, think that you have arrived at that degeneracy. The opinion of others is of scant importance to me. You're here for the love of vengeance and I can't imagine anything worse."

Rachel raised her head abruptly. She had promised herself to listen without responding. She spoke vehemently.

"Nothing worse, truly? Haven't you told me that you arrived at weeping in looking at my mother's face, because of what you saw there of pure sweetness and ideal tenderness?"

"Yes."

"Well. I've never been able to explain to myself how you were able, on the sand of Aguada, to look at the face of the woman who had done no harm to anyone, whom the crabs had devoured, without making an oath to punish those who were the cause of her death. Perhaps you can tell me how you were able to return to your house, to look at me, to witness a trial, to live, without experiencing the need to kill, justly, a deeply evil creature devoid of a heart, who laughed at your grief continued to calumniate you? If you can explain that to me, if I succeed in seeing in your conduct any other explanation that the one that my childish soul found then, you'll relieve me of a great weight."

"Because you thought your father was a coward, didn't you? That's quite possible, in any case. Perhaps he is; he surely is in the material domain. But I believe that men are mistaken in attributing more grandeur to courage than to cowardice.

They're mistaken above all in making use of their courage in the exercise of a justice that does not belong to them."

"To whom does it belong, then? To God. If that is so, if he exists, if he sees us, what is he waiting for? Why does he not exact that justice? Why has he put the inexhaustible thirst within us, if it is never to be satisfied? Anyway, what good is there in talking about God. I know, and have known for a long time, that you believed in him once but you don't believe in him any longer."

"God! God!" said Manoël Jehoudah, with a gesture that seemed to situate him at an infinite distance. "There's no need to make God intervene to understand that the world must disengage from hatred and travel toward love."

Perhaps he saw once again the cross on the boat, the beloved body lying on the sand, for he said slowly, as if he were seeing again his soul then:

"Yes, my first thought was to avenge myself. But it was at that moment, with the first flood of grief, doubtless because of it, because it appeared to me to be too great to be merited, that I understood what balances weigh good and evil and the measure of the law. Justice is commonly given the epithet immanent, because it accompanies every action, because it is the action itself. That is what I arrived at believing after your mother's death, as a tangible reality. If one does evil to another, it is to oneself that one does it. The man for whom you have come here and around whom you have woven a patient web had prepared his own punishment before you. He will be crucified in his turn. He will have a crown of nagahs hanging down to his eyes and his body will be exposed on a beach with the face devoured. There is no repentance, penitence or pray that can allow him to escape it. The law is ineluctable, the effect is engendered by the cause and once can no more stop it than one can make a river flow back to its source."

"And when?" cried Rachel. "When will this punishment happen? I've already read that in your books. There was question of future lives where one is born, it appears, with the recompenses and punishments of past lives to receive. But one does not remember anything. So what's the point? Me, I want to be there, I want to watch. I want to hear the man who has ruined my life and yours scream, I want to see a fear in his eyes of which I will be the cause, and from which her will suffer justly."

"But if you strike with a knife you will be struck with a knife. If you poison, you will be poisoned. The hand of the person who accomplishes the act inscribes to his account a similar act in his future destiny. And that is perhaps trivial in itself. But the knife, the poison or merely the evil thought will be transmitted in its turn. In the name of justice or vengeance, it does not matter—the evil will be perpetuated, as it has been perpetuated since the beginning of the world.

"I sometimes imagine human creatures as a great flock traveling from life to life, generation to generation, each of whose creatures bears a chain around the neck, the eternal chain, the chain of evil. Each can break it, liberate the captive human by the effort of intelligence. But instead of that, each one strives to render the chain of hatred more solid, to forge it in metal, to render it more durable in essence, in order that it holds the spirit bound to the flesh more forcefully.

"And then we are condemned eternally to be the slaves of evil, to bear and transmit than chain that crushes and holds down, unless there is a man of good will, a youthful hero possessed of true spiritual courage who dares to say: *I take pity on those who have done me harm, I um breaking the chain, perhaps I am a coward, but I forgive.*"

"Well, I'm not that youthful hero, and I don't aspire to be," said Rachel. "I've obeyed the counsel of masters less magnanimous than you. Except that I'm surprised to see my father professing now the morality that Christians preach and don't practice."

"Forgiveness is not the privilege of Christians. It's the secret of deliverance and all religions know it. But it's difficult to attain. No one can know that better than me."

Manoël Jehoudah lowered his head, and then walked slowly around the room. He sensed in his daughter the blind

143

force of a millennia-old instinct. He considered her momentarily. She had never resembled her mother as much. The mildness of her features was sometimes replaced by an expression of gravity and resolution. The sight of his daughter's beauty had always brought Manoël Jehoudah a tender emotion.

He perceived a cigar-butt forgotten in an ash-tray, and through the pandanus branches that fell back over the veranda he distinguished the silhouette of a cross in the depths of the garden. He imagined what his daughter must have suffered in imposing the lie upon herself and submitting to hatred. He felt pity for her. He extended his arms to her. They hugged one another, but without weeping.

Closer to one another, their hearts leapt as they had not done for a long time. Rachel recounted of her existence what she thought a father could hear, because she did not know that a father can hear anything. She could not hide from him her joy at being partly responsible, because of her influence on Castro, for the disorder and madness that had taken possession of the old city of Goa.

"Look where they are, the Christians," she said.

Manoël Jehoudah listened to his daughter in silence. "There are no good and evil men, as you seem to believe," he said. "That would be too simple. There are unfortunate men, tormented by their passions, who advance in darkness, God knows with what slowness, toward an unknown goal. They struggle with one another, they do one another harm, but there are some who are a little further advanced in the journey, to whom a small part of enlightenment has devolved. Those sometimes hold out a hand to their brothers, and help them, saying to then: *the road is this way*. That is all that we can hope for.

"But do you know what it is, Rachel, to lose one's soul? Have you read in the books the description, albeit almost always puerile, of damned creatures? That description hides beneath a romantic form an aspect of the truth. Oh, how the words Hell and the abysm, when one has ceased to believe in the Hell of religions and the abysm of space, can sometimes take on a redoubtable meaning! There are souls that are doomed, and it's not because of the crimes we believe."

"It isn't by doing evil consciously, even lovingly?"

"No. Evil is the small change of life. We want the happiness of others in order to enjoy ourselves. We kill animals to eat them. We kill our fellows in wars. But there is a crime far greater. Remember the old Biblical word. *The only unforgivable sin is the sin against the spirit.* That is what dooms the soul. That is what you are about to commit."

"Me!"

"To stop the impetus of the creature, no matter what stage it is at, to reawaken passions when they are dying down, to blow out the shadow of the ideal that might have appeared to it, to draw it down, toward matter, far from the spirit: that is the sin of which it speaks, from which I want to save you, my daughter."

He had lowered his voice. It was in a voice equally low that Rachel said: "Do you know where the souls of the dead go, Father"

"I believe so. Near to us and far away. In an intermediate region devoid of form and color. I'm not sure of knowing."

"And you don't fear that there are souls doomed, not by their crimes, but by their goodness, souls that are wandering and desperate because they have been precipitated into death abruptly, unjustly, who are calling out to dear beings, a child, a husband, souls who are gazing in amazement at the darkness and asking themselves: *What have they done for me? They have done nothing. They did not love me enough to avenge me.*"

"Shut up. I've often said that to myself. But no. She is resting in peace, Dolça Jehoudah, until the day when she will wake up in a birth devoid of memory."

"You're not certain of that. You're not certain that it wasn't her who guided me one evening, who whispered in my ear: *That is the man. Render to the Christian the offense he committed against the Jewess. Deprive him of happiness as he deprived me of life.*"

"We're certain of nothing. In ignorance, abstain from action."

Rachel shook her head. The father and the daughter gazed at the garden. The rain had stopped but the wind was blowing in gusts with an extraordinary violence. They both fell silent now. They were experiencing the lassitude of a sleepless night. They only exchanged a few more indifferent words.

"You'd better wait here until the storm ends," said Rachel.

"It's less than two miles to Abdullah's house near Ribandar. He lost his parents last year. He'll be glad to see me. I'll go that far."

On the threshold, Manoël Jehoudah said: "When do you want me to come back?"

She hesitated. "Oh, well, tomorrow."

She followed him with her eyes. He had difficulty struggling against the wind. His silhouette was outlined at the end of the street, and suddenly seemed to Rachel to be immense.

The Death of the Archbishop

The tempest seemed to rise over the sea at the same time as the sun. It was unleashed with such violence on that Mary Sunday[8] that no one in Goa believed that a ship would dare to approach the coast. The captain of the *Resolution* was a pious man. The idea that he was transporting a vicar apostolic, an extraordinary envoy of the Pope, made him think that his ship was inaccessible to the fury of the elements and that even the rocks would part before him. Fortunately, in addition to that conviction, he had a perfect knowledge of the coast of Goa. He succeeded in dropping anchor in the little bay of Cabo, almost within sight of Fort Mary Magdalen.

The certainty that everyone in the fort had that a disembarkation was impossible during the tempest had suppressed all surveillance. In less than two hours the *Resolution* succeeded in disembarking the contingent of troops sent from Portugal in launches, through the mist and the rain. The poorly-informed government, ignorant of the extent of the revolution, had only sent five hundred soldiers. They were young recruits, almost children. Their delight in escaping the lower decks of the *Resolution* and seasickness was so great that it was difficult to prevent them from starting to sing. The new governor, Senhor de Ribeira and the papal envoy, who was accompanied by two Dominicans, disembarked with the soldiers.

Fort Mary Magdalen put up no resistance. It was taken, amid lightning-flashes, without a single rifle-shot being fired. Commandant Carrillo, who was a shrewd officer and well

---

[8] I have translated *Dimanche de Marie* literally, although the festival in question is not celebrated in Occidental churches. It is the Sunday of the last week of Lent and celebrates Mary the Egyptian, the penitent prostitute—a celebration intended to demonstrate that it is never too late to repent.

aware of the derisory number of the forces he commanded, thought that it would be wise to take advantage of the initial enthusiasm of his men to take possession of the port and the new city before the resistance could be organized.

The inhabitants of Goa who looked out of the windows on hearing the regular rhythm of footfalls thought at first that it was some troop maneuver that the weather did not justify. They did not recognize the young faces to which the sentiment of an unexpected success added a heroic pride. Cries of alarm were uttered, but it was already too late. The governmental palace, the telegraph office, the officers of the *Abelha* and the house of the Navy, where Marcora and his daughters were asleep, were occupied in no time. Only a few shots were fired, at the inoffensive Chinese, whose group was mistaken for armed revolutionaries.

In the distance, on the other side of the river, Fort Aguada remained silent. It might bombard the city, cut off the road to old Goa or sweep the marching troops with fire. An officer crossed the river with a clarion and four men. He headed for the fort in order to summon it to surrender. He almost reached the door, which was closed. But he waved a white flag, in order to negotiate, in vain. The fort remained mute and enigmatic. The officer came back.

"Castro must be in the fort," said the inhabitants. "He'll fire when the moment comes. The game isn't lost."

It was after midday. The rain ceased falling. The wind eased. A ray of sunlight even pierced the clouds.

Commandant Carrillo decided to set forth at hazard to march along the road to old Goa. In order to have an impact on minds, the vicar apostolic intended to arrive in the cathedral and pronounce the solemn excommunication of the archbishop at vespers, when all the faithful would be assembled. Fifty men had been left at Fort Mary Magdalen and guards dispersed throughout the city and the port. Only three hundred soldiers remained disposable.

"Castro knows what he's doing," people murmured. "He's just waiting for the propitious moment to fire."

The soldiers gazed in surprise at the silhouettes of palm trees and monasteries, and the distant extent of the pools. Puddles of rain water splashed underfoot, and their delight augmented as they marched. They were penetrated by a sentiment of fortunate and facile conquest, of service rendered to the fatherland. They were the heirs of the conquistadors of Albuquerque, the ancient masters of India.

Immediately after the advance guard marched the papal envoy. He had an ascetic visage with a large nose; he was particularly thin and paltry, but he raised himself up to his full height and religious fervor was blazing in his eyes. He was clad in a simple Dominican robe and was holding a wooden cross devoid of ornamentation in his hand. For want of great religious pomp, he thought it best to act with an excess of simplicity.

The news of the disembarkation of the troops had barely reached old Goa and sown terror therein when the soldiers began to pass through the triumphal arch. They did not seem very frightening. They gazed at the old houses with puerile expressions and advanced in good order toward the cathedral.

Panic swept over the city. A cortege of children clad in white, guided by nuns, took flight like a swarm of moths. Everyone remembered stories of rape and pillage committed by troops who captured cities. Some barricaded themselves in. Conception Colaço leaned pensively over her balcony, in order to vanquish the danger by seduction.

The aged Senhora Mascarenhas ran to put on her low-cut crimson dress with the long train, believing that she would then possess an incomparable majesty. She reassured her family by saying: "They wouldn't dare. Leave it to me." And she appeared on her threshold, where she stood immobile, like a fairy in an operetta, before the stupefied soldiers. Meanwhile, her husband put on a top hat and a black coat, saying that he wanted to die in ceremonial costume. His sons did likewise.

But those to whom the morning's events were recounted said: "Castro must have emerged from Fort Aguada and recaptured the new city. He will advance as victor toward old Goa, and there will be fighting here in the streets." They prepared weapons and listened for the cannons to announce Castro's victory in the distance.

The rumor also ran around that Jéronime Caval had arrived at the head of a troop of boatmen from the port and that Father Vincent was arming the slaves of Boma. But Jéronime Caval was sleeping off the night's drunkenness and Father Vincent was praying.

The soldiers were deployed in the large square in front of the cathedral. The papal envoy climbed the steps solemnly. He gave a few curt orders. An officer sought information as to the location of the bell-ringer. The two Dominicans headed for the altar and took the lighted candles therefrom.

Then the crowd that was filling the church for vespers moved aside, huddling against the pillars and the altars, gripped by horror. Everyone had understood. The monk with the big nose was about to launch the mysterious malediction; he was about to caused occult forces coming from the occident to emerge from his bony hand; he was about to excommunicate the Archbishop and those who had separated themselves from the Church with him.

A fear greater than that of pillage and rape took possession of souls. There were cries of despair and hectic flights. The cortege of white-clad children, which had formed up again, fluttered hither and yon. Doors were heard slamming shut. Conception Colaço, who was swooning with emotion at seeing so many young men in uniform gathered together, uttered a great sigh and fainted, letting her hair fall like a sheaf along the wall. Somewhere, Juana de Faria, struck by a crisis of hysteria, began to utter a savage and regular plaint, an incessant animal howl.

The Archbishop's door opened and a priest with an illuminated face announced that the Archbishop was about to emerge and go to the cathedral. And at the same moment, the bells, as is prescribed by the ceremony of excommunication, began to toll the knell for the dead.

Emotions came and went with an extraordinary rapidity. The news of the imminent apparition of the Archbishop flew from window to window, and circulated from street to street. The great spiritual battle was about to be delivered. Miraculous possibilities were glimpsed. The power of a Saint animated by the spirit of God, was infinite. What could that Antichrist of small stature, surrounded by the soldiers standing on the threshold of the cathedral, do against it? Assuredly he was about to be changed into a statue or suddenly start running on all fours, displaying the frightened muzzle of a beast. Like an annunciation of the miracle, the sun was completely disengaged from the clouds and illuminated the square.

The bells fell silent. The silence became extraordinary. The papal envoy stood between the candles of his assessors and raised his cross. With soldiers bordering the square around her and facing her, Senhora Mascarenhas, protecting her family with his outspread arms, was standing on her threshold like an enormous colored caricature. In the shadow of the corridor behind her, the silhouettes of bulging silk hats and obsolete coats were immobile.

From the lungs of the sickly Dominican emerged an unexpectedly formidable voice, which filled the square, caused the stones to vibrate and terrified hearts. That voice recited the sentence by which the heretical Archbishop was expelled from the Church.

"He can no longer receive nor administer the sacraments, nor participate in the divine offices, nor fulfill any ecclesiastical function..."

The voice swelled further with every syllable. The extraordinary envoy had been preparing for the proclamation of that sentence during the long crossing. The ancient joy of chastisement radiated from his entire person.

"If he refuses the penitence of seven years that is imposed on him, let him be anathematized..."

The faces of the audience went pale. In a fearful dream they glimpsed the cardinals processing like crimson waves

151

under a gigantic golden dome, around and old man motionless beneath a radiant tiara.

"The ordinations he has made are annulled. We retrench him from the holy communion...."

As a symbol of the spiritual death of the excommunicate, the assessors blew out their candles. The papal envoy looked with a terrible satisfaction at the city of ruins over which he had just spread the papal malediction.

An extreme dejection weighed upon everyone. The houses seemed more dilapidated, the towers more unstable. The pillars of cloisters were inclined, on the brink of collapse. An exhalation of death emerged from the decrepitude of chapels. Conception Colaço awoke from her faint, and when she stood up, twisting her hair beneath the stone frame of her window, the flesh of her armpits had tints spoiled by putrefaction.

Gazes were turned toward the Archbishop's palace, the portal of which remained open. If the Archbishop had appeared at that moment, if he had raised his transparent hand to bless his people rejected and accursed by the Church to say to them: *I am here, I have not abandoned you, I am sufficient to lead you to God*, the entire city of Goa would have flooded the square, the soldiers and the papal envoy would have been swept away like miserable dust blown from the Occident.

But the Archbishop did not appear.

The priest who had announced his emergence said that he had donned his episcopal garments but that he had desired beforehand to receive a few directives from God. He had asked to be alone and he was sitting in his armchair in the room where he usually received his revelations

When it was decided to open the door of that room, Monsenhor de Silva was found rigid, fixed, sculpted, beneath the miter and the dalmatic, under the flash of the pectoral cross, like a figure of stone, like a phantom archbishop. He was dead.

His pride, his resolution to struggle, was legible in his attitude. He had, however, obeyed God, who had summoned him. His gaze and his smile attested an ecstasy so radiant that those who saw him immediately fell to their knees.

The death was announced in whispers, like a pious fuse. Everyone knelt down on the spot. The papal envoy, who was advancing to signify the sentence to the Archbishop, reached by the communication of the prayer, stopped to pray himself, and his large nose remained inclined toward the worn paving-stones for a long time, as if he understood the defeat that his victory hid.

A slow recitation, a sobbing lament, went up in the streets and inside the houses. Ecclesiastical silhouettes appeared with candles on the thresholds of churches. Thick mulatto faces were transfigured by dolor. Hindus ignorant of the Christian religion shed tears. Caricaturish figures became sublime. The prayer for the dead, sung by all, swelled desperately, like the canticle of a man who has just lost his part of the ideal.

The last clouds had dissipated in the sky and a more placid dusk fell over the kneeling city.

The Sons will be Punished for the Sins of the Fathers

When the officers of Fort Aguada learned, on the Sunday morning, that Portuguese troops had occupied the new city, they fell into a great perplexity. Castro came to Fort Aguada every morning and went to the new city thereafter. Doubtless the violence of the tempest had retained him. Then too, it was admitted that on feast days the discipline was less rigorous. The evening before, many soldiers had slept in the new city under the pretext of celebrating Mary Sunday.

It was Castro who had to give the orders; it was up to him to assume responsibilities. The officers were all irremediably compromised in the Goanese revolution, but they could not think without anxiety about the reprisals of the metropolis, and secretly envied the fate of their comrades who had passed into English territory in order to remain faithful to their homeland.

In addition, they had links with the leaders of the revolution. Lieutenant Altaïde was the lover of Juana de Faria, the sister of a member of the Colony Council, and Lieutenant Oviedo was the lover of a young niece of the Mascarenhas, of fiery temperament. He received her by night in the fort, via a small door situated in the ditches of the keep. Inès de Mascarenhas had come the previous evening, had been retained by the storm and had forgotten herself in her lover's arms.

The officers gathered and invited the sergeants to deliberate with them. A violent dispute began. Those who had invested their hopes in the future of Goa wanted to attack the troops, scarcely disembarked, under the command of Lieutenant Oviedo, who was the oldest, or to bombard them when they advanced toward old Goa, which would inevitably happen.

Lieutenant Oviedo did not lack courage, but at the very moment that someone knocked on his door to announce the redoubtable news of the disembarkation, he was falling asleep beside the ardent Inès. Exhaustion was legible in his features. He asked for two hours' respite, of which he counted on taking advantage by sleeping.

Castro's arrival would have removed the responsibility of action from everyone. Someone watching from the top of the keep with a telescope finally recognized his silhouette. He had the habit of coming on horseback and crossing the river on the ferry shortly before the place known as Reis Magos. It really was him. Extraordinarily, he was advancing on foot, and running. He was recognized by his uniform and his huge belly.

At that moment, a boat traversing the river in spite of the waves deposited the negotiator with the white flag and four soldiers on the beach of Aguada.

Until the moment that Castro arrived the best thing was to stay silent and wait. That was what they did. The negotiator's voice remained without response and he was seen to cross the river again.

But Lieutenant Altaïde, who had picked up the telescope again, uttered an exclamation of surprise. He could no longer see Castro on the road. He searched for him in vain. Perhaps he was hidden in a dip in the ground. They waited, futilely. That enigma threw the garrison of Aguada into consternation. Lieutenant Oviedo fell asleep seeking to resolve it.

The hours passed, but the fever of combat had faded away. Anxiety had invaded souls. Since they had seen the four young faces of the men who had arrived from the distant fatherland, the soldiers had softened. Some were talking about spiking the guns. They began to fear the arrival of Castro that they had desired.

Even the sergeants were of the opinion that if he came back, the door should be left closed, as had been done with the negotiator.

With the aid of the telescope, the place where Castro's image had appeared and had dissipated so mysteriously was scrutinized again, but in vain.

Rachel had lain down on her bed after her father's departure. She could hear the vague noise of her servants' footfalls.
They resided on the first floor, and they were going to mass.
She was drowsy, and that noise became in her agitated brain
the murmur of a cortege in flight. It was a Jewish quarter in a
dream city fleeing Christian persecution. Rachel glimpsed
resigned faces, children on donkeys, the sacred books of the
synagogue carried by old men. They all appeared to be submitting to the misfortune of exile with a perfect tranquility.
She was about to cry out: *It's necessary to resist, to seek revenge*, but the servants closed the entrance door with a click as
they left, a silence followed., and her slumber became more
profound.

Rachel woke up with a slight warmth on her lips. It was a
heat that spread throughout her body and inflamed it lightly.
The sensation was so sweet that she kept her eyes closed for a
few seconds in order to prolong it. Then she sat up with a cry
of fright.

Joachim was beside her. He was holding her in his arms.
He explained, volubly, that he had come in via the garden, as
he had done the previous evening, that he had not found anyone, and that he had perceived her, lying on her bed, through
the door to the drawing room, which she had left ajar.

Rachel looked at him without hearing him. She was still
enveloped by the light tissue of sleep and the delightful heat
was running through her body. Her eyes widened, her lips
became moist, and a frisson ran through her. Her arms knotted
around the young man's neck and she let herself fall against
him with the unique desire to recover the transitory intoxication of her awakening.

She found it multiplied, and in a matter of seconds, the
forms, the powers and the mysterious speech of instinct surged
from the depths of her being. She remained pressed to Joachim's breast, palpitating, surprised and glad.

He did not lose sight of his objective. He explained to
her, with a sudden authority in his voice, that he wanted to
save her at any price. The project that he had explained the

previous evening could be realized immediately. According to approximate calculations, the ship sent by Portugal could not be far away. He had made an arrangement with boatmen on the river. He would take her with him immediately. They would wait for the tempest to end on the deserted coast of Siridao or that of Aguada. In the meantime, the boatmen would set out in quest of a boat of sufficient tonnage to reach the nearest English port. They would embark as soon as the wind had calmed down somewhat.

Rachel shook her head to say no, although Joachim's words filled her with joy. There was no resonant guitar to intoxicate her as before. An internal music was speaking within her, as imperious as the appeal of the senses, as lacerating as the pleasure glimpsed. And her father's words returned to her memory. She saw him again, with his face so benevolent and so sad. What did he want, except her departure? A door suddenly opened which permitted her to escape the drama prepared for the evening.

Her head felt empty, and she was moist with languor. She would have liked to go to sleep on the young man's breast, without thinking about anything.

She was still saying no with her head, but she got up, mechanically, and picked up her mantle. Then he took her by the shoulders, and without adding anything, he drew her away.

It was raining. The streets were deserted. They did not encounter anyone, all the way to the river.

"My father has gone to the forts, as usual; he won't be back before two o'clock," said Joachim, in order to extend an atmosphere of security over the departure.

The boat had a kind of wicker lattice cabin at the rear, over which a tarpaulin had been thrown to protect it from the rain. They installed themselves within it.

In a corner of her mind, Rachel saw a Jewish community fleeing, backs curbed, faces resigned, confident in the justice of God.

Well, I'm like the daughters of my race, she thought, *like the oppressed whose history I read in the old book. I'm resigned, I'm fleeing.*

But when the oars began to strike the water and the boat slid rapidly along the worn stones of the quays, she was suddenly seized by the charm that came from the perfume of the trees and Joachim's presence. When he explained to her that the tide was going out and that they would reach the sea all the more rapidly, she could not help replying, with a smile, that it was a pity, and that she was greatly enjoying the pleasure of being there.

She looked at him with eyes whose green had become brighter, suddenly cleansed, and they savored together the infinite voluptuousness of desiring one another in the movement and the danger. They perceived that they had brought nothing that was necessary, like linen and toilette equipment, and they laughed about it at length. The nearest port was Ratnagiri. They would find all that they needed there. Was there a hotel? Undoubtedly. If not, they would have the resource of spending the night in the travelers' bungalow, or even under the stars. Great storms were always followed by magnificent evenings.

The broad-leaved mango-trees and the rustling palms seemed to run along the bank. On the other side of the river, on Divar Island, pools were glittering, and in the distance they saw a flock of aquatic birds striping the air.

"That's a sign that the sun will soon pierce the clouds," said Joachim.

A canoe transporting a man of whom they could only see the beard amid the folds of a green kaftan crossed their path. One of the oarsmen stood up and shouted something they did not understand while waving his arms. At the same time the man in the kaftan pointed in the direction from which he had come; but they did not turn their heads. Neither the words they heard nor those they pronounced had any importance for them. They were only preoccupied with sensing themselves beside one another, and the horizon of waters and damp plains appeared less vast than the one they were discovering within themselves.

Joachim had taken Rachel's nape in his hand, and he gently brought her face closer to his own as if to see the emerald gleam in her eyes at closer range. She did not resist. They united their lips for a long time, and then they disunited them in order to gaze at one another again, and recommence.

They were laughing together when one of the boatmen turned round to say that the wisest thing to do was to stop at Reis Magos. There were a few fishermen's houses there, where they could wait for the arrival of the boat that he would make every effort to find. In any case, it was no longer raining and the wind was calming down.

At Reis Magos or elsewhere, what did it matter? Rachel and Joachim felt increasingly tranquil as they went forward. They did not pay any attention to a rumor coming from the new city, nor to the men running back and forth along the road that led there.

Pedre de Castro was in a hurry. He was in a bad mood. His duties obliged him to make futile journeys. He did not like following that road along the river Mandavi. When he had the time he reached the new city by making a long detour by way of Banguinim, but this morning he had stopped at Mascarenhas' house and had had a long argument with him about the means of expelling the Chinamen from the quays. Many of them had died of malaria. All day long one heard the sound of coffins being nailed shut. They were becoming a public danger.

The best thing would have been to poison that vermin, he thought. If they had settled on that means he would not have wasted precious time that morning. Certainly, he had time to reach Rachel's house before the end of vespers, but he feared that he might be retained either in one of the forts or in the port.

His thoughts took a more cheerful turn, when he recalled that he had received a white flannel outfit the day before from

Bombay, which he believed to be the latest Paris fashion. He smiled.

One can't imagine how susceptible women are to elegance. As long as I have time to put the costume on!

Not far from Ribandar, he was struck by the appearance of a little man who was in the process of going upriver in a canoe.

What bizarre resemblance there are, he thought. And he urged his horse to a trot.

The approach to one place on the river was particularly disagreeable to him.. Almost involuntarily, he cast a glance at the waters and he saw a boat descending in parallel with him. It was not very far away. Two united forms were sitting under the leather roof of the cabin. He wondered who the people could be who were quitting old Goa on that rainy morning.

Leaning over his horse, he looked and he saw. He saw a forward inclination of a head and a hand holding the nape of a neck.

The fingers of the hand were buried into the hair, plunged therein. But what stopped the beating of his heart was the forward movement of the woman's head, the avidity revealed by the thrust of the neck. Yes, it was her who was leaning forward to press the lips, to drink the kiss more ardently.

He recognized the hair with the blue tints in which the hand was buried with a tranquility of possession, and the little he could see of the face of the man crushed by the embrace was sufficient for him to identify his son.

His son! Rachel! At first, he felt neither pain nor hated. He gazed at the astonishing scene with a singular power of observation. He diverted his gaze to the backs of the oarsmen and he remarked the musculature and the sweat. Rachel was bare-headed, his son too. Where were their hats? That thought preoccupied him, and he stood up in his stirrups to see whether he could perceive them in the bottom of the boat.

But suddenly, laughter rang out, fresh and musical, such as he had never heard before. He believed for a second that it was not Rachel who had laughed. Where did such laughter come from? But the truth appeared to him. Rachel laughed like that with his son, while with him she was always grave and sad.

Then a lock of the desired hair came loose and Rachel twisted it, raising her arms like the handles of a vase. Joachim rested his forehead lightly on the white flesh above the wrist. That gesture unleashed Castro's fury more than the kiss. Joachim had made it with a young, charming impulsiveness of which he was incapable. He pictured his son with his narrow shoulders, his gauche manner, and his myopic eyes. How had he been able to please? He was a hypocrite, a worthy pupil of the Jesuits. He knew full well the amour that his father had for Rachel, and he had put everything to work to make her love him.

He shrugged his shoulders at the thought of that amour. A whore like Rachel! He had a desire to call out to them, to shout to Joachim that the Jewess had an interest in playing that comedy with him, that she was one of Antonia's boarders, anyone's creature. But what if they went to land on the other bank, to escape him? No, it was better to follow the boat, to know what they intended to do.

A light wind caused damp nagah flowers to fall.

As before! Castro said to himself. Oh, the naked Jewess on the boat going up the river after the pogrom, whom he had not possessed! That would have avenged him in advance for this Jewess!

He started to laugh bitterly.

The boat was going in the other direction and he was following along the bank, but he was on the cross all the same. Jealousy was crucifying him. Of the crime that he had once imagined, and which he had not contrived to commit, he was now the victim.

Then he had a bizarre impression. That Manoël Jehoudah, whom he had subjected to ignominious treatment and then soiled with his calumnies: he had never heard mention of him. Doubtless he had died somewhere. But half an hour before, at the place where the road to Ribandar ended at the river, he had seen, or thought he had seen, a little man resembling that Jehoudah going upriver in a canoe. Was it not his double, materialized, who had come to witness his misery and to rejoice therein, in the measure that the dead can have joy?

He shivered in terror. Then he wondered whether he was losing his mind. Did a dead man have any need of a canoe? He did not look back, however, in the confused fear of seeing a Jewish physician in the distance, aboard a phantom boat.

At the place where the river widened and the road ceased to run alongside the water in order to zigzag toward the city, Castro saw Rachel's oarsmen head for the other bank. In order to follow them, he had only to cross over on the ferry, which was in any case his usual trajectory to go to Fort Aguada.

He called the ferryman, whose house was a few paces away. But the ferryman was absent, the house deserted. Castro dismounted, consumed by rage. A broad extent of water separated him from Rachel and Joachim, whose boat was diminishing visibly.

Through the fog that enveloped his ideas, he then had the notion that something abnormal was happening in the new city. He heard the sound of a clarion coming from the direction of the port, and then the echoes of a few rifle shots. In the distance, on a path, a few silhouettes seemed to be fleeing an inexplicable danger. An impressive silence fell thereafter.

But one single image occupied Castro's mind: that of the hand in the beloved hair, those two faces stuck together by the lips.

He finally discovered a canoe at the water's edge, wasted time unfastening the mooring-rope, and then leapt into it and rowed with all his might. Fortunately, the current drew him along. When he reached the other bank, near Reis Magos, he was exhausted by the effort. He started running along the road that went along the coast. It was at that moment that he was seen from Fort Aguada.

Rachel, standing up, gazed at the river and the distant horizon of the sea. The sky had become clear again.

The Malabaran who possessed a boat with a deck capable of going along the coast as far as Ratnagiri was a little further away, with his boat anchored in the little inlet of Aguada. The fishermen had assured them that, in order to convince him to make the voyage, the presence of Castro's son was necessary. As feet sank profoundly into the wet sands, Joachim had insisted that Rachel wait for him at the place where they had disembarked.

Wrapped in her cape, Rachel took a few steps, and the vision of the Jewish community in flight returned to her mind. She was leaving too. She was fleeing the Christians who had done her harm and renouncing her vengeance. There was an interior force of resignation in the race.

She heard heavy footfalls behind her and, on turning round, she perceived Pedre de Castro. Her surprise on seeing him was attenuated by the greater surprise of observing the extreme redness of his face; it was the color of wine-dregs. He was breathing heavily, His voice had an unusual timbre. He did not know at first what he ought to say.

"Where's Joachim?" he cried. "I saw you together. You're leaving, aren't you?"

Surprise gave way to humiliation in Rachel. So, she depended on that man. He had the right to pursue her.

"Yes, we're leaving," she said. "So what?"

Pedre de Castro sniggered. "That's what we shall see! You belong to me, you hear?"

Perhaps her father's words had influenced her involuntarily. Rachel did not feel the anger she would have felt the day before at the informal address of that affirmation. She saw Castro look to the right and the left, take a few steps and return, like a wild boar about to charge hunters, and repeating: "Where's Joachim? Tell me where he is!"

She was afraid of what might happen; she was animated by a sincere desire to stoop him. She thought that she was still able to do that.

"By what entitlement do you claim that I belong to you?" she said, softly.

He considered her with amazement. His eyes moistened, his arms fell back. He searched the utmost depths of himself for words that were not familiar to him, and which he pronounced in a voice suddenly broken by emotion.

"Because I love you, now. I need you. Life appears impossible to me without you being there."

The stammer of the fat, red-faced man, his derisory effort to pronounce tender words, seemed more frightful to Rachel than anything she had feared.

"Pedre de Castro," she said, gravely, "you don't even know who I am."

He was not listening. He lowered his voice. "I'll behave as if nothing had happened. Stay with me. We'll be married whenever you wish. You needn't convert if that's what's stopping you. I don't care what anyone might think. But don't go. I need you too much."

"Once again, listen to me. I'm not the woman that I've made you believe."

He shook his head. He thought that she was about to confess former liaisons of which he was unaware. He made a sign that that was of no importance.

"When I've told you my name, you'll renounce me of your own accord. It would be better for you to renounce this immediately and go back."

He shrugged his shoulders at the idea of voluntary renunciation.

"When you met me for the first time, you were struck by the resemblance I had with another woman, and you were even frightened by it. Do you remember?"

He became suddenly attentive.

"That resemblance was natural, because I'm Rachel Jehoudah, the daughter of Manoël Jehoudah and..."

"What!" he cried, He uttered a little laugh of doubt. "Get away!" But suddenly, swiftly, in a low voice, he murmured: "And why didn't you tell me then?"

164

"Why? That's another matter. It would be better for you not to ask me the reason, and we can leave it there."

Pedre de Castro took out his handkerchief and sponged his brow, which was streaming. He breathed in deeply. He gazed at his shoes. A few seconds went by.

"I'd like to understand," he said. "When I've understood, I'll be satisfied."

Rachel placed her hand on Castro's shoulder with a gesture that was almost amicable.

"There are instances where there's more advantage in not understanding, in never understanding."

But he grasped her wrist brutally, saying: "I want to know why you deceived me. I understand, anyway. You were seeking a situation in life. You wanted to be married and you thought that the name of Jehoudah wouldn't be a famous title. So, as you're a Jewess, you lied, you invented a story, you humbled yourself before me, you would even have converted. What wouldn't I have done, if I had wanted to! Only you found my son. You thought you could get more advantage from that. Oh, Jewesses! You're all the same!"

All that Rachel had planned, her effort, her calm, her hope of making Castro leave before his son arrived, vanished in a second.

Her heart was beating rapidly. She was facing the enemy, she no longer experienced anything but the need to strike him. She became his equal in her fury.

"No, no, you're mistaken. We're not all the same. I differ from those of my race at least in that I'm capable of wanting and organizing my vengeance. I wanted to avenge myself on the odious man who had caused my mother's death, the coward who had attached my father to a cross, the perjurer who had accused him of the death of a child whose body he had thrown into the water himself with a stone around his neck. First I thought of killing him, but that was too simple and too good for you. Personally, I believe that there are good and evil men. You attached yourself to the good when you repented in the church. You risked going to find them afterwards, somewhere, I don't know where. I wanted to make you descend again among those whom hate devours, among those who are irredeemably damned, your peers. It appears that that is a crime too, but I assume it. I have only to look at your face to see that I've succeeded, to see that I've brought you to the point where you were before, when you love evil for its own sake."

"Enough! Enough!" Castro cried.

And Rachel did not know whether he was about to weep or, on the contrary, to throw himself upon her to strangle her. But anger carried her away.

"You want to know why I'm leaving with your son? You want to know the truth? Well, it's not so much because of him. He has only been the opportunity that arrived. In reality, if I'm leaving, it's to spare you, by virtue of a sort of belated pity, and fear of my own vengeance, because of the disgust you inspire in me, which you have always inspired in me, such that I would not have been able to resist, and it would have been necessary for me to see your blood and feast on your pain. From that, I wanted to preserve you. But it was necessary not to pursue me here…then, it became necessary to remind you of my mother Dolça and thank God, since you risked escaping me."

Rachel was not unaware that she was lacerating the heart of the aging man with a cruelty greater that any of which she had ever dreamed. Castro, deep down, had believed that he had inspired in Rachel, if not love, at least an attraction to which he could not give a precise name, but which surpassed amity. For him, that was perhaps better than amour. And that all disappeared, abruptly. He was alone, abandoned. He paraded his eyes over the sands of Aguada and was frightened by their desert appearance, which he had never noticed. The idea of remaining there when Rachel and his son had left appeared so frightful to him that he uttered a cry.

It was at that moment that Rachel, who had turned toward the coast of Aguada, in the direction in which Joachim had drawn away, perceived the latter advancing along the waterside.

Thus, she could not prevent, as she had hoped momentarily, prevent the encounter of the father and son. The tragic scene she had imagined was about to take place. She had thought with such force and for such a long time that the event might be avoided, even at the last moment, by the will of its creator. In vain, she had fled the house in which she had counted on asking the son for vengeance and protection against the father. The circumstances had come together anyway, like obedient matter in the unchangeable mold created by vengeful thought.

Castro could not see his son, who was behind him; he could scarcely see Rachel, who was before his eyes; he could only see within himself.

"You've been able to do that! It's true, there was one morning—perhaps only one—when I was pure. At the church of the Magi, I had returned to God. And then you were able to steal from me what you had given me. Anyway, it went. Thief, you've taken everything from me. You've succeeded fully. You were the demon!"

And suddenly, he seized Rachel by the front of her dress. He shook her, and then he drew her to him and shouted in her face: "You're going to be mine right away. I didn't have your mother, but I'll have you in spite of you, here, on the ground."

And he tried to tip her over. A hand seized his wrist. He saw Joachim beside him. Then his fury redoubled.

"You've come to take her. You think you'll take her away. You're forgetting that I'm the master."

He had released Rachel and he turned to his son.

"Wretch! She's made you believe her stories! She's told you that I murdered her mother, hasn't she? And that I put her father on a cross? It's possible! It's true; I ought to have done worse to that vermin. But has she told you that I picked her up in a brothel in Bombay?"

He started to laugh frightfully. Then, as he suddenly calmed down, and he said, almost in a whisper: "Go away. I order you to return to Goa. She belongs to me. Get into that canoe and go."

And he made a gesture to seize Rachel again and pull her toward him.

But Joachim stepped between them. He was pale and resolute. That brought Castro's exasperation to its peak.

"You're refusing to obey me? Be careful. I can force you to do it!"

On the sand, a few paces from Castro, there was an oar broken in two. The stump formed a club, which Castro seized. Perhaps he was only thinking of threatening and terrifying his son by exaggerating the image of violence. Perhaps he was carried away by the blind force that was unleashed within him.

Joachim did not recoil, and replied: "Rachel has only hatred for you, and you've just voiced yourself the reasons she has for hating you. So, it's for you to go away."

"She's been my mistress!" Castro cried.

"You're lying."

Scarcely had Joachim pronounced those words than the oar his father was holding fell upon his face. The blow was so violent that he found himself on his knees, supporting himself on the ground with his hand. In the same second, Rachel leapt to his side to support him, and Castro, in his rage, was about to strike him a second time.

He only stopped because of the sound of footsteps that he heard behind him. A man was marching alongside the river. He had seen the gesture, recognized Castro and Rachel, and thrust himself between them.

"Pedre de Castro, go home," he said.

The latter, agape with astonishment, recognized the physician Manoël Jehoudah. The oar fell from his hand, and at the same time, Jehoudah said: "Do you know that it is on this same spot, where you're standing, that I found my wife Dolça's body?"

And as Castro remained immobile and mute, he made a sign to the boatmen that he had brought and were watching from a distance, fearfully. He thought that they could lend him assistance to master the furious man.

But he saw the wine-dregs color of Castro's face accentuate suddenly. The latter was no longer occupied either with Jehoudah, nor Rachel, nor Joachim; he was only occupied in drawing breath, and he tried in vain to loosen the collar of his jacket. He fell to his knees, as his son had done, straightened up, turned his back in order not to allow the effort he was making to breathe be seen, and then fell full length.

It was only then that the Hindus decided to approach. They transported the father and son into the house of a fisherman of Reis Magos. There, Manoël Jehoudah recognized that Joachim had a grave fracture of the skull, and that his father, struck by an attack of apoplexy, was paralyzed on the left side. He hastened to bleed the latter. He thought that the best thing to do was transport them both to the new city without delay.

As they were getting ready to do that, Pedre de Castro came round. It appeared that the bleeding had returned his full consciousness. He expressed himself with great difficulty and the sounds only emerged from his immobilized mouth with a bizarre deformation. Contrary to what might have been thought, it was not to talk about Rachel or his son. He emitted a desire, patiently; it as that of being transported immediately to Father Vincent in the Church of the Magi.

It was necessary for him to repeat the name of the priest and the church for a long time to make himself understood.

There were several boats. Manoël Jehoudah decided that he would go upriver as far as old Goa and the Church of the Magi with Pedre de Castro, while Rachel took Joachim to the new city, where she would have a choice between several physicians.

Castro was laid in the largest boat, the one in which Rachel had come. He took his place beneath the wicker lattice, where her perfume still lingered.

Jehoudah noticed that Pedre de Castro, lying in the boat, was making a great effort to turn his head away and not to see him. He thought that his sight must be odious to him, and arranged himself during the journey in order not to be perceived.

At the place where the ferry was, he saw a solitary horse, which was whinnying, and further on, a long file of soldiers with youthful faces, among whom three monks were marching. Castro must have seen them too and was astonished by their sight, for he made a movement to sit up. Manoël Jehoudah moved closer to him then, but only heard the name of Father Vincent, repeated several times. It was that name that he repeated again, but with a desperate intonation, when they passed the place on the river where the nagah flowers, moistened by the rain, extended their inverted calices toward the water.

The boat went very slowly because of the ebbing tide. The soldiers were lost to sight. It was necessary to stop at Ribandar to let the oarsmen rest. The contrary wind further delayed the arrival in Goa.

Thus, the two men followed during the long afternoon that trajectory they had followed on another occasion, in very different conditions.

Castro had a fever. Things were losing their precision and their value.

It's only now that I'm on the cross, he thought, confusedly. *Perhaps I'm dead and condemned to go up this river incessantly with Jehoudah. Perhaps a guitar will start to play. Perhaps Dolça will slip between the oarsmen, naked, and throw herself into the water. I was afraid of death, but, behold, it's done!*

And he extended his arms as if he were on a cross, docile to his punishment.

Lord, be not redoubtable to the wicked! thought Manoël Jehoudah.

And, as he believed in the action of thought when it is projected forcefully, he strove to envelop Castro in the beneficent atmosphere of his forgiveness.

Having arrived in Goa, the boat was moored to the last quay. Dusk had come and the prayer for the dead, sung by sad voices, was rising over the desolate city.

I really am dead! They're praying for me, Castro said to himself in his dream.

It was necessary for Jehoudah to set out in quest of a palanquin and porters. At the same time, he learned about the day's events. When Castro was transported from the boat to the palanquin, the nascent obscurity prevented anyone from recognizing him.

Jehoudah ordered the porters to head as rapidly as possible for the Church of the Magi. In order not to impose his presence on Castro he followed the palanquin on foot. He had short legs and was obliged to run in order not to be outdistanced.

The old parish priest of Good-Jesus had a great deal of trouble explaining to Father Vincent that he was no longer a priest because his ordination was posterior to the moment when Monsignor de Silva has entered into conflict with the Pope.

Father Vincent left Goa at a slow pace, seeking to understand. What a mystery the perpetual ardor of men to do evil to one another was? What a mystery the death of the Archbishop was! God had taken away the life of his messenger when his word seemed to be most useful, and he would no longer wear the robe that was his sole interior glory.

Perhaps I've sinned by pride, he said to himself. *Yes, I haven't been humble enough.*

It was dark when his timid shadow emerged from the city and glided along the avenue of mango-trees that led to the Church of the Magi. When he reached the point where the path descended again, and from which one could see the horizon, he suddenly stopped and passed his hand over his eyes.

He could not see the fortress tower protruding from beneath the compact mass of stones like the solid force of faith. The church had disappeared.

The diluvian rain of the previous night had shifted the mobile sands and determined the collapse of the ancient monument. That had happened at the hour of vespers, perhaps during the excommunication, and no one had heard the sound of the collapse.

When Father Vincent went down he realized that at the same time as God had removed his protection from his saint, his active will had withdrawn from the ground where the church was built and abandoned it to oblivion.

So, there would no longer be any mass for the most wretched! What an unfathomable abyss the divine will was! He gazed at the expanse of shining pools, where the familiar canticle of the frogs was beginning to rise up, and then, further away, at the circle of mountains and the vast earth.

Well, it was necessary to try to comprehend. He would climb back up to his hermitage, in the midst of the most solid stones of the mountain of Boma, in the eternal cathedral that God would not ruin before the end of the world. But before then he would take off the robe that he ought not to wear any longer.

And, suddenly struck by the idea of some grave unknown sin that he had perhaps committed in conserving it, he took it off in the darkness, amid the sadness of the demolished blocks.

You have been proud, he thought.

But no matter! Would not a cross made with two knotted branches be sufficient? Would there not be, up there, on the edge of the great forest, a larger vault, from which the prayer of his pure heart might be launched further?

"It is in yourself that you will find Christ," Monsenhor de Silva had said to him one day.

He tried to penetrated those mysterious words. Henceforth, he would live with the savage men, he would be naked, like his brethren. He would love them more now that they no longer had a church. He would say mass for them without an altar and without sacred objects, and God would be there all the same.

He knelt down to pray one last time.

It was at that moment that the palanquin on which Castro was lying appeared between the mango-trees. The cool nocturnal air woke him up and rendered him consciousness of things. He made a great effort to get up, but could not do it, and it was Jehoudah that sat him up.

"The church?" he murmured, looking around him with widened eyes. "It's not here. Let's go to the Church of the Magi."

It required time for him to recognize the line of mango-trees and to take account of the fact that somber mass of stones at his feet was all that remained of the church where he had still hoped to find forgiveness.

He fell back, and closed his eyes. There was no longer any forgiveness for him. They could take him wherever they wished. Everything was finished henceforth.

Lord, be not redoubtable to the wicked! Jehoudah repeated, internally.

And he ordered the porters to resume the road to Goa.

Neither he nor Castro had noticed a naked man who was weeping silently in the shadows, beside a torn-up robe.

The Penitentiary

The Portuguese government had decided only to pursue the members of the Colony Council as responsible for the Goanese revolutionary movement, but it had given orders that that should be done with the utmost rigor.

With the exception of Castro, all the members of the Council were able to cross the frontier of Portuguese territory before being arrested. It was in a suit and a white cravat that Mascarenhas, followed by his sons in the same attire, departed on horseback for Visapour. His wife, who had not taken off her crimson dress, had said to him on the threshold of the house: "Don't worry. I shall maintain the hearth of the Mascarenhas."

Marcora, who had been found asleep at home, had been able to flee thanks to the initiative of his daughters, who had actively sympathized with the young soldiers charged with guarding him.

A search was made with particular care for Deodat de Vega, but doubtless he had not lost the memory of his years spent at Port Jackson. No one ever heard any further mention of him.

Castro's trial was held rapidly. Shifts of opinion were feared, and a revolt in his favor. That was mistaken. A bizarre apathy had taken possession of Goa. As if a mysterious order had been circulated, the gambling dens were closed, the pianos and guitars had fallen silent, energies were dead. Many priests had left. In the Franciscan convent only one monk in five remained. He had lost his mind. He was obstinate in singing the prayer for the dead all day long, in spite of the efforts that were made by the convent's neighbors to make him shut up. The last two shoeless Carmelites nailed the door of their Church shut with planks. The bell-ringer, who had been obliged, regretfully, to sound the knell during the excommunication, secretly unhooked the clappers from the cathedral

174

bells. For matins and vespers it was perceived in the agitated tower that pulling the ropes with all one's might could only produce silence.

Abruptly. Juana de Faria's skin disease became manifest with unexpected force. Milky crusts appeared on her forehead like a crown. That infection spread, and became commonplace in old Goa. The Chinese were accused of having propagated a new malady, to which effects were attributed all the more redoubtable because it came from distant China. It was also thought that the cause might be the humidity, greater that year, and the ambient putrescence. The rains that had destroyed the Church of the Magi had raised up a former charnel-house in a suburb. The bones of past centuries had been carried into the streets by the water. One poor man who had a cabin at ground level found a skull in his fireplace on returning home. The pools disengaged a more pestilential odor. The decomposition of vegetation was more active. Poisonous exhalations emerged from old monasteries and dwellings eaten by termites. The half-demolished towers had a more melancholy appearance, and it was believed at every gust of wind that they were about to lie down full length like exhausted old men, so much were ruination and death present in Goa.

There was not even a crowd around the tribunal in the new city when the judgment was pronounced that condemned Castro to twenty years of public labor. He had scarcely recovered from his attack during the two months of detention that had preceded his trial. He had only retained a kind of stiffness in the left arm that made him raise his shoulders slightly. That harmed him, however, for his judge, seeing him at an angle while the list of accusations was being read, believed the gesture to be a affectation of scorn.

Castro had been cared for in the infirmary of the prison of Goa. It happened, without anyone being able to explain why, that the two best physicians in Bombay, who were Jews, were installed in Goa during the time of his illness, and even more surprising, they obtained, by virtue of an intervention by the governor of Bombay, permission to care for him in the prison. At the same time they cared for his son, whose condition was more serious.

Senhor de Ribeira had hesitated over whether to have Rachel arrested. Her presence in the new city beside Joachim de Castro provoked popular hostility. He had her expelled from Portuguese territory after three days. She went to live in Cochin in her father's house.

As for Manoël Jehoudah, his active life had just begun.

Manoël Jehoudah perceived that he enjoyed an esteem and authority with regard to his coreligionists greater than he could have supposed. It came from his correspondence with erudite rabbis, students of the Kabbalah and the religious science of ancient Jewish books. A discreet renown as a disinterested scientist and an honest man had been constituted around his name, unknown to him. Those in the Jewish colonies of the Orient who had situations or fortunes immediately put themselves at his disposal. They were slightly astonished by the choice of the man that Jehoudah had chosen to protect, but they did not ask him any questions and they acted in his favor in the full measure of their power.

From the first evening, Manoël Jehoudah had resolved no longer to show Pedre de Castro a face that was odious to him. He explained to the prison physician, when the latter was transferred to the prison in the new city, the circumstances of the attack that had struck Castro and the first aid that he had given him. Then he left for Bombay, from which he brought back the two physicians who devoted themselves to the father and the son.

Castro refused during his convalescence to confess, or even to see a priest. He insisted several times that the crucifix above his bed be removed. It was the sole desire he expressed during that period. He paid no heed to his defense. He spent entire days in grim silence. He greeted his condemnation with an absolute indifference, as if to say: *What does it matter what happens to a man as manifestly abandoned by God as I am?*

The public works were to be carried out in penitentiaries in Mozambique. The passage of the boat carrying convicts from the colonies of Macao and Malacca and were to collect those of Goa coincided with the end of the trial. Castro was embarked on it. Powerful interventions had already acted on the captain in order that he should be treated with care during the crossing.

Manoël Jehoudah took passage on an English merchant ship and arrived in Mozambique three days before the ship carrying the convicts. The Jewish colony there was not numerous and his influence was limited. Jehoudah made use of it anyway. By that means he entered into relations with the director of the new Mozambique Company, which had just obtained immense land concessions and the exploitation of the ports. The Company had the right to utilize the labor of the convicts of the penitentiary as it pleased. It was waiting impatiently for the ship coming from Goa in order to employ the new consignment of men in the clearance of sand from the port of Beira. The work there was crushing. Jehoudah obtained from the Company director that Castro would not be employed in it and would stay in Mozambique in the offices or the infirmary. He installed himself in Mezuril, on the coast, in order to watch over his protégé.

Castro did not see him and did not know of his presence. He thought the owed the advantages he had to his name and the situation he had had in Goa. But he deliberately indisposed everyone by his taciturn humor and his arrogant scorn. When he requested to be occupied in clearing wild land near the river Mocambo, along which a road was projected in the direction of the Namouli Mountains, it was immediately granted to him. The convicts that were about to brave hostile tribes and wild beasts were promised a reduction in their punishment. It was the punishment of his life that Castro wanted to abridge, by death.

The Company had a steamship that went up the river and resupplied the convicts, distributed at intervals, every week. Fever had killed one of them in a little wooden cabin. It was necessary to replace him immediately. Castro left with the steamer and Jehoudah was only informed in the evening.

He fell into a great sadness. He had thought that he had time before him. The work that he was pursuing, and for which he would gladly have given his life, was perhaps unrealizable. He knew, by virtue of information obtained since his arrival, that a sojourn in the marshy regions of the west was almost always fatal for Europeans. Castro risked dying out there, alone, amid thoughts of hatred, with a soul plunged in despair. He resolved to join him. But the course of the river was difficult, and dangerous to travel. In order to depart it was necessary for him to wait for a long week in Mozambique for the return of the Company steamer.

The heat was overwhelming and he began to have bouts of fever every night, which caused a profound dejection. The governor of the colony and the director of the Company came to see him in order to deflect him from his project. It was not without anxiety that they saw that debilitated old man confronting the climate of a region that brought more robust temperaments to an end in very little time. They divined confusedly that it was for reasons of moral encouragement that the physician wanted to join Castro.

"The best thing to do is to abandon him to himself," they said. "The almoner who saw him quit him with a very bad impression. He's a creature that seemed utterly doomed."

But their efforts were vain. They obtained a promise from him, however, that he would only stay with Castro for a few hours. The steamer would wait for him and he would come back to Mozambique with it. Jehoudah did not know then how he would be welcomed by Castro and he envisaged the hypothesis that the latter might refuse to exchange the slightest word with him.

After three days of slow navigation between desolate scrub, and then between the walls of virgin forests, the ship stopped beside a long sandbank. There was a narrow trail at its extremity that led to a broader trail opened with the ax in the entanglement of wood and lianas. A little further on, in a clearing, a miserable hut of planks represented the most advanced outpost attained by the Company for the Exploitation of Mozambique.

The captain of the steamer accompanied Jehoudah as far as Castro's hut. He supported him, for he had a fever and had difficulty walking. Behind them, a sailor carried, as well as the week's provisions sent by the Company, a package of various objects bought by Jehoudah with Castro's intention. The captain recounted afterwards that he had observed with surprise that the Jewish physician's package contained a rather large crucifix with an ivory Christ. It was, he said, the best of the genre that could be procured in Mozambique. And he added that it was the first time in his life that he had seen a Jew making Christian propaganda.

Contrary to what had been agreed, the steamer did not bring Jehoudah back to Mozambique.

"When we arrived," the captain said, "Castro was sitting at his door staring at the forest. He darted an indifferent glance at us and turned away, exactly as if we had not appeared at the end of the path. Jehoudah asked me to leave him alone with Castro, which I could not do without some anxiety. The hut is only a few minutes from the river. He promised to rejoin me on the boat alone, a little later.

"I saw as I looked back that the physician was sitting beside Castro, still motionless, and talking to him. I stayed long enough to consider them. The convict continued to give no evidence of attention. In the end, I went back to the boat and spent the night there. In the morning, Jehoudah joined me to tell me that he was not leaving with me. He had the face of a man who has not slept, but who is satisfied. When I persisted, he told me not to worry. He intended to spend the whole night there. The provisions he had brought in the package containing the crucifix, combined with those destined for Castro, would be sufficient for two. He would come back down to Mozambique when the boat next returned the following week."

In reality, he was to undertake a much longer voyage.

The captain of the steamer had received a formal order, when he went upriver again, to bring Castro and Jehoudah back with him. The governor of the colony and the Company director had thought, with common accord, that the sole means of preserving a man of Jehoudah's age from a sojourn in the forest that might prove fatal to him was to recall the convict who was the cause of his departure.

This is the story the captain told on his return. He repeated it later to Joachim de Castro and Rachel Jehoudah when they came to Mozambique together and went upriver with him to see their fathers' graves.

"We went along the great sandbank that marked the end of our voyage. We arrived at the usual hour—which is to say, the end of the afternoon. I distinguished the forms of two men, sitting on the sand and sustaining one another. They were clasping one another like two brothers. The elongation of their bodies emphasized the disproportion of their height. What struck me, however, is that in spite of his extreme smallness by comparison with his companion, the physician Jehoudah had, in his manner of holding Castro by the shoulders, something broad and protective that made him appear the larger.

"Doubtless they had hoped to see the boat arrive sooner than usual. They must have been struck almost at the same time, several days before, by the malaria typical of the region, and the arrival of the boat coincided with their last moments. Perhaps Castro was already dead when I disembarked. Jehoudah stood up, took a few steps in my direction, and fell down again. When I arrived beside him, he handed me two letters, the addresses of which were written with extreme care, and I understood that what had enabled him to live that long was the necessity of giving me the two letter in my own hands and obtaining the assurance that they would reach their addressees. One of the letters was for Joachim de Castro in Goa, the other for Rachel Jehoudah in Cochin.

"When I had given him the assurance he demanded, he uttered a great sigh of relief and closed his eyes. Nevertheless, he opened them again and stammered: 'If Castro's letter does not reach his son, take charge personally of making Joachim de Castro know that wanted ardently, before his death, that he marry my daughter Rachel.'

"The necessary cares were lavished, but he didn't recover consciousness. As for Castro, he was dead. When I approached him, I had difficulty recognizing him. He was truly another man. His grim expression had disappeared, to give way to an almost joyful calm. He was wearing a chaplet around his neck that I recognized for one of those the missionaries of Mozambique sell.

"I went as far as the cabin. It was in perfect order. There were two glasses side by side, two axes, but only a single crucifix. All that I saw attested that the two men had lived and worked side by side for a week in perfect accord, in truth like two brothers who loved one another dearly. We dug their graves side by side."

In accordance with his father's desire, Joachim de Castro married Rachel Jehoudah. They never returned to Goa. Rachel often reread the last letter that she had received from Mozambique, and which concluded thus:

...It is not your happiness that I have considered, for happiness is not the goal. It is not even the reparation of the wrong that you have caused. I wanted to bring back the man that you had deliberately driven back on the road of humanity, to the straight road where everyone has similarly to gaze at the beyond with a resigned tranquility. And thus above us, in the domain of causes and effects, I have interrupted a current of shadow, the chain of evil that is eternal if active forgiveness does not intervene, if love does not replace vengeance.

While I am finishing this letter, he is praying. We do not know that either of us will live until the boat arrives, but that scarcely has any importance for us any longer. Soon we shall lie down on the same bed of leaves and my companion's slumber will be peaceful. You are doubtless wondering how I have given him that peace, how I was able to render hope to a man who had been deprived of it. It was not with ideas. He did not listen to me at first. He continued staring into the distance, in the direction from which night was coming. Nor was it with the objects of his religion. I had thought that there was a benevolent force in their usual matter that aids the spirit. I spread out the chaplet and the Christian cross on the ground, with a clock and a compass, in vain.

I did not take account immediately of what was acting in his soul. It was only at length that I understood the force of the thought of love that I had within me. I placed that thought of love like a light in the miserable convict's hut on the sand of the river, in the forest where I cut trees with him at dawn. And when I saw the desperate heart suddenly melt and the stone mask of the face of hate fall, it seemed to me that the forest fell silent, that the vapor of the pools dissipated, that a light arose around us brighter than that of the rising sun.

I did not weep then, because I had exhausted long ago the sum of tears that a creature can shed, but I experienced a delight so pure that I wished a similar one for all the beings on earth, and especially for you, my child.

Love is the great force of the earth. All my years of study and my experience have only taught me that secret, which I bequeath to you.

Here men are buried in the place where they fall. If you do not see me again and I die far away from you, do not be saddened by my solitude. I am no longer alone. I shall repose beside a man that I have arrived at loving and to whom I have communicated that love. We are two. We have struggled fraternally against the trees, the torrid sun and the fever. We have decided not to quit one another any longer. We are content and tranquil at the thought that our bones will be mingled, that we shall sleep side by side. And if there is another voyage to undertake, if there is an awakening, it is together that we shall get up to depart again.

LOTUS BLOSSOMS

FACING THE WOODEN BUDDHA

Facing the wooden Buddha that a traveler brought back from China for me, and which was sculpted by the bonze of a pagoda on the mountain of Cao Bang, I sat cross-legged for many an evening on the carpet with arabesques and colored flowers, the carpet where my dreams awaken like as many serene little lamps.

And as I had long requested the intermediary spirits that populate the invisible realms to grant me clairvoyance of my previous existences, I saw images flowing and familiar eyes peeping through lowered eyelids, forms emerging from the shadows of days long past.

But because of the imperfection of my soul, those forms were indistinct, those eyes immeasurably veiled, and I only contemplated scattered fragments of beauties and dolors that are no more. For it is only given to those who are pure to escape from the prison of time.

And I knew that through the countless ages the justice of the law had always made a mediocre man of me. Never, like the more favored or more prideful men who remember their past lives, had it been given to me to be a person remarkable for his talents and illustrious in his nation.

Nothing but a collector of grass at the foot of a chalky cliff who incessantly makes the same gesture of puling with his rake! A sort of juggler who travels the roads behind a donkey and gives performances in villages! A man who tans hides, married to a delicate creature whom he tortures by his vulgarity!

And always on the other side of the world, in the luminous Orient where the forests rustle, where the sands sparkle, where the pagodas extend their circular domes and azure mosaics toward the sky! And because of that I am solitary in the land where church bells resonate and wheat grows instead of rice.

Finally, I have seen my last incarnation, the one in which it was given to me to be a poet who touched the beauty of forms, who loved things with his heart, who glimpsed the verities hidden beneath appearances. Thus, in a subterranean grotto, the colorless rainwater, after having filtered for thousands of years, condenses into crystalline stalactites.

Into stalactites of thoughts of love, the rain of my quotidian thoughts has mutated, during the life of an Indian poet who lived in Delhi and Benares. He loved charming faces and perfect forms, and the love of beauty led him to the love of knowledge as an amorous young woman leads a stranger to her fiancé.

And that is why, in memory of that fraternal predecessor in the innumerable voyage, I have written the book of Lotus Blossoms, the book whose characters I have deciphered in the depth of the mirror, the mirror set above the wooden Buddha that a traveler brought me from China.

For it is taught by ancient Sages that a magic can be gestated in certain expertly varnished woods, and that that magic, with the reflection of the mirror, recreates the lost word what was pronounced in the depths of the soul and engraves it in the crepuscular mist of the mirror, engraves it for the eyes that see.

And I say, having concluded the transcription of the ancient work: May I be worthy of the man that I have been, I who am unworthy of the man that I shall be. May my spirit launch itself higher, may my spirit launch itself more rapidly toward knowledge and toward amour, may my actions be in harmony with my thoughts, may my feeble voice resonate far away and transmit to other humans by the mystery of writing the teardrop of beauty that I have wept.

THE BLACK SERPENT THAT BRINGS LUCK

Dawn is rising. Thank the God who has enabled you to discover in his gilded court the black serpent that brings luck to the house.

It is necessary to bring him milk in a flat earthenware bowl and put dry foliage alongside in order that he may repose there.

No face of evil augury will appear at the door today, no sad thought will stand on the threshold of the soul.

An entire day of good fortune, with no quarrel among the servants, no bitter memory to trouble the purity of your gaze!

O black serpent, I shall put milk in the flat bowl every day and I shall prepare the dry foliage, back serpent who visits me so rarely!

LITTLE LIGHT

An interior spiritual suavity puts on the features of her face a delicate expression that is reminiscent of the flight of a swallow on the edge of a pond in a spring twilight.

She does not know how to play the cithara, or compose verses, but everything in her is natural poetry and invisible harmony.

She liberates butterflies from the hands of children and helps the good God's beasts to find they way. Everything that is small and fragile excites her tenderness.

She does not accomplish any great deeds of goodness and she dreams more than she acts. It is even claimed that she is slothful.

One cannot define the exact hue of her dress, of a blue intermediate between that of the sky and that of the water. Who can say, too, whether she is cheerful or sad?

She does not like fêtes, long journeys, solemn gatherings or the external appearances of wealth. She dreads poverty and gladly goes for walks in the garden.

She has been nicknamed Little Light. But for me she has a secret name in the depths of my heart and I never pronounce it. I like her because of the interior spiritual suavity that is reflected in her face.

THE EMPEROR OF CHINA
AND THE EMPEROR OF JAPAN

The Emperor of China and the Emperor of Japan met one beautiful evening on the calm sea. Two flag-decked ships advanced solemnly from either side of the horizon, and thousands of junks, with their colored lanterns, were motionless on the waves, like as many great stars, while countless stars were motionless in the sky, like as many minuscule junks.

The Emperor of China and the Emperor of Japan sat facing one another under a silk parasol with a golden handle, and beside them there were a Chinese dwarf with a square bonnet and a Japanese dwarf with a miter of peacock feathers, who presented them with tea in a hollow block of crystal. The two emperor drank a few mouthfuls of it and gazed at one another in silence. Their robes were streaming with precious stones and they resembled two timid gods who dare not engage in conversation.

The courtiers on the decks of the ships formed a respectful circle of embroideries and armor. There were mandarins there of the nine different ranks, from the Tai Four who wears a red stone to the Tai Tchao who wears a golden globule. The Shogun was there, surrounded by the Lords of the Earth, and certain religious functionaries bent double by the discipline of rites, radiating veneration as a lamp radiates light. And on the shores of China and Japan the peoples were amassed, gazing at the calm sea.

The two emperors were going to discuss the imminent invasion of the Tartars, and the potency of the epidemics that had fallen mysteriously on certain provinces. They were going to seek together means of making rice circulate rapidly over land and sea, in order to remedy famines; they were going to study the causes of the fabulous typhoons that, in certain epochs, raised up the sea. They were going to enter into communication with the Spirits, listen to the voices of the ancestors. From their meeting the lightning would spring forth that enables the Gods to descend.

The Emperor of China, the more resolute, spoke first, and the conversation was rather animated. They were both great lovers of lacquer and were astonished that a certain shade of violet could not be obtained.

"The polishers of Canton do not bring as much care to their work as before. The colcothar is too calcined. One no longer finds absolutely pure cinnabar. As for the rose, it's even more terrible. The cultivation of safflower has been abandoned. The secret of the ancient masters is lost. In truth, the world is in decadence."

The two emperors were very unhappy, and when the conversation was concluded, they almost wept, bowed down behind their fans, while the two ships drew away solemnly over the calm sea.

THE CHARITY OF PADMANI

I found the torn robe of a pauper on my garden fence. The pauper himself, leaning on his staff, was drawing away along the road with a singular lightness, clad in an embroidered mantle with fringes, which resembled my most beautiful mantle.

"I enabled the pauper to eat and I enabled him to drink," Padmani[9] said to me, with a serene visage. "I took him to the bath and he smoked his hookah. And as his mantle was torn I gave him an embroidered mantle with fringes, for it is appropriate to be charitable."

"Everything you have done is well done," I replied.

"When I had given him that," Padmani went on, "I saw that the pauper was as poor as before. It gave me so much pain that I wanted him to carry away an unusual wealth, the wealth of a good memory, and I gave myself to him."

Thus spoke Padmani, with simplicity, and she went into the house, occupying herself with little things.

Then I meditated upon charity and the knowledge of good and evil, which it is not given to women to have.

"How old might that pauper be?" I asked, sadly.

Padmani burst out laughing. "How could I remember that? I only saw his eyes, which were weeping."

I mediated again upon charity.

---

[9] Padmani is a variant of Padmini, which means "She who sits upon the lotus" in Sanskrit, usually with reference in ancient sources to the goddess Lakshmi.

THE GOD OF BENEVOLENT INTELLIGENCE

O god of benevolent intelligence, who is depicted with the large bare forehead of a mature man, the ingenuous gaze of a child and the creased mouth of an old man, you who hold a crystal ball and a closed Lotus, you who are motionless, you who see, you who know.

O god of benevolent intelligence put on my face the smile that comprehends, enable my hand to make the gesture that excuses, give all my attitudes the agility that daily indulgence brings to the body.

Take away from me the anger that blinds and envelops us with a red mist, do not permit frantic desire to possess me, for it forces a man to walk on all fours in the manner of beasts.

Give me the measure with which one weighs one's actions like black pebbles, the measure with which one weighs one's thoughts like grains of luminous wheat.

Give me the judgment by means of which the truth is discerned from error and the clairvoyance that enables one to know that a man is good even beneath a vulgar or unpleasant appearance.

Enable me to stand up between good and evil as one stands up between two enemy brothers. Show me the part of the lie that the mildness of the white mask hides and the part of human necessity that there is beneath the grimace of the black mask.

Do not make me laugh because of the pleasing character of pain, nor make me weep because of the spiritual emotion that beauty procures, and permit me to understand death, that entry into the land of immaterial humans, subtle landscapes and delicate vibrations.

Give my mind an inexhaustible thirst for knowledge, my heart an unlimited faculty of cherishing the various forms of creation, and permit me to climb with the agility of a runner the steps of knowledge that lead to the portal of amour, O god of benevolent intelligence!

PADMANI'S MOTHER

She had told me such delightful things about her mother that I resolved to accompany he when she went to pay her a visit in a village lost in the foothills of the Arvalli Mountains.

Our horses died in the sands of the That desert and we nearly drowned crossing a river that had flooded. But all those dangers were unimportant, since it was a matter of going to see a marvelous creature full of wisdom and beauty.

"It would be vanity on my part to claim that I resemble her," said Padmani, "she has so much natural majesty and superior nobility." Her eyes shone and she became a little girl again as we drew closer.

Outside a wretched hut, a semi-savage old woman was sitting. She did not get up to kiss her daughter and contented herself with moving her jaw to the right and left as a sign of confused satisfaction. And my soul as full of shame for the charming Padmani, whose tears flowed like pearls over cheeks the color of the moon.

And when we resumed the road of return, I held her tenderly by the shoulders, striving not to think any longer about that unfortunate visit. But she laughed, an enchanted music was in her voice, and she repeated: "What did you think of her? I haven't lied to you, have I? It's sweet for me to love such a mother."

Then I was full of shame for myself. O marvel of the purity of hearts!

THE SECRET DRAWER

In the ivory casket encrusted with gold where her jewels are and the souvenirs of our amour, we discovered a secret drawer in which there was a yellow parchment of sad aspect, with characters in the Zend language.

"Perhaps it's a curse or an indication of a hidden treasure," she said to me. "It's necessary to go to the mullah who known everything, to discover what these characters mean." But I shook my head because I knew full well what the parchment contained.

It contained the history of our amours, that of all human amours. It said that in the beautiful ivory casket there is always an unknown corner with a secret history, and that in the soul of the beloved there is always an incomprehensible bitterness that neither the mullah nor anyone else can explain.

DIVINE WISDOM

Perhaps there is a delicate garden at the summit of a savage mountain, with a kiosk of porcelain and lacquered wood, from which one can perceive in the far distance the cities in which humans agitate.

Oh, to live there, with the perfect certainty that no visitor will appear at the minuscule door of the kiosk, that I will not hear any formula of politeness or affectionate testimony.

There I will walk slowly, I will examine the design of a leaf, the veins of a pebble, the brightness of a drop of water, or the nuances of a memory.

There, in sum, neither a family, nor amity, nor amour, will envelop me with its gray, blue, or pink cloud, and I will not be like a gleaner searching for a grain of pleasure in a field of ennui.

I will sit down under a mulberry bush that is not cultivated for silkworms, I will pick a rose that will not be destined for a bouquet, I will follow a path that will not retain the imprint of a female sandal.

And there, like a perfumed essence falling into a golden urn, wisdom will filter from the silent sky, brought by the speechless wind, and slowly fill the spiritual urn of my soul.

I will be surrounded by relatives, attentive because they will be silent, friends faithful because they will be motionless, and mistresses tender because they spread sweet perfumes without wanting to. O family of trees, amity of stones, amours of flowers!

And if one evening I see the black silhouette of some counselor, or the incarnadine veil of a woman with beautiful eyes, walking by my side I will cut a willow branch and I will hurl the leaves toward the crescent moon, in order that they will understand that a sentiment of the vanity of the world has penetrated me, and they will turn around.

And at the hour when the stars are exhausted and the dew makes a shiny crown in my hair, after a night of meditation, perhaps I shall know, in the vanishment of ecstasy with the birth of the dawn, the perfect amour of everything that raises a man to the rank of the gods.

THE PEACOCK'S PLUMES

A very beautiful woman was standing on a balcony. Beneath the muslin the milky flesh of her shoulders was visible; she was covered with jewels like an idol, and she hid part of her face behind a fan of dazzling peacock plumes.

And I looked at her for a long time, forgetting Padmani, who was walking beside me, for the beauty of a woman is greater on a balcony because of the mystery of the room that is behind her. And I would have liked to be noticed by her, and I drew myself up to my full height and turned in her direction.

Padmani said nothing, but with a ridiculous affectation she remained taciturn, and a little later, I thought that she was afflicted by my long gaze, and I said to her: "Are you sad because you're jealous of the beautiful woman on the balcony? Tell me your thoughts so that I might console you."

"I'm sad," she replied, "because of the dazzling plumes of the fan. The peacock that bore them will no longer design a multicolored wheel in the sunlight. How cruel people are to birds! Don't you know that the peacock is the bird I love most of all?"

THE YOUNG MAN OF THE NIGHT

He made the dead leaves in the garden crackle softly. The dog did not bark when he passed by. The moonlight did not project his shadow on the sand of the path. But I knew that he was there.

I stopped playing the cithara. I placed the instrument of the cushion. I remained still, I did not look in the direction of the window. But I knew that he was looking at me through the gap in the shutters.

How did the oval of his face appear? What were the color of his eyes? What form did his turban have? In the end I turned my head slightly in his direction. There was a light mist on the window pane.

I did not hear the crackle of the dead leaves in the garden and the dog did not bark. I picked up my cithara again and I began to play again slowly, for I understood that he had gone.

THE CHINESE POETESS AND THE WHITE POPPIES

I

I am in love with the poetess Tchou Chou Tchenn who lived in China several hundred years ago. [10] Her father had married her to a vulgar man in order to punish her for going by night to take a bouquet of white poppies to a deserted mountain.

Since her childhood, it had never been possible to cure her of that habit. As if a mysterious voice were calling her, it was necessary that she went, one certain nights, to make that nocturnal homage to an invisible Spirit.

The vulgar man beat her and she swore not to do it again. But when the time came, she slipped out furtively at the hour when everyone was asleep, by a path that led nowhere and was lost in the midst of stones.

One morning, she was found dead on the summit of the deserted mountain. Her body was covered in dewdrops and shining, as if she were dressed in a tunic of diamonds. Had the Spirits of that solitude stolen her soul? The white poppies were not found beside her.

II

I am in love with the poetess Tchou Chou Tchenn who lived in China several hundred years ago. The vulgar man she had married was a currier by profession and had a shop in a street in Rae-Ning.

In the midst of heaped-up hides sat that delicate individual with eyes the color of green jade and hands the color of

---

[10] Chu Shu-chen, as her name is usually spelled in English sources, was a Sung poet active in the early twelfth century, famous for her employment of *kuei-yuan* [boudoir-plaint] poetry, bemoaning the fate of neglected wives.

white jade. And tanned leather emitted a perfume sweeter for her than that of lilies or roses.

She read her verses to her husband when he was in the shop with his apprentices and other vulgar men, his friends. No one understood, but they all remained still, full of bliss, sensing the invisible breath of beauty drifting over the house.

And once, a traveling mandarin listened through the crack of the door and marveled greatly. And he prepared a troop of cavaliers and armed men with a gold and crystal palanquin in order to remove the delicate and subtle individual from the currier's shop.

She would have liked to go far away from the company of vulgar men, to live in a palace in the midst of rare substances, to enjoy the music of lutes, the conversation of literates and the possession of manuscripts laden with thoughts, but something retained her there. It was the voice that has no sound, the path that leads nowhere, the mysterious nocturnal task to which she had devoted herself; it was the presence of the deserted mountain, to the summit of which, on certain nights, she had to carry a bouquet of white poppies.

III

I am in love with the poetess Tchou Chou Tchenn who lived in China several hundred years ago. She spoke very rarely, on seeing flocks of storks decrease in the sky from the balustrade of her house.

She only encountered once, in the midst of other powerful mandarins, the father who had consigned her to poverty by marrying her to a vulgar currier in order to punish her and to cause her to retrogress among beings.

As it is prescribed, she prostrated herself on the road before her father and took the hand of the malediction and kissed it. And he, who was an evil man, was astonished to see in his daughter's eyes such a beautiful gleam the color of green jade and the star Ki.

He did not know that the soul is made of a substance more inalterable than virgin gold and that a person who gazes internally is only purified by contact with vulgarity.

And in his pride he said to his daughter: "Give me the white poppy that you have in your belt." She handed it to him respectfully, but she did so in such a way that the petals fell off and that nothing remained but the stem.

"She hasn't changed," said the mandarin to the other mandarins. And the currier must not receive any more from her than her father received. She gives everything to the Spirits."

IV

I am in love with the poetess Tchou Chou Tchenn who lived in China several hundred years ago. When she died, al the curriers of Rae-Ning were in mourning and her husband, the vulgar man, who was fat, became like a willow in winter.

He wept incessantly, thinking that he had not loved her enough, and he repented of not having made fur robes with his hides uniquely to cover her.

He said: "When she spoke, I was transported to a marvelous land, but we were a long way from one another. How can one love, to that extent, something that one has lost without having understood it?"

And perhaps, in a previous life, I was that vulgar man, and that is why I love the poetess Tchou Chou Tchenn, and I still weep for her after centuries. I have searched for her on the balustrade of my house when I see storks drawing away, and if footsteps resonate on the road, I imagine that it is her, going silently to carry her white poppies to the deserted mountain.

THE LOTUS AND THE DEVAS

As I pushed the garden gate she was in the middle of a bed of roses and, her eyes raised to the sky, she had a finger over her lips and seemed to be saying "Shh!" to someone. But there was no one there.

I remained silent then. But she said to me: "It's in order to hear you saying words of love to me more clearly that I made a sign to a group of devas clad in white to remain silent above the garden."

"O Padmani, how I would like to see those devas. Can you not ask them to come closer and show me the beautiful ovals of their features, and their robes, doubtless woven of clouds?"

She shook her head, and replied: "They've just gone away, because they breathed in the aroma of certain lotuses of a rare species that have just blossomed a thousand leagues from here on a mountain in China and they'll be intoxicated for several days."

THE ASSEMBLY OF SILENT MUSICIANS

Having climbed an interminable stairway, I suddenly found myself in an assembly of musicians in black robes. There was lacquer on the walls, the ceiling was dull gold, everything was faded and everything was veiled in the room where those musicians of genius were gathered.

The faces of those musicians were illuminated by ecstasy and they were touching their instruments with light hands, as in a dream. But even though I listened hard, I could not perceive any orchestral music: nothing but a great mysterious silence.

And that silence was so anguishing, so charged with unexpressed thoughts, that I began to tremble. But the person who had brought me touched me between the eyes with his finger and said: "In this room without reflections, it isn't with the ears but with the heart that one hears."

And I began to understand the music of the musicians in black robes. It was the hidden harmony of the earth, the language without words, the resonance without vibrations, the beauty that is perceived by the interior senses of the soul, and it is since that day that I have possessed the knowledge of the real life.

THE CARAVANSERAI OF MELANCHOLY

The caravanserai had a long immense corridor. I knew that her husband had just arrived and that she was with him somewhere in the vastness of that place of brick. From the depths of the dusk I heard dogs barking, camels crying and camelteers and liter-bearers quarreling. And sometimes there were dragging footsteps in the long immense corridor of the caravanserai of melancholy.

I did not emerge from my room, in the hope that she would come by, that she would chance to come by and stop for a moment. But the hours, as inexorable as regret, ended up passing with the barking of dogs, the quarrels of the litter-bearers and the slow scent of the moon in the indifferent sky. The hours passed and she did not come by in the endless corridor of the caravanserai of desperate expectation.

Then I went out to see again the little road that descends among the gray-tinted cinnamon trees, the little road where I had walked so happily beside my beloved. I had not gone out for long, the time of a glance, the time of an amorous thought; I had not gone out for long, but just long enough for her to come for a minute to say hello in passing, in passing along the long corridor of that caravanserai of separated lovers

She has pushed the door, she has gone in, she has embalmed the chamber with her robe and, not finding me, she has left in clear evidence a very tiny handkerchief, like a sign of divine fidelity, like the presence of her heart, and she has gone into the long corridor, she has gone never to return, and that handkerchief is all that remains to me henceforth of the woman I love, in the caravanserai of life.

THE STAR OF MERCY

Padmani's eyes are raised toward the star-studded sky and she is looking with extreme attention... A drop of silver is shining on her cheek.

She believes that every star corresponds to an emotion of the soul and that every soul is under the influence of a star in the sky. The drop of silver is descending slowly.

Oh, how anxious she is before the thousands of characters traced in the enigmatic blue book.

"What are you looking for with so much ardor, O Padmani?"

"I'm looking for my star. I know its name, but I don't know where it is. It doesn't shone brightly. Its name is the star of mercy."

"I know it," I told her. "There is it." And I showed her a star at random.

"It's the most beautiful," she murmured. And on her cheek, the drop of silver had disappeared.

THE BEAUTY OF REFLECTIONS

One evening I shall quit the earth of humans and you will remain alone. That is why I intend to tell you that essential word of life. Light the lamp, my beloved, in order that what the furniture and faces enunciate will have their vestment of clarity.

All things have a reflection, which is the true substance of the world. Motionless waters are phosphorescent, eyes shine, and there are luminous particles that float at the level of tiled ground, and which are not engendered by the moonlight. Matter strives to disengage the soul. All gleams are beautiful except that of gold.

In the world of apparent forms it is necessary only to love the reflections, the sheen of lacquer, the polish of crystals, the dormant dullness of jade, the glimmer of precious silks and hair. Good and evil are in the reflections, and some are pure and others impure. O my beloved, never take gold in your divine hands.

For Ahriman, of whom there is mention in the books of Zend, Iblis the tempter, and Satan with whom Christian priests menace children, are only incarnations of the spirit of gold, the evil spirit that causes humans to retrogress on the route. March forward, O my beloved, guided by the spiritual reflections and turn your face toward the sun.

In the garden, where the brambles and the nettles are, dig a big hole and bury the gold. Remain in your house without gold, or clad in a robe without fringes, with hands devoid of rings, go far through life. There are many fewer evil deeds that is believed, if one has elevated thoughts. Live in a temple or in hovels, with sages or beggars, give your body to all men if it pleases you, but do not receive a gold coin for it.

Seek the reflections, O my beloved, they are substance, they are beauty. The more you seek them, the more of them there will be, and in the end, you will walk enveloped by gleams, like a princess entering a city in the midst of a rain of blue lotuses. And if you should happen on occasion, in the splendor of a dwelling or before statues of the gods, to be gripped by the attraction of gold, remember this thought, which I am bequeathing you, and which is the best of my spirit, the reflection of myself, which will accompany you, O my beloved.

All gleams are beautiful except that which comes from gold.

THE TERRESTRIAL PARADISE

I lived in the terrestrial paradise for a long time. There was a tiny jet of water there in a porcelain basin as large as a hand. The tree of knowledge was a peach-tree, and as its wood bears happiness I, the first man, had cut a branch, which I had folded under the arch of the door while the first woman clapped her hands.

Beneath the circle of the peach-tree branch, the first woman often stood in the sunlight, without any visible costume. It was me who handed her the fruits of the tree and she bit into them, laughing. Then she threw the stones over a little pink hawthorn hedge that separated the terrestrial paradise from the road where God doubtless came in the evening to spy on us.

No irritated angel holding a flaming sword expelled me from the terrestrial paradise. I left it for no reason, guided solely by my own folly. Scarcely had I left it than the notion of god and evil tormented my soul cruelly, and I knew how bitter it is to go all alone over the hard earth.

All alone, because the first woman continued to live in the terrestrial paradise. I sometimes go along the pink hawthorn hedge. Then I hear her laughter resounding, and I understand that someone is offering her fruits. I would dearly like a few parcels of the former happiness to fall on me inadvertently, but I only receive the peach-stones that she throws on to the road, as before.

THE MARVELS OF THE VOYAGE TO CHINA

I recounted to Padmani everything marvelous that I had seen when I traveled in immense China. I described to her the Palace of Immortal Joy, the Fountain of Dragons in the labyrinth of the gardens of Jehol, the Silver Lake with its seven hundred crystal kiosks at the foot of a hill of azure mineral, the Isle of Silent Pagodas and the tomb of Confucius, as harmonious as the excellence of ordered thought.

I recounted to Padmani the festivals that I had witnessed: the Festival of the Seventh Evening, in which an envoy from the heavens descends bearing an orchid, and the Festival of the Lords of the Three Worlds, in which the spirit that presides over vital force is born. I described to her the corteges of the Festival of the Old Man of the Moon, who determines marriages, the dazzling costumes of the masters of ceremonies and those who regulate the genuflections and reverences, and I told her how the Festival of Kites is celebrated on the mountain of Fou-Tcheou Fou.

Padmani listened to me in silence and I sensed that she had a question to ask me, and that, of everything I had said, only one thing interested her, which caused her slender neck to extend and her eyes of somber jade shine.

"What color were the kites?" she asked.

"All the colors of the rainbow, Padmani."

Then she lost herself in a dream.

Then I told her about the mysterious reveries of opium, the strange superstitions, the extraordinary miseries, and the dangers I had run, the menageries of wild animals I had seen in Macao, the arrival of the Portuguese fleet that I had seen at Liampo, and the pirates I had avoided, and the whales that had passed in the distance, and all the astonishing marvels that the man who makes a voyage to China can contemplate.

Padmani listened to me in silence, but the sounds struck her ears without reaching her soul. A problem was tormenting her and weighing more heavily on her head than the crepuscular helmet of her hair.

"Does the mimosa of China have another perfume than the mimosa that grows in our garden?"

I replied to her: "Exactly the same perfume."

Then she uttered a great sigh of relief, as if I had liberated her from a disturbance, and she said: "What's the point of going to China? The two of us are so content here."

THE NAKED YOUNG MAN

There was a naked young man who came to bathe and advanced in the sunlight over the sand of the Jumna. He was very handsome, he was agitating a liana negligently, and he smiled at he gazed at Padmani.

"Why is that young man smiling at you?" I asked.

"What young man are you talking about?" replied Padmani. "I can't see anyone."

And she widened her eyes in the direction of the naked young man, who passed close to her.

"I'm taking about the young man who has just gone past you with a liana in his hand."

And Padmani, belatedly lowering her eyes, replied: "Doubtless the devas obscured my vision momentarily. That happens sometimes."

But the next day, as I had discontented her by my taciturn humor, she was sitting outside the door of the house and she was gazing at a deserted path in the garden with a singular and joyous fixity.

"What are you looking at so attentively, Padmani, in the deserted path?"

"Doubtless the devas have obscured your vision," she replied, with a hint of impatience. "I'm looking at a handsome young man who is coming along the path, negligently agitating a liana."

And I said: "I can see him too. He's been there since we were on the bank of the Jumna. How fortunate he is to be handsome, that invisible young naked man."

And Padmani stood up, with a moue of tenderness; she pointed her finger at the path and said: "Look. He's running away, and he'll never come again."

THE IMPATIENT CREATURE'S THREE RAPS

When someone knocked three times on my door I was in no hurry to open it. I corked the bottle of rosé and I closed the manuscript of the poet Mir that I was in the process of reading. Who will ever know whether I was wrong not to hurry?

There was no one on the doorstep of my house. An impatient creature had knocked and had gone away without waiting. But must one run when good fortune presents itself, and how, in any case, can one distinguish the three raps of good fortune from the three raps of ill fortune?

And the street was almost deserted. I asked a water-carrier who was passing whether he had seen anyone drawing away, but he contented himself with smiling without making any reply. Was it an opportunity I had wasted or a chagrin that I had given time to draw way?

However, a picked up among the weeds of the pavement a rose that had been dropped. I sniffed it, but it did not emit any odor, as if it refused betray the secret of the woman who had worn it.

I went back inside and I reopened the manuscript of the poet Mir at the place I had marked with the bookmark. But I was distracted and the poems fluttered around me without reaching me. I listed to the noises of the silent street. I closed the manuscript and replaced the bookmark with the rose. Oh, how can one distinguish the three raps of good fortune from the three raps of ill fortune?

THE DIAMOND OF THE DEAD

There is a funerary custom of Nepal that requires a diamond to be placed in the mouth of dead people in order that they retain the beauty of their visage in the darkness of the tomb.

The gods who preside over the decomposition of the molecules of the form stop work because of the brightness of the precious stone, which interrupts the effort of their sovereign will.

The poor man who only clenches between his teeth the dust of his terrestrial regret, will sense the contours of his face disappear and an active destruction will remove the flesh from his bones.

Even the gods of the dead, those subaltern instruments of the passage from one world to the other, are the slaves of wealth. Their advent is delayed by a sumptuous dwelling that preserves from cold and the sun, by the abundance of remedies that cause malady, the sister of death, to recoil.

The diamond dazzles those mercenary gods by means of the facets of its gleam, and, crouched in silence around the possessor of precious stones, they respect the rigid visage of the rich man, marked with the seal of authority.

However, O poor man, the law is just, the superior law, for which the gods of death are only obedient phantoms, blind and mute larvae submissive to their orders.

For the more rapidly your poor carnal form perishes, and your form is worn away by their labor and thinned by lack of nourishment, the more rapidly you will acquire the subtler and better life in which you will only be clad in the bright form of the spirit.

And there, finally, you need not fear the attack of any corruptible and tenebrous god. There, everyone brings the treasure that belongs to them, everyone keeps the spiritual property that he has accumulated by means of wisdom.

There is no diamond pure enough to immobilize the changing features of the soul if they are not sculpted themselves in the marble of moral beauty. It is only in the realm of the spirit that humans measure the rhythm of justice.

THE BITTER ALMOND

To have water pure of all pollution it is necessary to rub the interior of the jar into which it is poured with a fresh almond and then expose it to sunlight.

With the almond of resignation I have rubbed the jar of the soul, in order to make the slime of evil sentiments disappear and the crystal water of virtue shine.

And behold my soul. It is devoid of passions. The sunlight shines through that transparent water, that water of immaculate perfection. It is necessary not to drink it, however. The jar has been rubbed by a bitter almond.

THE SUPERIORITY OF KNOWLEDGE

She said to me: "I'm very knowledgeable. At thirteen I knew how to weave, and fourteen I knew how to tailor garments, and fifteen I played the lute, and at sixteen I learned to dance. At eighteen I directed your servants, your gardeners and your litter-bearers."

And I replied to her: "I'm very ignorant. I've tried to pierce the mystery of hidden things and it remains impenetrable. I've tried to discover the secret law of poetic rhythms and I haven't succeeded in doing so. I don't understand anything of what I see around me. I don't know why you laugh and why you weep, and you remain by my side as the greatest enigma of the universe."

Then she uttered cries of joy in thinking about the superiority of her knowledge and she started whirling around in the bedroom. But she stopped, looked at the ceiling and, as if she had a regret, she came toward me, saying: "There's something else that makes you even more ignorant: I know that I love you, and you don't."

THE EMPEROR OF CHINA AND THE SUN

The Emperor of China thought he had observed that the sun did not obey his will. He was inconvenienced by its heat during the summer and he reproached it for having caused a singular tulip that had been brought to him from the barbaric Occidental lands to die. Then too, he cherished a profound love of darkness. He resolved to stop the sun in its course and he summoned his entire court in order that it might witness his unlimited power.

Toward the shore of the ocean where the sun rises, a great cortege set forth during the night. In his palanquin, the emperor had placed a magic jade wand over his knees that had belonged to Fo-Hi, the inventor of writing and the twenty-seven-stringed lyre, and the love of darkness shone in his blinking eyes.

Mandarins of high rank followed him, bearing lighted lanterns, which they lifted up very high. A few were weeping at the idea that they would no longer see the beautiful light of day. Others were thinking that they had always been asleep at daybreak, and they regretted the idleness that had deprived them forever of that spectacle. The soldiers had put on black armor as a sign of mourning. Only the minister of rites was smiling perfidiously behind his silk fan.

One the shore of the sea, a little man clad in white was praying. "What are you doing here, O holy Buddhist?" the Emperor asked him. And the little man clad in white, seeing the thousand lanterns, the tears and the minister's smile, understood what was happening and thought that the Emperor as about to lose face by virtue of the sun's disobedience, all the more so as a slight pallor was already perceptible over the water.

"Great Emperor," he said, "I was praying on the salty sand because I know, thanks to my knowledge of celestial things, that the sun will no longer to rise over the earth of humans in order to fecundate it. But astronomical laws are rigorous. The only hope that remains to us is that you can make it obey, O omnipotent one, by extending the magic wand to Fo-Hi toward the Orient."

The Emperor harangued the mandarins, but the saint tugged his sleeve, because of the slight blanching of the sky. It was necessary not to permit the sun the slightest delay.

No one would have believed that Fo-Hi's wand had so much power, for there had never been a dawn so splendid.

Thus imperial face was saved. All the lanterns went out simultaneously. The minister of rites grimaced. The little man clad in white resumed his prayers on the salty sand.

THE BEST PART

There are remarkable actions to accomplish on earth. I could make myself illustrious in several ways: in the arts, in war or in commerce, but I am so content next to my beloved.

I am told that a caravan is about to set forth through the mountains for Kabul, and will then go on to Ispahan. What a reception the poets of that city would give me! Pick up your fan, my beloved, in order that I can see how your eyes close when the cool air caresses your face.

The Emperor of Delhi has just summoned me to him. It is a great honor, to which I am very sensible. Quickly, my embroidered robe! Ali, who will see me go by from his balcony, will faint with jealousy. But my beloved has undone her hair over her shoulders and I must contemplate it until tomorrow. Ask the Emperor to pardon me.

All the Sufis assembled this morning in the mosque to discuss the purity of the doctrine. It is the prophet of Allah himself who is summoning me. But my beloved has baked a cake of almond milk and cinnamon, and she is so charming when I praise her because I find it to my taste. Oh Sufis, ask the Prophet to turn his face away from an insensate man!

Caravans are setting forth for distant lands, Emperors are sitting solemnly in the midst of the courts, sages are intoxicating themselves with divine wisdom, but we, my beloved, are reading books of poetry, sharing the almond cake, and looking at one another silently in the little house that shelters an immense happiness. We have chosen the best part.

THE MIRROR THAT CONSERVES DREAMS

When she goes to sleep, she places a polished silver vase beside her filled with limpid water. She does not remember her dreams, she only remembers their beauty, and she believes that the mysterious image remains in the mirror of polished silver.

As soon as she wakes up, she leans avidly over the matinal water. "Oh, come quickly and see, my beloved! There are palaces in an amaranth mist, there are bouquets of lemon trees and young men clad in white walking under marble porticoes."

I lean over too, I rub my eyes, but I see nothing, nothing but her charming face alongside mine. But then she is annoyed with me and accused my mind of dullness, which is not able to disengage quickly enough from the dense shadow of sleep. And who knows, perhaps she is right?

Once, I leaned over the clear water of the silver vase first, and I said: "I see a young woman with bare breasts, a young woman who is dancing with a scarf the color of the moon. She resembles the bayadere of the temple of Parvati I saw last year in Benares, she resembles the beautiful dream that I dreamed all last night."

But she smiled without emotion and replied to me: "If there is a bayadere and if she danced in your dream, it is not in the bottom of the silver vase, for in the limpid water resides a charm, a secret correspondence with the soul that sleeps alongside, and that marvelous mirror is polished with an artistry so magical that only a certain quality of dream can leave its subtle trace therein."

But all the same, she stirred the water with the tip of her fingernail.

THE INTERIOR MOSQUE

There is a fraternity of builders who move from city to city in order to build mosques of marble and stone with profound cupolas like forests and delicate minarets like young women.

Are those builders pious men? It does not matter. They know the place in the mountains where the beautiful stone is hidden that resists time and the marble as immaculate as the forehead of a virtuous young man. They come and they erect the place of prayer that puts humans in communication with God.

O my soul, be similar to the fraternity of builders. If doubt is sometimes within you, do not listen and build. Discover, in order to build, the solid thought in the mountain, the marmoreal song in which the blue veins of harmony run. Build the tower incessantly higher.

The spiritual tower that is launched toward the sun! For everyone must extract the authentic white stone from the soil of errors, everyone must labor himself on the cupola that sustains the minaret that springs forth, everyone must build in his soul his own interior mosque.

THE DESIRE TO BE LOVED

She talked, she talked incessantly, sitting outside the house. Her joyful voice covered the sound of the fountain in the garden, and while I listened amorously, I gazed into the warm evening air at successive flocks of white birds rising up and scattering slowly.

And then she suddenly fell silent and gazed for a long time at the tops of the palm trees motionless in the ash of the dusk, so long that I said to her: "Why aren't you talking any longer, Padmani?"

She uttered a great sigh. It seemed to me that the fountain in the garden stopped making its secret sound. She put her hands together and said, from the depths of her heart: "I would so much like someone to love me!"

And she continued to gaze at the tops of the palm trees, increasingly drowned in the ash of the dusk, as if she could not see me beside her. Then a black bird traversed the sky and traced a long horizontal line, as if it were cutting the sky in two.

THE MAN FROM THE LAND OF SITTIM

The man from the land of Sittim, she said, would come back one day to look for her. She would take off her necklaces and march on foot beside that tyrannical master along the roads that go toward the high plateaux.

Take advantage of the caresses of my body, she said, for as long as I can give them to you. Clasp yourself against me until your head is designed in my skin. There will be a time when I shall no longer dance and when I shall no longer love, for the man from the land of Sittim will come and he will take me away with him.

I picture that man with a stall stature, cracking a large whip of rhinoceros hide. The footsteps that resonated behind us in the night were his. When she reposed in my arms I heard him behind the door like the respiration of a nightmare and I held a naked dagger in order to fight with him.

One spring day when I felt that I loved her more than usual, a spring day when the aloes and cinnamon trees embalmed the garden, as I was at her feet, my head in her knees, and I asked her whether she loved me, she replied in a low voice: "I think the man from the land of Sittim will come soon."

And one evening I saw a very small old man with a very benevolent face who made a signal of the hand to her. He was clad like an itinerant lama and I paid no attention to him. But a little later, when I found the necklaces and silk dresses that she had left in the bedroom, I understood that the man from the land of Sittim had come to fetch her.

THE SILENT ARMY OF THOUGHTS

My thoughts have started marching toward you like the silent army of the Emperor Aureng-Zeb, with its thousand elephants with felted feet, toward the fortress of Paromisus.

You cannot see them, you cannot hear them. They envelop you, however, launching thousands of arrows toward the nocturnal beacon that shines above the inaccessible tower.

But can one touch a distant soul with the reeds of light thoughts? Is your veil of mauve silk not more impenetrable than the millennial stone of ramparts?

O tower the color of bronze, bathed by the gilded vapors of the Afghan mountains, tower of good and evil, tower of the separation of frontiers, go on, you are right, keep your gates closed to the silent army that is marching toward you.

For in every light arrow there is a hidden poison, the poison of words that lie and amour that betrays, and of that poison, the soul always dies.

THE SEED OF GOODNESS

There is a particle of hidden goodness in the depths of every soul. It does not shine, it does not radiate any heat. And no one knows that it is there. Sometimes, a man travels the road of life from dawn to dusk without letting anyone see his hidden treasure. Unfortunate man, who keeps that particle secret, hidden in the depths of his soul!

He accomplishes evil deeds, he betrays his friends, he sells his spirit and he is ashamed of something luminous that would like to be exhaled from him. And the further he goes, the more evil he does, because reprobation and punishment harden him with their evil strength. "He's a soul forever doomed," people say of him. Are there souls that can be doomed, since there is a particle of hidden goodness in the depths of every soul?

The soul is like a seed of wheat that has been thrown upon untilled ground, where there are stones and the roots of nettles. Worms roam there, avid for nourishment and it is the place where the scorpion makes its bed. The seed is utterly black, miserable, obscure, covered with corruption. It bears the weight of the earth upon it. But by virtue of the power of divine genius, it silently molds its form, it pierces its route, it triumphs over beasts and substance and launches forth toward the sun.

O my God, I bear my seed of wheat buried beneath a thousand stones and a thousand shadows. Preserve me from the worm of treason, the scorpion of envy and discouragement, when the tears of the rain fall. I only have a tiny particle of goodness and I am afraid of seeing it perish at any moment. O my God, give me the strength to grow and radiate, and enable the particles of goodness in the souls of all my human brethren to grow and radiate at the same time, in order that there will be no longer anything, in the end, but a single great light!

THE SWALLOW IN THE LINEN CHEMISE

She gets up before daybreak and wants at any price to convince me that I have slept longer than usual and that it is high time I got up too.

"Can you hear the dahi merchant passing out there with his baskets?" she says to me. But I recognize the screech of the old owl in the garden.

"Now, there's the water-carrier in the courtyard arguing with the servants." There is only a swallow in a linen chemise fluttering in the bedroom.

In vain she agitates the paper curtains. It's dark outside. It's dark...and yet... I'm mistaken, my love. Since you are up, dawn has broken.

SOMETHING UNIMPORTANT

She said to me: "You'll push a wooden gate. You'll traverse a garden as big as a hand, at the end of which is a little bamboo house. I'll be waiting for you at midnight on a blue-painted rush mat. But go, you're attaching too much importance to something that's hardly worth the trouble."

I had begged her so much to be mine! I had suffered so much the day when she left with an Afghan from Kabul who had thrown his mantle of striped wool over her! I had wept so bitterly when the three Ganges boatmen had lain her down in the bottom of her boat and had rowed away singing.

"Is that my fault?" she had said to me afterwards. She was so weak. It was never her fault.

How slowly the hours succeeded one another! I saw processions going toward pyres and the smoke of pyres rising toward the sky, and clouds in the sky that the wind carried away. Vultures were circling over the Parsi cemetery. The night deployed like a cloud of vapor emerging from an immense and invisible cassolette.

I pushed the wooden gate, traversed a little garden between two beds of white poppies and looked into the bamboo house through the door, which stood ajar. She was naked on the blue-painted mat, she had her fan over her face and she was tapping the ground with her hand. I kissed that hand and lay down beside her.

As first light appeared, I stopped, as I was going toward the wooden gate, and saw that the white poppies of the two flower-beds had wept tiny tears that were running down their stems. Standing in the doorway she was putting up her hair, and she said to me by way of adieu: "You can see that you attached too much importance to something that was scarcely worth the trouble."

225

THE DEATH OF THE EMPEROR OF CHINA

In the middle of the silent night, in the Palace of Supernatural Brightness, the Emperor of China heard in the distance the light footsteps of Death, which were coming toward him. She walked along the Avenue of Divine Dragons and then she came through the Garden of Blue Jade Fountains, the Garden of Sunflowers, in her black armor and her bronze mask, agitating her fan of crow-feathers, in the midst of the sleeping eunuchs, and traversed the mute halls, the halls of thrones and gods, the halls devoid of candlesticks and resonance. She stood behind the curtain of violet silk, which was stirred by an imperceptible quiver. Then the Emperor of China became aware for the first time of the great solitude in which he had always lived.

He could have struck his brazen gong. The Minister of Punishments, the Minister of Rites, the mandarins of the Great Council and the Manchu princes would have come running from the four cardinal points of the Forbidden City. The three hundred wives would have torn their robes and uttered the despairing moans prescribed by millennia-old ordinances. He would have contemplated on the faces the surge of new ambitions, long-contained hatreds, and evil delight, launching forth from souls like a flock of black birds liberated by death. But no! It was better remain alone, as he had always been, in the ice of his silver robe, beneath the snow of his diamond-studded crown.

And from the shadow of the past he saw the face emerge of the woman who would not come, the only one whose presence he would have desired. Her name was Lost Swallow and she had the custom of bring her hands together like closing wings. Oh, the Festival of the Lanterns, in spring, on the mountain of Emoui, the pilgrim path where peach-blossom was falling, and the eyes of the daughter of the poor, so rich in amour! What had become of her now? Doubtless a pinch of dust under a stele devoid of an inscription. And he, at the summit of the universe, had lived in the midst of the rhythm of ceremonies, in the majesty of imperial feasts, isolated in a perfect solitude like a geometrical figure, as rigorous as a law, as exact as a verity. And he watched the violet silk curtain quiver, slowly lifted by a hand gloved in black metal.

No Occidental ambassador, no traveling sovereign, had ever been better received than that Princess of the Afterlife with the somber bronze mask. He buckled on the war-sword of the first of the Han, he threw the sacred standard of the Celestial Empire over his shoulders, and he took in his right hand the crystal globe that was transmitted from dynasty to dynasty because it reflected a particle of the unknowable. He would rather have seen the image of Lost Swallow there than that of God. But for lack of memory of philosophical spirit he perceived neither one nor the other. O solitude! Such was the sense of his destiny.

Through the violet curtain the sword of death attained his heart. All alone! In the great mirror, he perceived a road of dream where peach-blossom was falling, an ideally solitary road. And he started marching along it, holding aloft the crystal globe, in which there was nothing.

THE JUDGE AND THE EXECUTIONER

You lifted the perfume-burner and you lowered it, by turns, and you pursued with your open arms the beautiful mauve and blue smoke that swirled slowly and faded away mysteriously in the darkness of the ceiling.

And you said to me, laughing, but nevertheless with a slight dread, in showing me the perfumed air: "Look! There's a judge with a long red robe and a black turban, and behind him, carrying a curved sword, I can see the executioner of the King of the Mahrattes."

And I replied to you: "For a very long time I've been followed by a judge, a judge in a black turban, behind whom stands an executioner. Even when the setting sun doesn't redden the blue of the smoke, he's always beside me, that eternal judge.

"The one you're showing me will dissipate suddenly if you open the window and let in the evening breeze. But my invisible judge will remain, and the executioner of remorse, a thousand times more pitiless than the King of the Mahrattes, will torment me with his sword."

THE PASSING OF THE BIRD SIMURGH

The bird Simurgh,[11] which lives on the summit of Mount Kaf in Persia, only passes once in life over the dwelling of a man. Fortunate is the man who has his face turned to the sky at that moment!

Is it not its golden plumage, my beloved, that has just brushed the palm tree? It is necessary not to close the window, for one cannot see the sky through the nacreous panes."

Once single time, and then it is over. Will it by on a night studded with stars or in the splendor on the rising sun? Ought I to place a bowl of milk at the top of the eucalyptus in order that it might come to slake its thirst?

When I sit down beside you in the evening on the terrace, I always lean toward your face and it is impossible to take my eyes away from yours. I am sure that the bird Simurgh will choose that moment to pass through my sky. I will hear the sound of its wings. Will I raise my head?

---

[11] Author's note: "The bird Simurgh was the symbol of divine thought among the sufis of Persia and India."

THE GENEROUS ILLUMINATOR OF BOOKS

Your father Betab, the illuminator of books, said to me in welcoming me: "Everything that is in my house between these four pillars of black bamboo, under the mantle of the white-washed roof, my guest, belongs to you.

"Here is the wine that contains the thought of God, and the flour cake in which there is the intimate substance of the material earth. Here are the cushions, here are the jewels gathered by the love that humans have for precious stones. All of them are yours, my guest."

And a little later he said to me, when I wanted to play the cithara in order to please him, and charm the end of the evening: "It's a great pity that my daughters cannot come to sit beside you on the carpet in order to see the guest playing the cithara.

"They will listen to you from the top of the stairs, behind that golden gauze. Don't be offended if they whisper and you hear the rustle of their woven silver slippers as they draw away."

And it was for you, whom I could not see, that I played the cithara. You whispered behind the golden gauze, your slippers slid over the fabrics, and I sensed my own genius.

And later, when I was alone in the guest-room, the door rotated silently, and without whispers and the friction of slippers, you both came to huddle beside me.

The lamp was dead and I was still unable to see you. You said: "O cithara player, can you feel how warm my lips are! Can you feel how firm my breast is against yours?" And the miraculous night sent guests of enchantment through the window. But with sadness I caressed your forehead with my hand and replied: "Certainly I would have liked to take from your father the illuminator of books the most precious of his possessions, but he has given me everything with such a generous heart! Go, young women. The cithara player will sleep tonight with the confidence respected."

PADMANI'S TERRORS

In the middle of the forest we have found the jade statue of an unknown divinity. Padmani began by running away, but she retraced her steps and I said to her: "The gods are inoffensive; it's only the human heart that is evil."

And on the road, returning to the house, we encountered vagabonds of evil appearance. Padmani started by running away, but she retraced her steps and I said to her: "These men are inoffensive, and there is nothing in them but obscurity and sadness."

And as we arrived at my door, a scorpion walked over the doorstep. Padmani began by running away, but she retraced her steps and I said to her: "Animals are inoffensive. See how I have driven this one away with the tip of my stick." And she put her hands together, saying: "How brave you are, my beloved!"

"Yes, I am brave," I replied, "incessantly to confront the eyes of the woman I love, your beautiful eyes, Padmani, without knowing the danger that they hide, instead of running away, far away from you, who are more redoubtable for my soul than the forgotten god, the wandering man or the scorpion on the threshold."

Then Padmani laughed, saying: "You'd do as I do: if you fled, you'd immediately retrace your steps!"

THE CEMETERY OF MELANCHOLY APPARITIONS

O cemetery of melancholy apparitions! The fabric of a white wall, the design of a lizard on the appearance of the door, the flagstones and the grass, a funerary checkerboard on which swallows perch like the jetsam of a dream, and the dusk deploys the vaporous muslins of its extinct blues and past amaranths...and the crescent moon on the edge of the horizon...

Ghazlane the Persian advances toward me, as light as a mist and holding a cithara as transparent as a cloud. Can one kiss your lips and grip your supple waist in the world without real form? And beside her I see a cypress that is launched toward the heavens like a dolorous prayer.

Azad the poet smiles at me from afar. He is leaning on a staff as of old. "Don't you like wine, friend? With what mouth do you drink?" He makes me a sign to approach...even closer. He wants to whisper a secret in my ear, the great secret, which makes living men dream. But a lemon falls from a lemon tree into a pool of rainwater and a star of water-drops springs forth. I draw way without looking back.

How beautiful the crescent moon is on the edge of the horizon! How solid the earth is! O cemetery of melancholy apparitions!

THE SILENCE OF MASKS

When we went to see the collector of masks, we saw samurai, emperors and gods.

Some visages had metal horns and others red beards and long sharp teeth.

There were some that resembled Vritra and others Ahi, and others that were like Naga the demon serpent.

You were afraid and you trembled in the midst of all those faces of lacquer and ivory, and you asked whether they were not going to come to life and click their jaws.

But the collector of masks said to you: "O my child! We are in the world of deceptive appearances, motionless passions and inoffensive evil.

"I live in the midst of these faces because, although they are terrible, they are mute, and I prefer the tranquil fury of masks to the hypocritical benevolence of human faces."

THE PRIEST UVASTRI

It was necessary never to tell the story of a murder in front of her. She started to tremble then, she pronounced incomprehensible words, her eyes became fixed and she followed a mysterious tragic scene in space.

"There's the priest Uvasti!" she said, fearfully. "It's necessary to have pity on me." And she sought to flee, or, on other occasions, she advanced with a threatening visage, and, turning toward the closed door she cried: "He's just come in; the priest Uvasti is standing there."

"And in the evening, when we were alone, she sometimes stopped singing, she huddled against me, she squeezed my hand for a long time and, looking at the door obliquely, she murmured in the voice of a little girl: "Do you know whether the dead forgive?"

Often, I thought I saw him walking around the house. He had strangely red eyes in a pale, sad face, and his teeth gleamed between his lips. He was clad entirely in white and dragged one leg slightly. He seemed weary and when he turned round I distinguished the bloody trace of a wound between his shoulders.

And she said to me on certain days: "O my beloved, how beautiful life is when one is in love. The priest Uvasti won't come any more."

She was mistaken, however. One does not kill the past with a dagger between the shoulder-blades. He will always be behind the door, that sad, terrible, pitiless priest Uvasti.

IN THAT OLD, THAT VERY OLD GARDEN...

It was an old, a very old garden. Autumn had taken possession of it and lamented there incessantly with the wind. And the dead were accustomed to come and wander there.

Why had they chosen that place, that very old garden? Because of the rotting leaves, or the exhalations of the pond? I don't know. But I saw them from my window.

I saw the dead in the pathways. They did not seem very unhappy. They stood motionless, obstinately looking at the ground, and they seemed deprived of intelligence.

Sometimes they strolled two by two. At other times they raised their arms sadly. I thought that they were going to lament but they remained as silent as the descent of dusk.

At first they had frightened me, but I became accustomed to their presence. The absence of a gleam in their gaze led to an absence of pity in my soul.

Sometimes I threw breadcrumbs to the birds, but they did not pick them up. Sometimes I threw them amicable thoughts; they slid through the middle of them and did not perceive them.

In that old, that very old garden there was a fountain full of youth. They were around it, passing close to it, but they never went to drink there.

In that old, that very old garden, I walked in the midst of the dead. I heard them drawing away when I went back into my house. And it took me a long time to realize the extent to which I resembled them.

BENEATH THE VEIL OF SIMULATED SLEEP

She had undressed and she had gone to sleep beside me. Her body seemed to me to be longer than usual. I had lost my reason in seeing my beloved undress and go to sleep beside me.

I dared not move for fear of waking her. The lamp had lost its reason, like me, for it was throwing out large flames, which danced on the silken fabrics and the naked body of my beloved.

Like me, and like the lamp, my beloved was intoxicated by slumber, for suddenly, with a mechanical and negligent gesture, she ran her hand over my body.

And the fabrics, the mahogany bed and the stars in the window became intoxicated in their turn and were whirling around me, when I saw that my beloved was not asleep and that her eyes were gleaming though her partly-closed eyelids.

TRUE PURITY

You tell me that I ought not to dress in garments of white wool, because I am not pure enough. But, O charming one, true purity is not in actions but in the heart.

One evening when I was standing on the threshold with slightly troubled eyes, you exclaimed: "My God, you've just seen the bayaderes dancing!" And yet, O delightful one, I was enveloped by the swarm of celestial thoughts that the dance inspired.

As I stirred thousands of minuscule shells in an earthenware vase you took a handful of them, which you dropped in the sunlight, and you said: "They're as numerous as your sins." And I replied: "O perfect one, how neat and pure my sins are!"

And the evening when I found you asleep and naked on the mat and I woke you up by kissing your lips, your first movement was to roll yourself in your veil. I asked you why and you simply said: "It's so that you can have the pleasure of unrolling it." O sincere one, true purity is not in actions, but in the heart.

IN PRAISE OF THE YEARS

Like wine, which, in growing older, is deprived of its bitterness, like the palm tree that sheds a circle of dry branches every year in order to send a fresher and younger spray skywards, so my soul rejects its impure thoughts on the regenerative contact of the years and throws toward the sky of death the juvenile bouquet of idea aspirations.

Old age is not terrible. It places on the head of the wise man a crown of roses collected from the mystic garden of thought. The sight of the physical eyes diminishes, but one perceives unsuspected gardens, silver rivers, the unfurling of the valleys and mountains of the interior land. One hears the resonance of human voices less clearly, but perception arrives of all the mysterious words that are spoken in the beyond.

O power that I feared when I did not know you, you are as benevolent as affection, as fecund as the potency of wheat, as transformative as spring. You have given me knowledge of measure, you have taught me the value of amity, and you have enabled me to weigh human actions in the balance of forgiveness. You are the treasure of the poor man, the clairvoyance of the blind, and the agility of the paralyzed.

I rejoice in advancing along your ineluctable path, in which every step I take renders my heart lighter and where I contemplate an ever purer light. It is thanks to you that I have advanced in self-knowledge, that I have discarded futile veils and deceptive masks and that I can contemplate things in their double aspect of good and evil. It is thanks to you that I shall reach the narrow door of death, purified by forgiveness, and illuminated by intelligence.

THE MINIATURE OF AMOUR

In Persia, Chapour painted miniatures so delicate that one could distinguish therein, on the robes of kings that he had represented, the design of each thread of fabric with its particular form.

And one also saw every grain of the flesh on the faces of the favorites, like a magical universe shaded by a dwarf down.

In the same way I would like to paint a miniature of my soul, with my amorous thoughts, which unfurl like threads of silk, and my hopes, more tenuous than down.

But I am not like Chapour, who looked at the material substance of form with a magnifying glass. Through my own mind I follow a thousand tenebrous colors and I lose myself in the subterranean palace of spiritual things.

I possess tender sentiments for you that I do not unveil to you, and the treasure of my amour you will never know, and you will not even receive a delicate miniature of me.

PADMANI'S EMBROIDERY

The three of them understood one another so well that they ended up resembling one another. They caused such sweet harmony to reign in the house that I sometimes heard something akin to real musical vibrations gliding from the ground floor to the terrace.

They were equally beautiful and their rooms were the same color. Their images, however, were not equally reflected in the clear water of a bucket in the sunlight. Without me being able to explain how, the face of the youngest, whose name was Padmani, only designed in the water a mobile double the color of ash. The youngest was the saddest of the three.

They were as cheerful as bees in spring and goats on the mountain slopes. Their laughter resonated in the stairwell like a cool stream.

The youngest was the only one who liked embroidery. She was embroidering the face of the Buddha in golden thread on wool, but she never finished it.

When we went out of Arcate together, they ran hither and yon, and cut large bouquets of wild flowers, the sap of which made stains on their garments. But the youngest said that she only liked the flowers that grow in the sky and are invisible.

What are the three of them doing at this moment? Are they smiling into the same mirror? Is one of them speaking my name? O my God, may my beloved savor the quietude of the soul, and may Padmani never finish her embroidery.

A LITTLE BLACK SMOKE

A little black smoke suddenly dirtied the white sheet on which I was writing a poem for you. I had painted an illumination all around it like those of Abdoud Samad and the masters of Samarkand. The lamp has gone out. The sheet is dirty.

The poem retraced the evening, the marvelous evening when you told me you loved me for the first time. The stars were high and silent and the forest leaning toward you seemed to be listening to your words. I have never forgotten those hours, and I reminded you of them in the poem

How beautiful you were, and how moving and profound the landscape that surrounded us was. I remember that, suddenly, you inadvertently uttered the name of a man you had loved before me. That is in the order of things. On the most beautiful poem of amour, a little black smoke always falls.

THE RAJAH OF GUNNAUR
AND THE SLAVE BOUNDI

I

The Rajah of Gunnaur had never shed tears, when he was afflicted by a strange dementia. He thought that he was summoned at night by the beasts in the shadows of the forest that loomed up, tall, menacing and inexorable, beyond the terrace, the garden and the river, facing the millenarian palace of Gunnaur.

He would have liked to read manuscripts, or play musical instruments, but he could not. In the distance, hyenas were laughing, snakes making a noise as they slithered, monkeys chattering in the branches and tigers mewling seductively, all the beasts saying his name.

Then he advanced on to the terrace and he saw the animal people waiting for him. Elephants raised their trunks, herons clicked their beaks, birds plumed like warriors flapped their wings, crocodiles emerged from the mud and insects rustled in the grass.

And a thousand eyes were fixed on him. The beasts wanted to make him retrogress in the scale of beings, to take away his human rank. Then he was afraid; he trembled. He thought of the course of his immortal soul. However, he did not weep.

II

And it happened that a slave, Boundi, who was secretly in love with him, slipped into the garden one night, to the foot of the terrace where he was standing, and played the lute in the shadow of the lemon trees.

And that night, the Rajah of Gunnaur did not see the tempting beasts, he did not hear the tempting voices of the backward return. And the devas floating around him brushed him with their delightful thoughts.

But when he was told in the morning that a casteless young woman had soiled the moonlit lemon trees with her presence, he gave orders that she should be beaten and expelled from the city Oh, how obscure souls are and how long their road is!

III

The beasts called to him so forcefully, from the edge of the tenebrous forest, that in the end, the Rajah of Gunnaur traversed the garden and the river in order to be a beast too.

And he was a beast in the forest. He barked with the wild dogs, he laughed with the hyenas, he climbed on to the back of deer, he lapped up water when he wanted to drink. He moved on the ground on all fours.

And sometimes, in the clearings and the wild jungles, he heard the echo of a lute, a lute similar to the one that the slave Boundi had played under the lemon trees.

And then the devas glided under the somber vault of the trees and touched him with the crystal wand of memory, the memory of beauty glimpsed. However, he did not weep.

IV

And because of the distant lute, because of the invisible devas, he eventually returned to the palace of Gunnaur. And as the soul has its tides, the flow of reason carried him away. He forgot the realm of the beasts in order only to reign over humans.

He was powerful and, he was clement, he had armies for war and he built temples for prayer. He was feared and he was loved. He practiced justice, but in the city or on the roads, or in the feasts in his palace, he remained enveloped by an interior solitude. And he never heard the lute, the aerial lute, resonate in the distance.

One day, when he was hunting with all the grandees of the realm, he stopped under a majestic old tree in order to rest, and he noticed human bones that the rain had whitened. He saw a delicate wrist with a sculpted iron ring.

"What can that iron ring be?" he asked.

"I recognize it," said one of his servants. "It's the bracelet that the slave Boundi was accustomed to wear on her wrist. Under this majestic old tree, a slave, Boundi, has come to die."

Then, for the first time, the Rajah of Gunnaur wept.

THE BUTTERFLY AND THE LAMP

She was kneeling on the prayer-tug. Beside her were a lighted candle and an uncorked bottle of essence of roses. A butterfly with miraculous colors was flying in the room. Her face was ecstatic.

When I came in, she made a movement like someone caught at fault. I leaned over her and I saw in her eyes the image of the young man about whom she was thinking. I snuffed out the candle. The butterfly had flown away.

THE SOOT OF VERITY

The man who loves verity, under his flat tresses and his robe of gray linen, advanced toward me in the vestibule of my house, and behind him stood a young woman who was always smiling softly. The man was radiant with virtue and the young woman with innocence.

And the man said a thousand things about all subjects, in a low and emotional voice, and the great affection he had for me returned incessantly in his speech. He even took my hand and shook it tenderly.

"Lie down on the cushions," I said. "Drink Shiraz wine."

The face of the young woman was like a moon of fresh milk.

And the man who loves verity and who gazes obliquely, suddenly had an impulse so amicable that he almost took me in his arms. "It's necessary that you know eventually. It's a matter of the wife that you love. She isn't worthy of that love." And he told me all the things that come to mind when one has not drunk the Shiraz wine that makes one forget.

The face of the young woman was so pure that I feared that it might fly away like a round bird.

And as the Shiraz wine was brought, I got up, I went to fetch a little bile and I spread it in the bottom of the cups before offering them. And the sincere man said after having drunk: "Doubtless a scorpion was asleep in the bottom of the gourd when this wine was poured into it to transport it to India, for its taste is very bitter.

I replied: "Is it not necessary to render to someone what he has given you?"

The bitterness put a grimace on to the virginal milky moon.

And when I was alone, I perceived an even greater bitterness between my teeth. The visitors' sandals has soiled the white chamois-hide carpet, the breath of the man, in escaping, had covered the mirror with vapor, the rose in the vase had shrunk, the water in which it bathed was turbid, and the true stars in the windows had gone out as the virtuous innocent moon had passed by, and on the painting of beautiful memories there was the soot of verity.

ON THESE RED SANDALWOOD TABLETS

On these red sandalwood tablets a poet of Gwalior whose name has been lost has written a poem that the centuries have effaced with their sand.

Perhaps it was a powerful king who traced those verses in the silken howdah of his elephant; perhaps it was ascetic sitting among the reeds of a marsh.

A great cry of amour or maxims of wisdom? Dolor, hope or renunciation? We do not know. How many things are forgotten forever!

I too, on paper woven with flax from Gwalior have written your name and the description of your beauty, and the inexorable sand of time will efface my verses.

What does it matter, Padmani, if people know nothing about us later, as long as you know at this moment how much I have loved you?

THE BLACK ROSARY OF LOST OPPORTUNITIES

In a street in Benares, a woman made me a sign from a window. She smiled and I made a semblance of not seeing her. I went back at nightfall. The window was closed.

In a street in Benares, a beggar extended is hand to me and I hastened my pace, turning my head away. But I suddenly remembered the teachings of the prophet and I went back. There was no longer any trace of the beggar.

In a street in Benares, a mullah showed me from a distance the sculpted door of a mosque. A little later, when I wanted to pray, I wandered interminably along the bazaars and bamboo walls.

And thus, all my life, I have left behind me a black rosary of lost opportunities. Insensate that you are, you who do not know that there will come a time when one no longer encounters a woman, a beggar, or God.

THE BLACK POPPY

Never was any kiss as cruel to me as the one she gave me outside the garden gate, saying that she was sad to be leaving me until the following day, and that she would always love me.

A dahi merchant passed along the street with his wicker baskets. Children in the dust were fighting over a fragment of camphor. And I saw her joy in departing, which radiated from her, like a mute angel clad in lies.

"Until tomorrow without seeing you!" she said, again. Her dress made a silky noise of new muslin. "What are you going to do while waiting for me?" She drew away slowly, without apparent haste. I followed her with my eyes, I picked a black poppy and I went back inside.

A WOMAN IN A MIRROR

Nothing is more melancholy than gazing at a woman in a mirror. One does not quite recognize the room behind the woman, and the candle in the background gives the impression of burning for the worship of a forgotten god.

It is an illusion of happiness that one savors in juxtaposition with the illusion of a creature. I would not be surprised if the woman suddenly flew away through the window like a bird, and the flame were detached from the candle and fell to the ground like a dead ruby.

The woman beside me might be another. I am not very sure of being in that room. A muslin bird flutters, a dead ruby makes a drop of flame on the carpet, and I am detached from my body, I cease to be myself, and I lose myself in the infinity of the mirror.

THE FESTIVAL OF BHAVANI,
KNOWN AS THE ONE WHO CAUSES WEEPING

Oh, why did you not come? I was waiting for you with so much impatience! I have prepared the shawls and muslins that you love. I have walked along the path whose detour pleases you. How sad the song of the nightingale is when your heart is aching!

Oh, why did you not come? It was the day of the festival of Bhavani, the goddess to whom fourteen different names are given, and I remember that one of them is Felicity. How sad the sound of the merriment of passers-by is when your heart is aching!

Oh, why did you not come? All the bazaars were closed. All the temples were mute. Every footstep that resonated in the distance was yours. I remember that the goddess Bhavani is also named The One Who Causes Weeping, How heart-rending the silence of the city is when your heart is aching!

THE MYSTERY OF HOLLOW PEARLS

In a hollow pearl there is a little sleeping princess. In her minuscule hand she holds a pearl invisible to our eyes, and in the bosom of that pearl reposes a sun, a moon, an Earth, and all the planets, in movement though a sky smaller than an ant.

Our universe also reposes in the hollow pearl of a giant princess whom we cannot see because of her immensity. How large we are and how small we are! Which of the two, in fact, and how many sleeping princesses are there?

THE STREET OF CHAGRIN

That street, such a short street, with its tamarinds above the walls, which cast a blue-tinted shadow, I call the street of felicity.

I crossed it with a single leap and I snatched a clump of foliage with my hand, which I scattered behind me.

Your house was to the right, a little house with a low roof and a black ebony door, and I called that house the house of happiness.

The room in which you reposed beneath the mosquito net had colored floor tiles and I had lived such hours of intoxication there that I called it the room of memories.

Your little house is still to the right. The tamarinds cast a blue-tinted shadow. But the street is interminable, and I call it the street of chagrin.

THE YOUNG MAN OF THE DUSK

The young man that I had seen passing had a saffron-colored turban and a white robe tightened at the waist by a golden cord.

I was sitting in front of my door at the hour when the watchmen on the ramparts are replaced and he did not make me any sign or dart a glance at me.

I listened to the trumpets resonate in the towers. I watched the stars lighting up and the young man in the saffron-colored turban drawing away.

And it was only when his silhouette had disappeared along the walls, when there was no longer time to run after him, that I understood, outside my door, the extent of my solitude.

IT'S BETTER THAT YOU DON'T COME BACK

It's better that you don't come back, since you have left the house once. Other peach-blossom is falling in the garden, other lotuses are opening on the pond. But it was the old flowers that were dear to me. It's better that you don't come back.

Since you're far away from me, may your voyage be pleasant. The world is large. There are other lamps in warm interiors, which light up faces filed with tenderness. People also play the cithara there, and read books. You'll be loved tenderly, since you're far away from me.

It isn't the departure that is the greatest sadness. One says adieu with a firm heart. At one crossroads you'll find an inn; at another you'll find a friend. And then, everyone knows that separations and chagrins form the quotidian weave of life. It isn't the departure that is the greatest sadness.

It's better that you don't come back, because of the gaze that is no longer the same, because of the hand that isn't extended with the same frankness. I know very well that the power of forgetfulness is unlimited and that forgiveness is the heart of God. However, since you have left the house once, O happiness, it's better that you don't come back.

THE TWO BAYADERES AND THE UNIQUE VISAGE

Two bayaderes, in the same moonlight, have seen, at the bottom of a well, the unique visage of their beloved.

They have sent down the metal bucket in order to bring it back up, but there was only troubled water therein full of broken reflections.

They have refused to dance on the three stones of the Temple of Ganesha and they have wept when the moon rose.

And the Brahmin with the flaxen hair and the parchment fingers said to them: "Such is the law, my daughters, and it is better...

"The beloved only appears once, the true immortal beloved, and woe betide those who try to snatch him from the mystery and distance of the well."

But the bayaderes continued to weep in the moonlight, for those who have glimpsed the visage of the beloved once never forget it again.

A FLEETING WHITE SILHOUETTE

"It was a light footstep that I had heard on the dead leaves. It was a white silhouette that I had seen fleeing at the end of the path. I had been alone all day," she told me, "and the hours seemed long to me." She smiled, showing her teeth as if she wanted to bite an invisible fruit.

I was so desirous that she should explain the white silhouette at the end of the path that I said to her "Didn't Taswir, the vina player, come to play with you a little while ago?"

But she replied to me, absent-mindedly: "No, it's been several days since I saw Taswir, the vina player."

She looked at me with eyes full of amour, and in the midst of the cushions I perceived one of the multicolored light muslin kerchiefs that the young men of Nepal have the custom of wearing around their neck. But she had already made me sit down on the cushions and she put her arms around my neck. O mystery of the heart of a woman!

"Are you not thirsty, my beloved?" she said then. And she took the jug of wine and I saw that there were two glasses on the tray and that someone had drunk from both of them. Her eyes were tranquil and her hand was not trembling when she held the glass out to me, and I drank for a long time, with intoxication. O mystery of the heart of a man!

THE ROOT OF UNIVERSES AND GODS

I see nothing but dolor everywhere. The people of poor villages will soon have no rice. Through the low streets of the city there are diseases passing that mark the houses for death to come and visit them. One man is torn by iron and another by chagrin. I see nothing but dolor everywhere. Everywhere, I see nothing but closed hearts.

I see nothing but closed hearts everywhere. There is no sincere pity, there is only an immeasurable pride. The sufi, the upright judge and the honest wife glorify themselves too quickly in being the foremost. As in a tower of stone, they enclose themselves in their virtue. And that virtue is truly made of stone. Human dolor breaks upon it. Everyone only believes in his own verity. There is no sincere pity. And yet there is a different path for everyone.

There is a different path for everyone, sometimes bordered by flowers and at other times strewn with stones. But all the paths rise upwards and the hardest is often the shortest of those that lead to the summit of the mountain. I have seen a woman calling to passers-by from a heap of stones and extending with the lassitude of her gesture an enormous measure of pity, and I have seen shining in the eyes of a thief about to be strangled the true light of God. But the true light of God is invisible for the blind.

The true light of God is invisible for the blind. Everyone closes his door at dusk and places the bar over the battens, for a beggar might pass by with his lantern handing from a black stick. No one wants to see the stars of pity that light up with the night and travel the length of inexorably mute ports. And yet the desperate carriers of stars are often the best and the purest. They knock on doors. "Open to us, just men, open to us, virtuous men! Is it not just that we have a small portion of wealth, a small portion of virtue?" But no one ever replies to them, and no one ever will.

For the sun of justice never rises in the narrow sky of the earth. The wicked are not punished and the good are not recompensed, and it is hypocrites who are the masters. Causes engender effects, but those who are subject to the effects do not know that causes and they curse God, with reason, because he gives enough intelligence to desire justice but not enough to comprehend the slowness of its progress and the mysterious extent of its law. And when one curses God, the heart closes more firmly and dolor increases, and that is why I see nothing but dolor everywhere, and nothing but closed hearts everywhere, and there is nothing for which to hope from human pity.

There is nothing for which to hope from human pity, and there is nothing for which to hope from the pity of God, since everything that we see of him is the unfolding of an impassive and immutable law. There is nothing for which to hope from anyone. But in the depths of the abyss of despair and injustice, it is permissible to contemplate the inalterable lamp of hope. For in oneself, in the radiation of one's own soul is the divine justice that never fails, that which needs no pity in order to shone, that which has within it an oil of amour, which is consumed without ever being exhausted. O interior force, root of universes and Gods, immortal human justice!

THE LOSS OF VERITABLE WEALTH

A ship laden with pepper and vanilla, drawing way from the port of Surat, carried away all of my father's heritage. It was wrecked not far from Goa. "May Allah by glorified!" I cried, when I was told that I was ruined. "The world is so full of wealth!"

Over the water of the spring that is between the fig trees near the port of Kadhmir, I leaned one evening and I saw two graying patches on either side of my forehead. Thus I learned that I had lost my youth, and I was filled with joy, thinking that there is more beauty in the dusk than in the day that is dawning, and that a traveler ought to be glad to be approaching the end of his journey.

But when I opened the door of my house and I saw the table empty of your boxes of make-up, and I understood that you had left me, I sat down on the threshold and I wept for my solitude, because I had just lost, for the first time, my fortune and my youth.

THE NIGHT OF THE DEAD POPPIES

The room was full of poppies and the wind had pushed the window ajar.

Lying in the midst of cushions I waited for the nightingale to begin to sing.

But that night, there was nothing in the garden but the whispering of the cedars.

I put my cithara down next to the half-full cup and I went to sleep when the lamplight declined.

Then the one that I would never see again moved the silk curtain aside.

She had a long robe perfumed with Persian musk.

She had silent slippers, mute necklaces and rings devoir of reflections.

She had the distant smile of those whose soul is absent.

She took the cup, she lifted it to her lips and she emptied it.

She picked up the cithara and she played a soft sad tune, which I heard without waking up.

She hesitated momentarily, looked at herself in the mirror and touched the lacquer panels.

And then she disappeared, like the memory of an evening of old.

When I woke up I saw the carmine of her lips on the rim of the cup.

And on a vibrant string of the cithara, the polish of her fingernail had left something like a drop of blood.

The wind was cold, the poppies were dying and outside, the nightingale began to sing...

TO AN INGRATE FRIEND

Praise be to you who have offended me, who has permitted me to contemplate at leisure the face of ingratitude. I have seen the gleam that treachery can give to the gaze, the hypocritical affection with which it is able to disguise itself, offering a hand loyally, making sincere confidences in order to deceive. Praise be to you who have offended me.

For I did not know the face of evil, I had not yet measured the force with which it passes through certain souls, uprooting good memories as a tempest uproots trees, devastating the field of amity where the crop has flourished with such difficulty. I did not know one of the two slopes of the mountain, the one that is in shadow, where it rains incessantly and where one is always sad.

I shall not remind you that I loved you with a true heart, and that, if I had not expressed it to you in vain words, my silence had often told you. Is there not, in any case, when a friend discovers a friend, a mystery in the gaze and the formula of greeting, which is the sign of fraternal pleasure? I shall not remind you of the fraternal pleasure that my presence procured you, but I say to you: Praise be to you who have offended me!

For I shall not render any harm to you. Not for lack of courage and not for lack of dolor. The finest courage is in silence, in the faculty of destroying within oneself everything born of evil, engendered by evil. And as for dolor, I have known it, I have measured it from the extremity of its profound root to the last distant leaf and I retain it jealously and egotistically for myself alone. And I say to you: Praise be to you who have offended me!

For you have made me a present of a magnificent wealth. The piece of lead was the soiled gold I have washed with my hands. I have taken your offence and I have kneaded it, I have polished it, and I have warmed it in my heart. I have transformed it in the secret forgiveness that enables me to comprehend life. That forgiveness is for me, henceforth, the key to all the locked doors that a man encounters in his journey. You have given me more than you have taken from me. Praise be to you who have offended me!

THE DESCENT OF THE RIVER

We'll never get there! Go more rapidly, oarsmen! Under the bamboo roof of my boat, by dint of having drunk wine, I can see nothing but a circular patch of sky in which the stars are dancing. Descend, descend the river, oarsmen, we'll never get there.

Where are we? I don't really know. But go more rapidly, oarsmen. Under the bamboo roof of my boat, I can only see, by dint of having drunk wine, a portion of my soul in which memories are dancing. Descend, descend the river, oarsmen. We'll never get there!

There is a house out there where a woman as beautiful as a piece of white jade is waiting for me. Go more rapidly, oarsmen. I have drunk so much wine that I won't be able to recognize her. Descend, descend the river, oarsmen, we'll never get there.

It's her! She's making signs to me. She thinks that I'm late. Go more rapidly, oarsmen! But I've drunk so much wine that it seems to me that her face has changed and that I'm in the presence of Siva, the destroyer of forms. Descend, descend the river, oarsmen, we'll never get there.

All the lanterns are going out on the bank. The cries of panthers can be heard in the distance. Go more rapidly, oarsmen. There's a solitary place where the forest commences. You'll set me down there and I'll go straight ahead, for wisdom is waiting for me at the foot of a banyan. Descend, descend the river, oarsmen, we'll never get there.

BLUE EYES ARE DEAD MIRRORS

I am afraid of blue eyes because they remind me of sapphires, and a sapphire is a fragment of a world anterior to the earth, which will never be seen again.

I am afraid of blue eyes because they recall a wine mixed with leaves that beautiful women made me drink in Bagdad and I shall never know the intoxication of that wine again.

I am afraid of blue eyes because they are those of closed souls and they reflect beautiful sunlit landscapes without seeing them and amour without experiencing it.

I am afraid of blue eyes because they are those that I see incessantly in the face of my beloved, and unlike other human eyes, those mortally blue eyes do not reflect my image, and resemble dead mirrors.

ON THE BANKS OF THE JUMNA

On the banks of the Jumna I saw a woman who was weeping. She was throwing flower petals over a cradle in which a dead child lay. The cradle was on the water and was beginning to float away.

"That is my child," said the woman, "my beloved child, who is dead. I didn't understand why he was always looking at the sky with eyes of wide and so sad, and why he turned away from the faces of the living. I understand it now.

"But what I shall never understand is why he was born to die so rapidly, why he was so beautiful, in order that love all the more tender grew in my heart; what I shall never understand is the injustice of the unique god."

And with a desperate gesture she threw flower petals toward the cradle that was floating away. The dead child could not be seen. The cradle was stopped by a branch. Nenuphars enveloped it and seemed to extend veer it the pious fabric of their leaves, and then it disappeared in the distance.

And I thought as I followed the bank of the Jumna: I too have lost a beloved child. She often turned away from my face and gazed obstinately at the sky. But I could not put her in a cradle and cover her with flower petals.

For although she is dead for me, she is alive for others. The river on which she is floating is more imperious than the Jumna. It is full of music that is playing and amorous kisses. It is the river of life on which my beloved has departed singing, and I am all alone on the bank.

We do not know why children are snatched from the arms of mothers, why there is that attraction in the faces one is going to lose, why the person who loves is not loved equally. Perhaps the unique god is unjust. But I envy you, you who can throw flowers over the dead child that you have lost.

THE THREE YOUNG WOMEN AND THE LOTUS

Three young women had just bathed in the pool and the water that moistened their bodies, as it evaporated in the sunlight, made an aureole of blue mist for them.

When they perceived me among the asokas, the first, the slenderest, uttered a cry and made the gesture of veiling herself with a invisible tunic, and she was like a reed bending in the wind.

The second, the tallest, started laughing and continued to walk tranquilly with a curious immodesty in the movement of her shoulders, and she was like a Ban tree when the force of its sap splits the bark at midday.

But the third, the smallest, gazed at me from a distance without seeing me. She bent down, picked a lotus and held it out toward the sky as if she were making an offering of her heart.

OLD BAD NEWS

You who are carrying a lantern on the end of a stick and a bouquet of dry leaves, why have you come to knock on my door, announcer of death? I know the news, she has just died in her house, which is on the other side of the city, at the end of a long path lined with tamarinds.

You are astonished by what I say, because the event has just happened, because her life only departed a few minutes ago with the fading light, because you are the first to have emerged from her dwelling in order to invite those who knew her to weep. You see, it is because I have received from the gods the gift of clairvoyance.

I have already seen her with a mute visage and eyes in which there is no longer a gleam, I have already walked along the long path lined with tamarinds, with a heart in despair, and that lantern on the end of a stick has already been agitated on my threshold by me. Oh, the blind man is a thousand times more fortunate than the clairvoyant!

There are different ways of seeing those one loves die, and the death that you are announcing, announcer of death, is far from being the cruelest. Go, continue your route. Night is advancing. She had many friends whom she cherished more than me, and you have still to knock on many doors. For many years I have been weeping, for I lost her a long time ago.

MUSIC, PRAYER AND SENSUALITY

The servant stood before me and he said to me: "Leave Agra and take the road that leads to the ruins of Kanoudje. Follow a broad path to the right and after a forest of mango trees you will see, behind a high wall, a house covered in ancient sculptures, which has the signs on the zodiac over its door, It is there that she is waiting for you and is tapping impatiently with her bracelet on the mosaics of her room."

Should I take my cithara? Should I hide in the folds of my black silk dopulta a small dagger on the golden hilt of which the name of Allah is engraved? Should I be preceded by six slaves clad in white with turbans as pink as the stones of Taj at dawn, with slippers as green as the lizards of the Ganges? Should I go alone bearing as a gift a Koran on Nichapour parchment with illuminations by El Moumen bound in the skin of an immaculate peacock?

I found the path, I traversed the forest of mango trees, I saw the signs of the zodiac encrusted in nacre in the ebony wood of the door and I respired a perfume in which there was such inexpressible sensuality that I fated and dropped the Koran bound in peacock kin. Three white dogs fled without barking as I approached and I heard the notes of light laugher spilling, as if an ivory wand were striking a crystal leaf somewhere—I did not know where—around me.

She was lying on a tiger skin and she was not wearing any garment or jewelry, nothing but a strange piece of jade on the forehead between her green eyes. When I gave her the book and the cithara her lips pouted disdainfully, as if music and prayer were nothing for her but the immaterial forms of ennui. I drank a dense wine that she held out and caressed a carnal substance more colorful than the illuminations of the Koran.

As I was returning home, I reached the edge of the forest of mango trees. I respired the balsamic resin of those trees and seeds fell upon me from the red clusters of their flowers. A snake was slithering through the grass. A monkey was eating a mango. It was hot. I saw in the distance the path that would have taken me back to Agra. But she had said to me: "You will come back to see me every day." And I sought through the trees the ebony door on which the signs of the zodiac were encrusted, and I did not find it...

And it is since that time that I am like a beggar, that I fight over mangos with the monkey, that I chase away the snake with a branch in order to drink from the stream. Never again will I take the path that would bring me back to Agra. Without the cithara and the book, I watch the bird of music flying in the distance and the cloud of prayer disappearing, and I seek, without ever finding it, the ebony door of the naked sorceress whose laughter was like the resonance of an ivory wand on a crystal leaf. I have lost the ideal and I have not attained pleasure.

THE TEMPLE OF THE SOUL

Like the Emperor Akbar, I went to pray in the mosque of Agra.[12] But the columns under the ogives of the cupolas were like files of pilgrims coifed with stone lace, who were walking and whispering, and did not kneel down.

Like the Emperor Akbar, I went to pray in the temple of the Brahmins. But one breathed the suffocating odor of nearby pyres there. The divinities were too numerous. Ganesha agitated his trunk and Siva spread his arms so wide that I was afraid of being seized before having concluded my prayer to God.

Like the Emperor Akbar, I went to pray among the Parsees. But the sacred fire always seemed to be on the point of extinction. I was enveloped by the immense shadow of Ahriman, and the Yatus with bat-like bodies fluttered around me, making a noise of muffled wings.

Like the Emperor Akbar, I went to pray in the Catholic church of the Portuguese monks. But a music of bells rose up from the tower and I came out again to see the bronze swallows that were making that noise as they flew though the azure.

Like the Emperor Akbar, I went to pray in the Synagogue of the Jews. But when the book of the Torah was presented to me I read so many mysterious characters that I was like a man lost in a millenarian forest and I recoiled before the enigma of cosmologies.

Like the Emperor Akbar, I sat down in the interior temple of the soul. There is no book there, nor columns, nor statues, nor sacred fire, nor harmony of belles. No window opens

---

[12] Author's note: "The Emperor Akbar went indifferently in order to pray into churches, mosques and temples. He attempted to unify religions and he thought that the true God is within us."

on the human world, and yet I was illuminated by the pure light of truth.

EPITAPH FOR BAGAWALI

Here lies Bagawali, who bore in the slender form of her body a strange genius always inflamed by the desire of sensuality.

That genius animate the dark clarity of her gaze, caused her nostrils to palpitate, moistened her mouth and rendered it parallel to the flesh of a fruit that one opens in order to bite it.

By the force of that genius, when she passé along the ramparts of Delhi, she left behind her a perfume that was neither burnt amber nor musk, but an indefinable and attractive wake that obliged you to follow her without thinking about it.

That genius cried through her mouth on a bed of grass in the shadow of cedars, it twisted her loins, it inflated her breasts, it extended her legs and it gave the impression of expiring, although it was eternal.

At present, the carnal form of Bagawali is dead, but the genius remains around this mound and this white stone, and if you do not hasten your steps, passer-by, it will take possession of you, and your existence will be devoted henceforth to the pursuit of pleasure, which renders sorrow and puts on the lips the bitter ash of death.

THE DELIGHTFUL FACE
OF THE FRIGHTFUL MONSTER

I had never seen a monster so frightful. Its body was composed of a substance intermediate between dead stone and living flesh and seemed to be perpetually decomposing and regenerating in a strange manner. Its limbs terminated in large hands, open in order to grasp. It gazed sightlessly though eyes full of glaucous liquid. Its jaw quivered, its horns were motionless, and its teeth were red and its fur blue-tinted. It was as heavy as an elephant, as long as a snake, as enigmatic as a sphinx, and it trumpeted all along the indefinite, ineluctable avenue between the centenarian cedars.

I experienced a great terror at the sight of that monster and yet I did not try to go backwards, and did not even preoccupy myself with it inordinately. I sometimes stopped in order to watch an insect walking over the sand or two admire the savant complication of the designs of a leaf. I knew that it would be necessary, at a given moment, to plunge my gaze into the eyes of glaucous liquid, to be seized by the large hands, to feel the contact of that substance animated by the seething of decomposition. However, I continued on my way in perfect unconsciousness, with my terror huddled in a corner of my soul, my terror to which I was giving no thought.

And gradually, under the shade of denser cedars, I drew closer to the frightful monster. But a singular transformation had taken place by degrees. What I had mistaken for horns were only the knots of a turban. In the glaucous liquid of the eyes there were flashes of sapphire. The quiver of the jaw was an illusion engendered by the promises of caresses emitted by the ivory of the teeth. What had been bristling fur have become delicate down, and what had been decomposed flesh had become a translucent pink substance. I saw the curve of shoulders, the circles of open arms. I drew alongside the monster that had seemed frightful. I was contemplating the delightful, divine face of death.

AT THE HOUR WHEN THE LOTUSES OPEN

There is, when dawn is breaking, a moment when the lotuses have just begun to open. They are slightly moist with dew, as if they have been weeping.

There is in the soul of a man who has advanced in life, a moment when he glimpses wisdom and at which he does not know whether or not his dusk might be his dawn.

It is at the intermediate hour that it is necessary to walk alongside the pool, gazing at the delicate mists that rise from the blue-tinted waters and take on imprecise forms.

For the greatest human beauty is in the landscape that one divines, the sky that one cannot attain, the uncertain aspiration of the spirit, the enthusiasm for the ill-defined ideal.

It is at the intermediate hour that he must formulate his desire, because the palm tree is only a phantom and the mountain only an apparition, because the world is no better designed than our soul.

At the hour when the lotuses have just begun to open and are weeping, he must go forth, his body glad in a white linen robe as light as the mist that impregnates its creases with the dawn.

At the quotidian hour of the birth of things, at the hour when there is not yet either good or evil on earth, he must go forth with his newly-born soul, he must go forth and he must say:

"O infinite power, subtle forces that are awakening, innumerable law whose mechanisms are invisible, treasure of spiritual thoughts that are scattered and would like to become captive,

"I request the clairvoyance that enables the penetration of the life of things and the soul of beings, I request the gift of awakening the beauty hidden beneath amour, as a sultan awakens a sleeping favorite under an orange tree in flower.

"I want to enter into communication with the intelligences that regulate us in order that they might pour their scintillating light into me as one pours an essence of condensed flowers into a jade bottle with azure veins.

"I want, until my death, to honor the spirit that enlightens and conform my life to the ideal of my youth. I believe, the lotuses have only just opened, but I know that my prayer will be granted, because the sun always rises."